SPEAR OF DESTINY

A riveting battle for survival in a hunt for the ultimate truth.

May 1942. In the sands of Libya, soldiers discover a tomb containing a crown of thorns and the devastatingly powerful Spear of Destiny. They've found the last resting place of Christ. Sixty years on, Gerald Usherwood and his old army pal Max 'Chips' Chippendale pay the ultimate price for the secrets they stole. Gerald, his throat slashed, is nailed to the wall in a crude impersonation of the crucifixion, and his old friend suffers a similar fate. Gerald's grandson DCI Ethan Usherwood is left to piece together the mystery behind the killings and uncover the treasure hidden for so many years.

SPEAR OF DESTINY

SPEAR OF DESTINY

by

Daniel Easterman

Magna Large Print Books
Long Preston, North Yorkshire,
BD23 4ND, England.

British Library Cataloguing in Publication Data.

Easterman, Daniel
    Spear of destiny.

    A catalogue record of this book is
    available from the British Library

    ISBN   978-0-7505-3174-0

First published in Great Britain in 2009 by Allison & Busby Ltd.

Copyright © 2009 by Daniel Easterman

Cover illustration © Jupiter Images/Michael Gesinger by arrangement with Allison & Busby Ltd.

The moral right of the author has been asserted

Published in Large Print 2010 by arrangement with
Allison & Busby Ltd.

Magna Large Print is an imprint of Library Magna Books Ltd.

Printed and bound in Great Britain by
T.J. (International) Ltd., Cornwall, PL28 8RW

To my wife of destiny, Beth,
with love from her ancient relic.

PROLOGUE

Woodmancote Hall
Near Bishop's Cleeve
Gloucestershire
England
December 2008

Christmas came to Woodmancote that year on wings of ice, amid flurries of snow that banked steeply against the stone walls and barn doors of Hamberley Farm. It had been a late winter in coming, but once its time had arrived, it descended with exceptional ferocity, turning autumnal skies to craggy ranges of arctic cloud. On Radio 4, they said it was due to global warming, and down in the Cap in Hand, old heads nodded and said it would get worse before it got better. They were droll old men, and they'd seen too many winters, lived through too many Christmases.

Snow covered fields and roofs and hedgerows with a solid sheet of white velvet, and for day upon day it would not melt. When the last flakes had fallen, there were nights of moonlight and starlight and shining lamps, nights when the whiteness of the countryside turned to silver, nights so crisp birds fell from the trees and berries froze and cracked on the branches. Animals died in their multitudes, sheep in the open fields, squirrels in their nut-filled trees, owls in the solitary darkness of the yews.

Throughout the week before Christmas, Woodmancote Hall was ablaze with light. Light from electric bulbs and candles, from twenty log fires, from a dozen chandeliers, from a thousand twinkling white fairy lights that sparkled on trees and mantelpieces. Softly from inside, music played: King's College Choir singing the carols of all our lifetimes, 'Once in Royal David's City', 'Silent Night', 'Remember, O Thou Man'...

Seen from outside across the east lawn or the vast expanse of Parget's Meadow, the house seemed like a liner sailing on waters of driven snow, a place of comfort and cheer, a haven from the bleak midwinter. Before the curtains were drawn across the tall mullioned windows, the lights inside each room would stream out across the untouched fabric of the snow, crisscrossing it with bars of light and shadow.

Old Gerald Usherwood, lord and master in Woodmancote, his family's home for seven centuries, had been a King's man in his day. It would be his eighty-third Christmas and, the day after, his eighty-fourth birthday. The lights and music were in his honour. A great party was planned, a party that would span the Christmas season and mark both his birthday and the Nobel Prize in economics he'd received at a ceremony in Stockholm two weeks earlier.

The family were there en masse. Though substantial, Woodmancote Hall was not a great house, and its ten bedrooms and hastily tidied attic rooms were far from enough to accommodate such a tribe of grandparents, parents, children, aunts, uncles, and cousins. Some late arrivals who could not be fitted in at the house or the lodge had to make do with rooms in the village or Bishop's Cleeve. The allocation of rooms had caused not a few headaches to Gerald's oldest son George, who, with his wife Alice, had taken overall responsibility for the grand gathering.

The house party was made up of four groups of Usherwoods, some Draytons, a handful of Cornwallises, the Canterbury Grevilles, one or two Ellises, the Naseby twins, and a pair of distant cousins from Madeira who hadn't set foot in England in over forty years. Some had travelled further, from the United States or Canada. Gerald's sole surviving brother, Ernest, was there, riddled with cancer but determined to see another year pass. 'Chips' Chippendale, his fellow survivor from his days with the Long

Range Desert Group during the North Africa campaign, was there and in fine fettle. Four of Gerald's five children had made it a point of honour to be there with their spouses and children. The party would be lavish. A great part of the prize money had been spent on it.

As the days passed, between preparations for Christmas lunch and the birthday bash, guests came and went like ghosts, now here, now gone again, half glimpsed through a closing door. They brought presents and clamoured for commemorative photographs with their host. The children among them, caught up in the spirit of Christmas and a party whose end was not yet in sight, romped timidly or brashly through the crumbling passages and winding stairways of the hall like the children of Alain-Fournier's lost domain.

One of the last to arrive was Ethan Usherwood, hot on the heels of his father, Guy, Gerald's youngest son. Ethan turned up on Christmas Eve after driving down from Quedgeley, just outside Gloucester. Of all the Usherwoods, Ethan lived nearest to Woodmancote, to which he was a regular and welcome visitor. But he worked as a detective chief inspector with Gloucestershire Constabulary, and had only been able to escape in time for the main party by dint of lavish arse-licking, some judicious Christmas presents, and a promise to put in some heavy overtime in January. The homicide case he was working on had gone dead, and he hadn't been in the least unhappy to put it to bed for the Christmas season.

'Sorry, Granddad,' he said as he walked up to Gerald in the Bentham Room, Woodmancote's illustrious central chamber, with its Elizabethan wainscoting and the remarkable Grinling Gibbons fireplace. The old room was festooned today with every possible decoration. Ivy, holly, mistletoe and sprigs of berried juniper hung in swags across the walls, their dark green colours setting off hundreds of golden balls suspended from them. Stockings hung from the mantelpiece. On little tables around the room stood bottles of home-made sloe gin, all lovingly laid down by Gerald several months earlier and ready, as in every year, to bring warmth, cheer and inebriation to the Christmas festivities.

'Got a mind to put you over my knee and spank you, young man,' Gerald replied. His eyes twinkled. Ethan knew his grandfather was unpredictable. He might have taken his late arrival as an affront. 'It's the same every year. Last to turn up, first to leave.'

'A spanking would constitute an assault on a police officer. You wouldn't want me to arrest you on Christmas Eve, would you? You wouldn't want to be hauled down to the nick, surely?'

Gerald cuffed him on the shoulder. He was clearly in a good mood this evening. Ethan smiled back. With a younger man, he'd have hugged him, but not with his grandfather.

'Come with me. Have some sloe gin,' said Gerald, grabbing him by the sleeve and steering him to a table on one side of the mantelpiece, right next to the nativity. 'It's better than usual this year,' he went on. 'Bigger berries and weeks early. Longer time to stew. It's got a bite to it.'

He poured his grandson a glass and waited to see his response. Ethan took a couple of sips and nodded enthusiastically.

'It *is* good,' he declared, and took a longer sip. 'Just the thing after the drive. It's freezing outside.'

'Didn't I tell you to bring your young woman along, boy?'

Ethan imagined a wagging finger, and remembered Christmases long gone. 'Why didn't you bring that chum of yours from school?' 'Where's your sister?' 'Where's that girl I've heard so much about?' 'Where's that wife of yours?'

Yes, Ethan thought: where is my sister? Where is that wife of mine? A verse of Byron's that had been used in Abi's funeral service drifted through his mind.

And thou art dead, as young and fair,
As aught of mortal birth;
And form so soft, and charms so rare,
Too soon returned to Earth!

They'd used the same verse at Pauline's funeral years before. His sister had died of leukaemia at fifteen, two years his junior. Before her illness, she had dazzled everyone in sight. A glorious future had been predicted. All in the grave now, her name chiselled in stone above it.

Abigail had been twenty-five when she died. It was eight years ago now. He'd been thirty. Now, almost forty, he could not bear the starkness of mornings or the oncoming of sleep. The thought of her at such times tunnelled through his brain like a worm that had no end.

'I don't have a young woman, Granddad.'

Gerald frowned.

'I'd understood–'

'You understood wrong. Women don't stay long with me. I'm married to my job, they all say that.'

'Man needs a woman, boy. You should know that by now. Even when we were out in the desert on some bloody awful trip, we'd head straight for the Berka when we got back. Or have a night out with one of those gals from the MTC. You don't have to

17

love them, you know.'

Ethan smiled and said nothing. Women were one of his grandfather's obsessions. He'd been married to his wife Edith for over forty years, but that hadn't stopped him taking up with a steady string of 'lady friends'. Edith had died fifteen years earlier, forgiving him, and it was said he hadn't seen another woman once since then.

One of the grandchildren, an Ellis by the look of him, ambled up and pulled Gerald away. Ethan stayed by the nativity, a fine Arts and Crafts job with Italian pieces. His father found him there, and dragged him off to join the melee of aunts and cousins, half of whom he'd never met before.

After dinner, the younger children, all in a state of high excitement, their thoughts fixed on chimneys and men in white beards, were sent to bed or driven off to the village. The rest of the party settled down in the Long Room, with its selection of battered armchairs, sofas, and window seats. Old friendships were revived, old animosities buried or given new life.

'You must be Ethan,' said a voice beside him. He looked round to find a woman standing next to his chair. A dark-haired woman in her mid- to late-twenties. He did not recognise her, and yet something about her was familiar. He got to his feet.

'Afraid so,' he said. 'You must be...?'

She laughed.

'You haven't a clue, have you?'

He shook his head.

'You're familiar, but I don't think we can have met.'

'Of course we have. Think hard.'

He scrutinised her features. Short black hair, green eyes that danced, pale cheeks, a full mouth that might have been made from cherries. As he struggled to place her, he realised he wasn't dealing with memory at all, but with the surprising clarity of her face, its beauty and the secret claim it seemed to make on him, whether from the past or the present.

'I'm Sarah,' she said. 'Your niece, in case you've forgotten. We last met when I was ten years old. Your parents brought you down to Canterbury. I thought you were terribly grand. In fact, I had a crush on you for weeks, you were my divine creature next to Mr Boko, my pony.'

He looked at her, and the memory flooded back. The pony had been piebald and short-winded.

'You've changed a lot,' he said.

'Thank you.'

He shook his head.

'I didn't say you'd changed for the better.'

'Ethan, when I was ten I was a geeky little girl with bad teeth. Old Boko looked better than I did. Surely I've improved since then.'

He thought back to the impression he had formed back then, when she was ten and he was twenty.

'You're right,' he said. 'You have improved. Quite a lot, actually.'

He looked at her admiringly. If only the rest of the family were as elegant and poised, he thought.

'Sit down again,' she said. 'I'll pull up a chair. We have eighteen years to catch up on.'

Two hours later, they'd gone about ten years down the line and were just settling in to the next eight when Ethan's father got to his feet.

'It's half past eleven, everybody. Those who want to go to midnight mass had better get a move on. St Benedict's isn't at all large, so there'll be standing room only if we get there late.'

As though summoned by him, a magus in tweeds, the bells of the parish church started clanging through the still night. As though angels had come to Earth. Or, some thought later, demons in the disguise of angels.

Hats and coats were fetched, galoshes grabbed from the hall, little groups formed. The road between the hall and the church had been cleared earlier that day. While the older folk cadged lifts, anyone below the age of sixty walked, and soon a crocodile of worshippers crept down the icy path, their way lit by the gentle fall of moonlight as it glittered on icicles and varnished the snow. Ahead, the lights of the little church shone out like beacons on a world become a virgin filled with God. Even the solid band of non-believers shivered, not from cold, but the mere beauty of the scene. As they drew near the church, the sound of singing reached them across the snow.

Sarah took Ethan's arm and stood with him at the rear throughout the service. The parish choir sang valiantly, carol after carol booming through the decorated nave, medieval songs mingling with modern lullabies, as though all was at peace in the world. They sang against the darkness and the cold, against grey misery and black grief. The coming birth of the new god seemed to exorcise all evil from the world, to draw a line between past and present, darkness and the coming light.

Ethan watched and listened, joining in the hymns when called upon, remembering, trying to forget. Sarah slipped her hand through his arm. She'd heard of his demons, of the night that shadowed his days. And though she did not believe in angels or powers or principalities, nor worship a god in a manger, she prayed for him.

Gerald and his old mate Chips had stayed behind at the hall, along with half a dozen of the seriously old brigade. Leaving the others to a round of bridge, the two old soldiers went upstairs to Gerald's study. Chips stepped for the first time into a cluttered room where the master of Woodmancote kept a lifetime's souvenirs, some scattered across desks and tables, others locked away in dark cabinets or shoved into drawers. The walls were lined from floor to ceiling with bookshelves, these latter crammed with a higgledy-piggledy collection of books. The volumes were of every colour, size and binding; some stood straight between the shelves, dozens were laid horizontally across their fellows. On the floor, piles of books had grown like stalagmites, some built into tall towers, others crumpled as though they had rested on a geological fault and come to grief. The study was the inner sanctum of the house, a hideaway to which few outside the family had ever been admitted.

On either side of a wide fireplace sat two easy chairs, old, battered and, to tell the truth, no longer very comfortable, save for the air of habitude and familiarity they exuded. To these the former comrades repaired. On his way, Gerald picked up a bottle of his beloved Benromach, which he sat on a low table between them. Two tumblers and a jug of water had been placed there earlier by Mrs Salgueiro, the Portuguese housekeeper.

It was over ten years since the pair had last

met. In that time, old friends had grown ill, and some had died. There were no more annual reunions, hadn't been in years. Memories once sharp as blades were blunted now, but if much of the past had blurred in their minds, the time they had spent together in the deserts of North Africa was as if it had been yesterday. As they talked between sips of whisky and puffs on their foul-smelling pipes, the past came alive for them, a living thing, as vivid to one as to the other, Gerald's recollections sparking off anecdotes from his friend, Chips's store of off-colour jokes bringing back long days and nights when death had seemed a likely thing, and a moment like this beyond all credence.

'Do you keep them by you still?' Chips asked after his third tumbler of whisky.

Gerald nodded.

'Here,' he said. 'Where they've always been.'

'Who will have them after you?'

A shrug.

'Don't know. Haven't thought. Maybe a museum. Couldn't say.'

'You know we ruled that out,' said Chips, raising the glass to his lips. He was a tall man, somewhat stooped now, but wiry, as if his muscles had not lost their flexibility and strength.

'And you?' Gerald asked. 'And the others?'

Chips shrugged.

'They're happy for you to hold on to them. But you're getting old; we're all getting old. It's time to find a keeper. We've talked of this many times before. We have to talk of it now.'

Gerald looked at his old friend. So many years had passed, it was hard to believe how close they had grown during the years of fighting. They'd stuck together, all of them, through the gross inhumanity of the war and its dreary aftermath. Someone had nicknamed them The Invincibles; but after Leary was killed by a landmine, the name had dropped out of common use.

'Do you mean tonight?' Gerald murmured. 'I thought perhaps to wait until the festivities are over. Till they all leave. Maybe Donaldson will come after all. Skinner possibly. They were both invited. The roads have been blocked, they may not have made it through. You were lucky.'

Chips ran a hand over his cheeks, his fingers scraping the stubble. He'd worn a beard when he was younger, but shaved it in middle age, once it started to show traces of grey and white.

'What about the girl?' he asked.

'Girl? Which girl?'

'Don't be provocative. The one I saw tonight. You know perfectly well which girl I mean.'

Gerald nodded.

24

'Sometimes I forget. There have been so many girls. In any case, she isn't a girl, not any longer. She's a grown woman. You can't have missed that.'

'Does she know?'

Gerald poured a little water into his glass and sipped anxiously. His liver had been playing up recently; Doc Burns had told him to ease up on the spirits. He shook his head.

'No,' he said. 'Not yet. Haven't told her. She's not ready yet. When the time comes, old boy. You know that.'

Their cheeks flushed, their hair coated in rime frost, their breath became plumes of mist against the lamplight, the guests returned to Woodmancote Hall. They came in groups of two and three, laughing, chatting earnestly, full of Christmas spirit. Ethan escorted Sarah again, and she held on to him tightly, her arm locked through his, fearful of a spill in the oversized Wellington boots she'd picked up for the walk. Her head was filled with carols and her lips, when seen in the light, were blue with cold. She talked volubly, answering his questions, piquing his curiosity. They spoke of books and films and journeys, of parents and cousins, of the numerous times their paths had almost crossed. It was too soon to speak of his dead wife or her brother, committed to a mental hospital at twenty-one and unlikely to leave it. By some instinct grown of adversity or conscience, they knew there would be time for all that later.

Indoors, there was much puffing and panting and stamping of frozen feet. Compacted snow fell on doormats and began to melt.

Senhora Salgueiro had warmed mince pies and set out mulled wine in the drawing room. The adults crowded round the table, ravenous from cold and the rigours of standing so long on the uncarpeted stones of the church. The older children, who had accompanied them, were sent straight off to bed, where hot pies, ginger beer, stockings, and fitful sleep awaited them.

The adults, with less to buoy them up by way of anticipation, felt the effects of age, overeating and a late hour more keenly than their offspring. For all that, sitting round a twinkling Christmas tree in such fine surroundings and in what was, for the most part, good company acted on their sense of nostalgia. They wanted sleep, yet were driven to prolong the moment. One by one, they gave up the struggle.

Ethan showed Sarah upstairs to her room.

'Thank you, Ethan,' she said. 'You've been very kind to a poor relation.'

'Sarah,' he chided, 'I'm a policeman, not a banker.'

'That may be, but I'm an academic, and that means poverty, as in church mouse.'

It was the first time she'd said anything about her work.

'I didn't know that.'

'I only finished my PhD a few years ago, so I'm a lowly lecturer with dismal prospects. I might get a readership when I'm fifty, if I'm lucky. Now, with your permission, I'll retire to bed. To be truthful, I'll crash out. And so will you. Which means Father Christmas won't visit us.'

He leant over and kissed her lightly on the cheek. She blushed and said goodnight before slipping into her room.

It is not known if Father Christmas arrived that night, for the house was woken prematurely, at about five-thirty, by a piercing scream, followed by a series of screams that descended in the space of several seconds to mere sobbing and, at last, to silence. In their rooms, all but the most heavily sleeping of guests sat bolt upright in bed. Ethan was the first to his feet and the first in the corridors.

The screams, he was certain, had not come from any of the rooms in his immediate vicinity nor, indeed, from the attic floor at all. They had been located somewhere below, on the second floor. Wrapped only in a light dressing gown and shivering in the bitter cold, he hurried for the narrow staircase. As he started down it, he heard other doors opening in the corridor behind.

As he came through the doorway that led onto the floor below, he became aware that a commotion had begun. Several of the bedroom doors stood wide open, and half a dozen guests, all men in pyjamas or dressing gowns, had gathered round a sobbing woman. Mrs Salgueiro, her hair in curlers, her quilted housecoat wrapped tight against the chill air, was being comforted by Ethan's father. From time to time she would exclaim in Portuguese, *'Ai, que medo! Que susto! Os pobres homens!'* then recommence her sobbing.

Guy Usherwood, not knowing what to make of these utterings, sighed with relief when he saw his son coming towards them.

'Father, what's going on?'

'Don't know. I can't get the woman to speak in English. She's had a bad turn, that's obvious. Look at her: she's as white as a sheet and shaking all over.'

At that moment, another door opened, and Sarah stepped into the corridor. She was wearing a black gown trimmed with gold, and her hair was sticking up in post-slumber spikes. Seeing what was amiss, she went up to the weeping woman and put her arms round her, uttering soothing words, trying to calm her.

Bit by bit, the sobs subsided, and the

senhora came a little to herself.

'Senhor Usherwood! His friend. *No gabinete* ... in study. Please...'

She burst into tears again, putting her hands to her face, as though to cover her eyes from some dreadful sight.

Ethan's father, the most senior family member present, made to enter the room, but Ethan stopped him.

'Dad, it's obvious something's wrong. Grandfather may have had a heart attack. I'm more used to this sort of thing than you. Let me go in first.'

His father hesitated, then backed off. Ethan put a hand on the doorknob and turned it reluctantly. If something had happened to his grandfather, it would cut him to the heart. He stepped inside and shut the door behind him.

A couple of lamps had been left alight. The fire had burnt down, however, leaving the room chilly and imperfectly lit. It took Ethan's eyes several moments to adjust to the low lighting. He reached for a light switch near the door, but could not find one. As he recalled, the old study had never been fully lit.

With his dark-accustomed eyes, he scoured the room. And he saw what Senhora Salgueiro had seen, saw what had come close to driving her insane. Hardened as he was to sights of criminal horror and gross domestic violence, nothing in his experience had prepared him for the sight that now met his eyes.

To the right of the curtained window ran a long row of bookcases, divided into narrow sections by a series of fluted oak pillars. To these pillars had been nailed the body of Ethan's grandfather. The Nobel laureate's throat had been sliced right across the windpipe, and his hands had been lifted above shoulder level, where they had been fixed to two pillars with small knives. These must have been rammed home with force, for they held his body hard in place. Ethan could make out signs of blood on other parts of his torso, suggesting that he had been stabbed several times before receiving the *coup de grâce*. Blood soaked the carpet all around him.

Chips Chippendale had been despatched in a different manner. His killer had decapitated him before suspending his body from cords attached to two wall lights, then set his head at his feet. The eyes had been removed and placed on a china plate that sat next to the head. A pool of blood had gushed from the severed torso, and now lay congealed and frozen in the light from a desk lamp.

It was Christmas morning, and Ethan fancied he heard in the heavens a sound of vast, harrowing wings. Not the wings of angels, nor the pinions of cherubim or seraphim, but the coarse leather wings of demons. He shook his head, knowing he heard nothing in truth but the rush of vital blood as it coursed dizzy through his brain.

Taking a deep breath that seared his lungs with the cold morning air, he went to the study door and opened it a fraction. He slipped through the opening, shutting the door firmly behind him, and turned to face the expectant crowd of relatives that had assembled in the corridor outside.

PART ONE

'The hidden city of Wardabaha is white like a dove, and on its gate is carved a bird. Take in your hand the key in the beak of the bird, then open the door of the city. Enter, and there you will find great riches, also the king and queen sleeping in their castle. Do not approach them, but take the treasure.'

From the fifteenth-century Arabic magical treatise, *Kitab al-la'ali al-makhfiyya.*

CHAPTER ONE

The Shifting Sands

The Western Desert
Libya
16th May 1942

The sandstorm came in from the south shortly after noon. It had been preceded by the hot wind the local Arabs called a *qibli*, a searing, all-engulfing torment that seemed to blow straight from the deepest pits of hell, burning and suffocating everything it came in contact with. They had sat out *qiblis* before now, wasted days during which all you could do was endure, grit your teeth, swear, sweat, and lie as still as possible in temperatures as high as 118°F.

They'd been struggling through this particular *qibli* for the second day when Corporal Skinner had cut loose with a string of profanities enough to scorch even this overheated air.

'I do not fucking believe this' were the first intelligible words he uttered. He'd said them so often, so many times before, that no one paid him the slightest bit of notice.

'Lieutenant,' he said, 'I think you should sit up and take a gander.'

Lt Usherwood groaned and crawled out from the low camouflage canvas under which they'd been taking shelter.

'Sorry, sir. Went for a pee, sir. Thought you should see this.'

'What's up?' the commander asked, his tired voice little more than a drawl.

Skinner just pointed. On the southern horizon, the light of midday was giving way to darkness, as black clouds roiled and tumbled across the desert sand. Gerald Usherwood snatched up his long-distance glasses and trained them on the clouds. Not clouds at all, of course, but huge billows of sand that stretched across the horizon from east to west, driven by a high wind that was picking up speed with every second it raced towards them.

'Get everyone back on board,' the lieutenant ordered. 'It'll be on us in minutes.'

'We're not too far from the RP, skipper. Should we try to head back while we can? Supplies are running short, and this could go on for days.'

Usherwood shook his head.

'There's too much risk of losing our way in this. We won't be able to take our bearings at night, and I don't trust the sun compass in a storm. There'll be time enough to head for the RP once this blows over. Hurry and get some canteens into the cabs.'

The rallying point for the two-vehicle patrol was just over one hundred miles away, at Rebiana. They'd gone out from base at Kufra Oasis as a full patrol of six Chevvys, but the two trucks under Lt Usherwood's command had carried on further west, deep into the Rebiana Sand Sea, on a search for wells. The others had gone north to Taiserbo, where there was talk of German forward units reconnoitring behind British lines.

Something big was coming up. It had been all the talk in Cairo two weeks earlier, and there was a buzz at Kufra, the western HQ for the Long Range Desert Group which had been taken from the Italians just over a year before.

The word was that Rommel planned a push on the Gazala line along the coast. The trouble for anyone trying to hold that line was simple: you could fix one end on the sea and defend it there against all comers, but down south it ran into open desert all the way down to deepest Africa. Jerry could slip down below your defences and twist round to spike you in the rear. R Patrol was probing for lightweight German manoeuvres, while Usherwood's Sandboys were trying to open a path further west than anyone had tried before.

They were looking for wells and hunting an oasis, a lost paradise called Ain Suleiman: Solomon's Spring. This secret place had long been the stuff of legend. The Bedouin said it had once provided the water for the magical city of Wardabaha, built in the sands by King Solomon, the source of all magic in Arab tradition. According to some blue-veiled Tuareg of the Fezzan, it still existed and was inhabited by a tribe of their brethren, a branch of the Kel Ajjer of Ghat. But no modern explorer had set eyes on the place. It was on no map, save for a map of the mind, where it floated, now here, now there. At the Royal Geographical Society, men in sober suits made fun of Ain Suleiman and its hidden city of magic. But Gerald Usherwood had believed in it. He'd learnt enough Tamasheq to speak with the Tuareg in their own tongue, something the men in Lowther Lodge were incapable of doing, and he had come to trust them. Ain Suleiman was there, they said, but no one knew the way. It was in the worst part of the sands, they said, it was unreachable by camel, it was probably silted up by now. He knew they were hiding something, and guessed they knew their way there well enough but thought it wise to avoid en-tanglements with the Italians or Germans or British. If they were hiding something, he reckoned that meant there was something to hide.

They had barely put their sand goggles

over their eyes when the storm struck. One moment the sky was bright blue, the next they found themselves in a thick haze that dropped visibility down to around twenty feet.

Closing the doors and windows kept the full blast of the sandstorm out, but the dust was like powder and crept in through every crack, chink, and cranny it could find. As time passed, a fine coating of sand covered every surface inside the trucks. The patrol wrapped their *gutras* tightly round their faces, but the sand was relentless. It worked its way inside the goggles, into ears and noses and throats, through clothing, down through ammo boots, where it irritated horribly.

Gerald had been through so many sandstorms now he thought his lungs had turned to desert. He knew there was nothing to be done but to grit your teeth, keep your watering eyes closed, and sit it out. This was a bad one, he knew it straight away, one of the worst he'd seen. It could last a day or a week, there was no telling.

All the other members of the patrol were old hands, and they'd seen their fair share of the desert winds. No one was chosen for the LRDG who wasn't able to put up with a bit of discomfort. Whether they were British, New Zealanders, Aussies or Indians, they were that strange species of human being for whom the empty wastes and searing heat of the Sahara was more home than the Home Counties, Wellington or Calcutta. They positively longed for the silence and the ever-present danger. So they sat and waited, keeping radio silence, singing the latest hits and telling long tales of battles they had fought and women they had bedded.

The storm did not let up for three days. When it ended, it did so suddenly, shortly after 6 a.m. on the third day.

'Thank God for that,' said Gerald. Back home in Gloucestershire, he had no time for a deity, and attended church only because he was the local squire and knew it was bad form to let the side down, the side being the Usherwood family. But here in the long vistas of the desert, beneath night skies thick with the eternal light of endless galaxies, he became a believer. Had he not been brought up in the C of E, he'd have made a happy Muslim ascetic, his heart grown fanatical from the harshness of the empty sands.

Each truck had a sun compass perched above the dashboard. Along with the latest RAF navigational tables by day and theodolites by night, the sun compass allowed patrols to navigate through uncharted territory. It took moments to get their bearings again, and longer to dig the trucks out of the blown sand, using sand mats. At last, they brushed themselves down and headed west again.

A barrier of *seif* dunes, all over three hundred feet high, pushed them further south, away from the route they'd planned to stay on. They drove through a waste devoid of life, beneath a cruel sky empty of birds or planes. Somewhere to the north, a war was in progress, but down here it seemed that the guns had fallen silent. It was as if the war had ended and all that remained was this desolation, this all-pervasive death.

Dusk had started to fall when Staff Sergeant Chippendale, who was riding shotgun on board Gerald's Chevvy, gave a low whistle. Max Chippendale's great talent – and his main qualification for the LRDG – was his remarkable eyesight. He'd been scanning the horizon ahead with glasses, calmly surveying the sands each time they reached the crest of a dune, before the controlled drop to the west flank.

He put his hand urgently on the driver's arm.

'Hold your horses, you great lummox,' he shouted. 'Weary' Leary, the Kiwi trooper Gerald had borrowed from T patrol, turned the wheel sharply, bringing the truck to a stop just short of the precipice in front.

'What is it?' the lieutenant asked from his seat behind.

'Not sure yet, skipper. Something out there. Give us a moment.'

Chippendale, an Oxford Classics don before hostilities began, scanned and re-scanned the landscape ahead. He pursed his lips and murmured something inaudible. That was about as enthusiastic as Chips Chippendale ever got. He passed the glasses back to Gerald, who jumped out onto the slipping surface of the dune.

'Middle distance, skip. Looks like we've found it.'

And so they had. They'd been heading straight for the oasis. Without the storm, they might have gone on further to the north, along their original trajectory, and missed it entirely.

'Ain Suleiman,' whispered Gerald. 'Solomon's Spring.'

Little did he guess what else lay buried in the great sand sea. A secret much greater than a mere oasis or a hidden city, more portentous than a desert route for the fighting and winning of a war, more deadly than Rommel's tanks or the battalions of Hitler's Reich.

A puff of wind lifted a plume of sand lower down the western flank of the great dune. Gerald climbed back into the truck.

'Let's go down and take a look,' he said.

Leary swung the wheel, engaged first gear, and let the Chevvy topple over the crest to start its slow descent back down to the desert floor.

Ain Suleiman waited for them, wrapped in its age-old silence, the most remote of human habitations.

CHAPTER TWO

Ain Suleiman

The Western Desert
18th May

As they drove down to the oasis, the sleepy settlement burst into vibrant life, woken by the roar of the patrol's engines. Dogs barked. Men rushed out of low *zaribas*, wrapping their blue veils over their faces. Others ran from further off, where they'd been tending to the camels. They were followed by women in black shawls, and children of all sizes, some clothed, the youngest naked.

With a jolt, Gerald realised he and his men might be the first outsiders these people had ever set their eyes on, and that the trucks, rushing down from the dune towards them, must seem objects of horror, grim monsters from the depths of whatever hell they believed in. He ordered Leary to stop, and signalled to Bill Donaldson in the following Chevvy to pile on the brakes as well. They slid to a stop, their tyres digging hard into the soft sand, where they sank almost to the axles.

'Switch off the engine,' Gerald ordered. In the car behind, Donaldson followed suit. A silence fell, as deep as the ocean and as wide, broken only by the braying of camels and the barking of the dogs. Above the oasis, hundreds of little birds flew in circles. In the west, the sun was changing hue as it began its descent to the heat haze that lay stretched across the horizon.

The skipper stepped out, calling on the others to get down too, without weapons.

'Don't do anything to startle them,' he said. 'Let me do the talking. Clark, stay here and cover us with the machine gun.'

They walked forward. Gerald went in front, striding confidently toward the group of Tuareg men who had formed a defensive line in front of their women and children. They all wore the *tagelmoust*, the elaborate indigo-coloured headdress that covers the head and face but for the eyes.

Gerald turned and beckoned Max Chippendale forward.

'Max, see the Johnny in front? He belongs to the Imashaghen, the ruling class. The shorter man on his right is their Anislem. The preacher. He's the one to watch out for. If there's going to be trouble, he'll be behind it.'

The Tuareg waited patiently for the five soldiers to reach them. They were tall men, lean, with the keen grey eyes of desert travellers. Behind a handful of Imashaghen stood their vassals, while a group of black slaves cowered with the women and children near the huts. Gerald made a swift calculation. The settlement must number around one hundred souls and some thirty camels.

Walking into the oasis, the soldiers, dry after so long in the open sands, felt the air around them change. The desiccated, searing desert heat turned moist and soft, washing their lungs as if in oil from the olive trees that grew on the far side of the little lake. Gerald breathed in deeply. He knew he would only have moments in which to convince the Tuareg leader of their honourable intentions. At the back of his mind, he calculated what proportion of their rations they could afford to hand over as a token of goodwill. Each of the Tuareg men wore a short sword slung across his left thigh, and Gerald knew they were fierce fighters who could use even these simple weapons to great effect. He noticed that two of the Imashaghen carried rifles over their shoulders, Italian Carcano M91/38 carbines.

If trouble did break out, he and his men had their service pistols, and Teddy Clark was a steady hand on the Browning. But the last thing he wanted was a massacre. If he had to choose between the lives of his patrol and those of anyone trying to kill them, he knew he could make the choice. But he wasn't sure if he could live with it afterwards.

'*Al-salam 'alaykum,*' he called out, using the universal Muslim greeting, and adding in Tamasheq, '*Ma toulid?*'

The man in the centre, inches taller than his brethren, continued to survey him from behind the blue veil, his eyes boring into him, looking neither to right nor left. Gerald stopped and waited for a response.

The Anislem, a Qur'an clutched ostentatiously in his right hand, bent sideways and whispered briefly in his lord's ear. Behind Gerald, the rest of the patrol had come to a halt. He could almost feel their edginess, or perhaps it was just his own. These were men with whom he'd shared the most intense days of his young life. They had fought together; pissed on the same sand; picked fleas from each others' bodies and lice from one another's hair; gone in search of women together in the Berka. They had headed into the desert together time after time, and come out alive again time after time.

Gerald waited patiently for a reply. The men of the desert lived an almost timeless existence, in a world where little changed from year to year, from century to century. No Tuareg would let himself be hurried.

But the headman had made up his mind.

"*Alaykum al-salam,*' he responded. '*Al-khayr ras, al-hamdu li'llah.*'

Gerald spoke haltingly, explaining who he was and where he and his men had come from. '*Min al-Qahira,*'he said, 'from Cairo.' Even this deep in the desert, Cairo was a legend. The Tuareg leader listened impassively, neither warmth nor coldness showing in his eyes. The other Imashaghen watched. No one fidgeted or shuffled or raised a hand to swat the flies that buzzed all round them. These were Kel Tamasheq: as straight as guardsmen, they looked ahead without visible emotion.

'A people have come to this land who are no friends of the Muslims,' Gerald said. 'They despise the Arabs because they belong to an inferior race, they hate the blacks because their skins are not white, they look down on the Berbers and the Tibu and the Kel Tamasheq because they ride on camels. In my language, they are called Germans. My people have come here to wage war with them. If they win this war, they will tear down the mosques, and kill the learned, and make slaves of the Muslims. They will send soldiers into the Ténéré, into the deep sands, they will carry off your wives and children to be slaves in the land they come from, where it is always dark and cold.

47

'My people are not a Muslim people, but we are the greatest nation on earth, and we have been friends to the Muslims wherever we have gone. We have come here to speak with you. We need your help to fight our war, and we bring tokens of our friendship.'

He went on like this for about ten minutes, and not once did the Tuareg betray their feelings. For all he knew, they might be laughing at him. Or planning how to kill him.

The Anislem, a man of learning who had studied the Qur'anic sciences and the Traditions of the Prophet in the now-decayed schools of Timbuktu, watched the infidels intently. His rank was clear from the leather wallets he wore slung across his shoulders, containing a copy of the Qur'an and other sacred writings. From his left hand hung an amber rosary, whose beads he turned and twisted through gnarled fingers. His name was Shaykh Harun agg Da'ud, and he had lived for many years among the Kel Adrar at Ghadames further north. He had long served the people of Ain Suleiman, performing marriages, burying the dead, writing down verses of the Qur'an to wear as amulets, inscribing talismans in the ancient Tifinagh script, guarding the secrets of the oasis. He knew that these strangers, like the Italians he'd met in Ghadames and the French he'd seen in Timbuktu, were a threat to his prestige and authority.

When Gerald came to a halt, the headman remained silent for a time. He had heard rumours of a war far to the north, but knew nothing of its currents and did not fear its outcome. Perhaps the stranger was telling the truth, perhaps he lied: he was some sort of unbeliever after all. These were the first unbelievers he had ever set eyes on.

Gerald whispered to Leary, telling him to go back to the trucks with Bill Donaldson, and to bring several items back with them. The silence continued.

When they returned, Leary and Donaldson carried an armful apiece. They laid their offerings on the ground in front of the headman, and stepped back. One by one, Gerald presented an odd mixture of military supplies: two pairs of chapplies, the desert sandals every trooper was issued with; a spare Jerry can; a pair of sand goggles for the headman; the desert stove from Donaldson's vehicle; a folding tent; and a selection of desert rations.

Last of all, Gerald unstrapped his Smith and Wesson .38 and handed it, holster and all, to the headman.

'I will teach you how to fire and reload it,' he said.

The headman did not move. Even the poorest Tuareg had his pride. Gerald waited. On the dunes, sand danced in a light breeze.

The fronds on the palm trees whispered. Somewhere, a child cried raucously. It would not be hard to take this place by force, thought Gerald. Each Chevvy carried two air-cooled .30 Browning machine guns. A Waffen-SS commander might have used them. Gerald fervently prayed he would not have to.

The Tuareg leader stretched out his hand and took the weapon.

'Thank you,' he said. 'It is much appreciated. As are all these gifts.'

'There will be more and better if you will give us your help.'

'My name is Si Musa agg Isa Iskakkghan. I am lord of this oasis. You and your men are welcome to stay. As for these other matters, we shall talk of them later.'

At that moment, a young woman who had been standing with the others in the rear came running forward. She was visibly distressed, and when Gerald looked more closely, he saw that some of the other women were agitated too.

'Si Musa,' she called out. 'Ask the strangers if they have brought medicine. Perhaps they will know how to save our son.'

Musa did not turn to look at her. The woman was dark-skinned and pretty, with flashing teeth and large eyes that were red from weeping.

'Go back to the women, A'isha,' her husband said. 'Shaykh Harun has prayed for our child. He will pray again later. If it is God's will, Yaqub will live. If not, he will die.'

But A'isha did not budge.

'Let the strangers prove their power, Si Musa. If our child lives, it will be God's way of showing you that they can be trusted. If he dies...' she sighed '...then they will have to leave.'

Back among the dwellings, the crying of the child redoubled in force. The later sunlight raked the oasis like a purple claw. In the distance, the sand shimmered, conjuring up a mirage, as if crenellated castles danced on the skyline where the dunes and the sky met one another.

Si Musa, inwardly as frightened for his son and heir as his wife, conceded. He turned on his heel and walked back to the encampment, his wife following. Gerald signalled to Donaldson. Donaldson, apart from his driving and navigational skills, was the patrol's medic. He was a Scot who'd been studying medicine at Edinburgh when war broke out.

'What's up, skipper?' he asked.

'Fetch the first-aid kit, Bill. Be quick about it. Their child is sick.'

In the headman's hut, it took only moments for Donaldson to make his diagnosis. The air was cooling as night approached, but he could still feel sweat trickling from his forehead.

'Tetanus,' he announced. 'Quite advanced, by the look of it. The jaw's rigid, and the bairn has lost weight, I daresay. Ask the mother how long it is since he got the wound.'

He pointed to a wide, unhealed cut on the boy's forearm. It was red and puffy, and the child – he seemed between one and a half and two – had clearly made matters worse by scratching it.

Gerald asked, but no one could tell him exactly how long. In the desert, they counted seasons and years and sometimes months; but days and weeks meant nothing.

In one corner, the holy man had insinuated himself. He watched, his eyes never straying far from the dying child. Beneath his breath, he murmured something, whether a prayer or a curse, Gerald could not tell.

Donaldson unwrapped a glass vial of antitoxin and injected it into the child's arm. The mother, already hopeless, made no protest. Si Musa agg Isa watched the priest, his shrewd eyes seeking out what was hidden in the old man's heart.

When they left the hut, the sun was setting like a ball of liquid fire, its hues of crimson, rose, gold and turquoise shredded by a billion spores of fine sand that turned them to greens and ochres, vermilions and russets. Fires were lit, using camel dung for fuel. The desert stove was rolled out, and Skinner got it going, surrounded by a bevy of giggling Tuareg women who had never seen a man sully his hands with domestic labour.

A camel was singled out and slaughtered, its hide stripped and set aside, its carcass cut into six parts, and everything that was not eaten preserved for other functions. Bread was baked on fires laid on the sand. Soon, a smell of cooking meat filled the cold night air. Leary showed his hosts how to grill the meat on the petrol-fuelled desert stove. Gerald ordered more rations broken out and made ready for the meal. Bully beef, tinned peaches, rice, potatoes, ten cans of baked beans – great sacrifices that they knew they would regret in the days to come.

In the hut, the baby fell asleep. Donaldson looked tense. He said it would be touch and go, and feared the consequences of his having attempted to treat the child at all.

Elsewhere through the encampment, families were preparing less palatable meals. Tonight's banquet was a sort of state dinner, reserved for the Imashaghen and their guests. The Anislem chose not to partake of the infidel fare, declaring it *haram* and forbidden to Muslims, but he was overruled by Si Musa, who said the food had come from Egypt and that the Egyptians were a Muslim people. Shaykh Harun slunk away to find food more fitting his status, but Gerald noticed that he moved back again under cover of darkness, and remained on the edge of the circle, no doubt listening intently to all that was said.

They ate well. What would have seemed poor rations in another time and place made a great feast for poor desert dwellers and soldiers. The camel was stringy, the meat was undercooked, and sand had drifted into everything. But no one complained. They washed the gritty food down with green tea, brewed three times, each brew weaker and sweeter than the one before.

The conversation was choppy, limited by the great linguistic gulf that separated the soldiers from the Tuareg. Questions were relayed through Gerald and Si Musa, answers given in the same way. It was cumbersome, but both parties gained a little understanding of one another. Throughout the meal, however, all participants were aware of a dull underlying tension, of the silence that emanated from the headman's hut, of the baby that did not cry and whose death might at any moment be pronounced. The Tuareg passed round pinches of snuff from little containers they carried round their necks, and Donaldson raided the cigarette ration, handing over packs of Senior Service coffin nails as though they were sweeties. Some of the Tuareg had smoked before, others subsided into fits of coughing.

There was music afterwards, and dancing, the men in one group, the women in another, their swaying movements lit by fires fuelled by dung laced with petrol. Beneath a sky so packed with stars it seemed a dome of silver and ebony, the sharp percussive notes of the *tindi* echoed through the sands like gunshots, softened only by the gentle scraping of two *imzads*. And then, out of nowhere, appeared a man wearing a white veil and carrying a flute. One by one, the dancers stopped and the instruments fell silent. The flute player began to play, softly at first, then with growing vigour, as if he wooed the stars; and as he played an ochre moon appeared above the horizon and rose into the shining firmament. As it climbed into the night sky, it shed its ochre tones and grew silver like the stars.

The music stopped, everyone clapped, and it was time for bed. The flute player came across to Gerald, and said he looked forward to speaking at greater length in the morning. It was Si Musa. Gerald said goodnight, and explained that he and his men planned to spend the night, as they always did, next to their vehicles.

They moved the Chevvys onto flat ground on the other side of the oasis from the

Tuareg huts.

'Time for a powwow, gentlemen,' said Gerald as soon as they'd checked things over and were rolling out their sleeping bags on the sand. It was bitterly cold: the day's heat had long vanished. Moonlight lay across the dunes, giving them the appearance of sheets of ice. Wrapped up in their Tropal coats, the men were tired and cold and looking forward to getting back to Cairo. A groan went up as Gerald spoke. Powwows could stretch into the night.

'We've got to radio back to base tonight. If anything happens to us, this will all have been wasted if we don't get the coordinates through. We'll take an astrofix now. The rest of you can be setting the aerials up.'

Skinner, Clark, Donaldson and Leary clustered round the radio car, setting two tall poles to front and rear, rigging the support lines, and stringing the dipole antenna between the poles. While they were struggling to get the aerial set up, Gerald and Max Chippendale took out the theodolite and screwed it onto its tripod.

Max put a wide wooden board beneath the tripod legs and spent the next five minutes with a plumb bob trying to get the instrument absolutely flat.

'Who the fuck thought you could use one of these on sand?' he swore, as he did every time he had to get it straight. He fiddled

56

with the legs, tightening and loosening, while Gerald lit the tripod with his Kemp-thorne torch, one he'd 'liberated' from an Aussie patrol.

'OK, skipper. It's as plumb as I can get it.'

He put his eye to the theodolite's telescope and picked out a star.

'Up,' he called out as the star moved across the lens. Gerald noted the time, using his chronometer.

Back at the radio car, Leary had his receiver buzzing. He twisted dials until the time signal came through from Big Ben, and Gerald confirmed the coordinates. He dictated a brief message to Leary, who encrypted it and transmitted the result to Kufra.

'Let's have a spot of swing, Weary,' someone said, and other voices joined in, calling for music before they settled down, a desert custom. Leary's wireless ranged from 4.2 to 7.5MHz and could pick up most short-wave broadcasts. He twiddled the dial and caught Glenn Miller's band halfway through 'In the Mood'. Clark found the rum pot and doled out rations to keep the cold at bay. No one declined.

Next thing, Peggy Lee was singing her new hit with the Benny Goodman sextet, 'Full Moon'. Above them, the moon moved majestically through its field of stars, the twenty-eight lunar mansions, through al-

Hak'a, al-Han'a and al-Dhira, past stars and planets named by the Arabs centuries ago. The song ended, and Leary moved the dial again, this time picking up Radio Belgrade. They listened uncomprehending to a barrage of German propaganda, but everyone knew what they were waiting for. They weren't disappointed. A record crackled briefly, then the airwaves were filled with the lush voice of Lale Anderson, the German Angel of the Soldiers.

'Vor der Kaserne
Vor dem grossen Tor
Stand eine Lanterne
Und steht sme noch davor...
Wie einst Lili Marleen.'

For all the English versions that had been recorded, the *auf Deutsch* original was the anthem of all the British troops in the desert. Some hummed, others listened silently. The desert swallowed the music and the silence equally. There was this moment in every day when they sat and thought of home and the nearness of violent death. The song ended, and Leary switched off the wireless.

Gerald drank the last sip of rum and put his mug back on the car. As he did so, he saw a dark figure coming towards the cars from the encampment. He reached for his pistol, then remembered what he'd done with it.

'Chips!' he hissed. 'Someone's coming. Maybe more than one. Tell the others.'

He jumped into the car and crouched behind the Browning. The figure moved rapidly across the sand, half shadow, half reflected moonlight. It didn't seem to be making any effort to conceal itself.

He let the shadow come within several yards of the car, then shouted 'Stop!' in Tamasheq. The figure came to a halt.

'I must speak to your lord.' It was a woman's voice. Relieved, Gerald told her to come forward.

'Is something wrong?' he asked. Donaldson had left the child sleeping after the dancing, and said there was nothing more he could do for him. Either the antitoxin worked or the child died. Had the woman come to tell them he was dead?

'My name is A'isha,' she said. 'Musa agg Isa's wife. Is the doctor here?'

'Donaldson,' called Gerald, 'I think you'd better come over. It's the headman's wife. She wants to speak with you.'

Donaldson's heart was thumping. He knew how much might hinge on this one small life. As he came out of the shadows that encircled the second car, the woman broke away and ran to him, throwing herself onto the sand at his feet and grabbing his legs, sobbing and laughing simultaneously. Amidst the tears and laughter, broken words escaped her lips.

'Bloody hell, Bill, I think the kid pulled through. She thinks you're a miracle worker. Next best thing to God.'

And so it transpired. When she finally collected herself, she told Gerald that her son had come out of his sleep hungry and asking for food. She'd given him some leftovers from the meal, and he'd kept them down. The doctor raised her to her feet and clapped her on the shoulders.

'No one else knows,' she said. 'Just my sisters. I came to tell you first. To thank you for saving his life. I am in your debt. My husband, my son, and myself will for ever be in your debt.'

Flustered, Donaldson said he would come to see the boy right away. But A'isha put up a hand and shook her head.

'He's sleeping again,' she said. 'Before you see him, you must come with me. All of you. You must be rewarded.'

They looked at one another awkwardly, assuming she meant that she would share her sexual favours with them. Gerald explained that they wanted no reward, that hearing of the child's survival was sufficient reward in itself.

She continued to shake her head.

'I know why you came to Ain Suleiman.

Everyone knows. Shaykh Harun says you must be killed before you find what you are looking for. But you have given my son back his life, so I will take you there. I will take you there tonight. It isn't far.'

Gerald looked at her, not understanding.

'We came to find Ain Suleiman. That is all we sought.'

'I know what you came to find,' she said. 'I will show you. The sands have moved in the storm. There is much to see.'

'What is this thing?' Gerald asked.

'It is not a thing,' she said. 'It is a city. The city of Wardabaha. I will walk there with you now. Before the moon sets. I will take you to the hall of the sleepers, where the Old Ones sleep. I cannot go all the way inside, none of us can. But you are angels. Come with me. Come to Wardabaha.'

CHAPTER THREE

The city of *Wardabaha*

Leary stayed by the radio in case base tried to make contact. Skinner had already been placed on sentry duty: he manned one of the Brownings, with a Very flare to hand if it turned out that the whole thing was a ploy on the part of the Tuaregs to raid the cars. The others set out with torches, following A'isha across the silver landscape. Not a word was said by anyone. Their feet sank in the soft sand, leaving impressions that were at once filled by moonlight, like mercury flowing into hollows. A white lizard, startled by the light, ran across their path and vanished.

They did not go far, a quarter of a mile at most. Their minds set on a desert city, on towers and battlements, on domes and minarets, on ancient stairways and the inevitable ruin of things once lovely and blessed, they saw nothing at first. When A'isha's voice rang out, telling them they had arrived, they looked and saw only dunes with more dunes behind them, moonlight with moonlight following.

Then A'isha took Gerald by the arm and led him forward. The others followed, all certain by now that they'd been tricked, that the woman had, out of treachery or high spirits, fooled them or betrayed them. Chips wanted to turn back, thinking the Tuaregs had duped them in order to loot the cars, fearing Leary and Skinner might already be dead. Yet there had been no shooting, no shouts, no hint of any activity behind them.

And then something altered, as though the landscape itself had undergone a great change or things magical become evident to the material eye. Just to his right, Gerald saw what looked like a human figure, a woman draped in clinging fabric. In a flash, he saw she had no head, and in the same moment realised it was a statue. Behind him Max Chippendale whistled.

'Holy Hercules!'

He walked up to it, content to let the moonlight serve for illumination.

'Roman,' he said. 'Roman and this far south, it doesn't make sense.'

'Over here, Dr Chippendale,' called Teddy Clark, reverting quite naturally to the don's civilian title.

Teddy had stumbled on a lion's head carved from marble, its nostrils flared, its eyes wide open, its luxuriant mane sculpted with great delicacy.

They went on, crossing between two dunes, and now a new world opened before their awestruck eyes. Pillars, some broken, others still topped by carvings of acanthus leaves, sprang from the sand. To one side, there was a fallen archway linked to another by a round face surrounded by what seemed to be long, wreathing curls.

'Medusa,' whispered Chippendale. Not curls of hair, he said, but serpents chiselled into it so finely they might yet have moved. Moonlight trickled across the face, blanching it, making it appear lit from within.

Max wandered among the ruins, mesmerised, at every step reminded of the great Roman sites to the north: Leptis Magna, Ptolemais, Sabratha. Libya, known then as Cyrenaica, had been one of the greatest provinces of the Roman Empire, producing grain, livestock, and a vast array of medicinal plants. The trade in silphium alone had made the province rich. Ancient Libya had boasted amphitheatres, baths, forums, villas – all the rich panoply of an imperial success story.

'I'm only guessing at this point,' Max said as he ran his fingers down the fluted side of a rose granite column, 'but I reckon this place dates from sometime after the imperial cult was brought here. Say around AD 70, up through Trajan's rule, maybe to AD 100 or a bit after. This is really a guess, though. There could be much later buildings. There might be anything buried in the sand. It just depends how long this place was active.'

'Is there really no record of a place like this?' Gerald asked.

Max shrugged.

'No idea. I've done my reading about Roman Africa, but I'm no expert. There could be a record, but I've never come across it. All the same, there's something at the back of my mind. Maybe it'll come to me.'

It was Clark who stumbled on the doorway. Young Teddy Clark, a fair-faced lad from Kent, a farmer's son, barely out of school, and lost in a desert of stone and gravel, far from the green fields of his father's farm. His sharp eyes picked it out from the sand, and he ran to it, calling the others to him.

The half-open door lay on the sheltered face of a dune, protected from the prevailing winds. Two fluted rectangular columns stood to either side, rising to over six feet, where they were crossed by a stone lintel on which had been carved an inscription in Greek, partly obscured by sand. At both ends of the lintel the engraver had placed a rosette with six narrow petals, flanked by stylised palm trees.

But it was the door itself that took Max Chippendale's breath away. It was a bronze door made of two halves. On the right-hand panel a skilled hand had limned in gold a faithful likeness of a seven-branched candlestick, and on the left side, matching it in skill and fidelity, the embossed image of a cross, and on this latter, writing in Hebrew. The left-hand side had been pushed back, leaving a narrow opening that a child might have passed through.

Astonished by this incongruity, Max raised his hand to the entablature and brushed away the sand that had stuck to the lintel. One by one, the letters came into view, each chiselled neatly into the stone.

Gerald came up close and stared at the inscription. The others gathered round. A'isha stood to one side, as though frightened to go any closer.

'I don't understand,' said Gerald. 'I thought this was a Roman place. What's a Greek inscription doing up there?'

'Can you read it?' asked Max.

'Not without a dictionary. Never was much good at Greek in school.'

'Well, you might also ask yourself what that Hebrew writing is doing on the cross. That, I'm afraid I cannot help you with. But the Greek's more straightforward. The Romans still used Greek in Egypt and Cyrenaica. There's nothing odd about it at all. It's the Hebrew that's bloody odd, and the candlestick. Jewish obviously. Next to a Christian symbol. Most peculiar.'

'Yes, I can see that. Can you read what it says?'

Donaldson had brought an oil lamp from his car and now held it up. The flickering flame cast light and shadow across the square epigraphy.

Max ran his eyes across the Greek letters, thought for a moment, then translated.

In the second year of the emperor Marcus Ulpius Trajanus, on the seventh of Tammuz, this doorway of the proseuchê was erected by the congre-

gation of the Ebonyim of Ain Shelomo by order of the archisynagogos Dositheos, son of Ammonius and the archiprostates Zenion, son of Zoilos.

'That's about it,' he said.

'When was that?' asked Teddy Clark. 'The second year of Trajan.'

Max did a quick calculation.

'Sometime in 100 AD. Trajan became emperor in January 98. The month is odd, though. Tammuz. It's a Jewish month. If I'm not mistaken, *proseuchê* is an alternative word for a synagogue. This Dositheos would have been the leader of the synagogue.'

'It can't be a synagogue,' commented Donaldson. 'There's the wee matter of a cross on the door.'

Max shrugged.

'I think you may be in for a surprise,' he answered.

'What's that mean?'

'I'm not sure. But I think we have to go inside, don't you?'

They looked at one another, at faces dim in the moonlight, then at the darkness in the doorway.

'Will it open, do you suppose?' asked Gerald.

The door seemed frozen in place, trapped ajar beneath a mountain of sand, its interior buried for ever under the weight of the desert, its secrets hidden in permanent shadow.

Max brushed sand away from the embossed images on the door, then ran his hand softly along the open edge. He felt old sand, old dirt, an accumulation of grime that century upon century had laid there.

'There's one way to find out,' he said. And he began to push the left-hand wing inwards. The others lent a hand and, to their surprise, the door offered little resistance. The gap between the bottom edge and the floor was wide enough to let the wing travel, grinding on sand, yet pushing whatever sand lay behind it away.

When the opening had been enlarged enough to let them enter, Max took one of the torches and led the way inside. A moonbeam followed him, a pale, milky wash of molten alabaster flowing across a dark layer of sand. Gerald told Clark to stay on guard duty outside.

'Keep an eye on A'isha,' he said. 'I still don't trust her.'

But when he looked round, the young woman was no longer there. He swung the beam of his torch around the nearest dunes, but there was no sign of her.

'Call us if anything happens, Clark,' Gerald ordered. 'Anything.'

He stepped inside.

It was as if, in that single step, he had been

transported from one world to another, like a man who, falling from the gunwales of a ship at sea, passes at once into the waves and is taken by water down to infinite depths. In the first moments of falling, he has no sense of the transition that is to come, and no true picture of how deep and cold the ocean is. Thus it was for Gerald Usherwood and after him his companions, as he stepped from the desert into a sea built of stone and the webs of small incessant spiders.

The room he stepped into was lightless. No opening existed in its roof that might have let moonlight or starlight through. It had, he realised at once, been dark like this for centuries, lit only partly in the day by the passing rays of the desert sun. It was no colder here than outside, and no warmer. But as his torch picked out walls and the shadowed recesses of a high ceiling, the vast spaces of the desert, through which he seemed to have been travelling for years, dwindled to the confines of an ancient room, an antechamber that would lead him deeper inside this inner place, this inmost of all places.

For centuries, the legs of orb-weaver and sheet-web spiders had crossed and re-crossed the chamber, leaving everywhere fine cobwebs in the darkness. As the moving light of Gerald's torch caught them, living spiders scuttled to whatever shadow they could find. A camel spider six inches long scurried from its nightly hiding place to a crevice between wall and floor. Gerald held to the centre of the room, knowing there would be scorpions in the cracks and interstices of the walls.

Max joined him silently, and together they began to pick out the features of the entrance hall.

The hall was supported at either end by four Ionic columns. One side wall carried a stone plaque inscribed in Hebrew, and its counterpart, opposite, a similar plaque bearing an inscription in Latin. The walls behind and in front were decorated with dozens of elegant mosaics. Among them all, one right ahead stood out. It glistened in the cold beams of their torches, burning with tesserae of white and red and blue and gold. It showed a great building set on a hill, a building of white stone that rose upon steep steps on every side. It was sur-rounded by battlements, with towers on each corner and a great courtyard in front. The central edifice towered above these, tipped by gold along the roof, and sup-ported on columns whose capitals were of gold. A tall doorway led into darkness. In the sky above, angels flew on golden wings, and in the silence they could almost hear the wings whisper.

70

Gerald went up to the mosaic and touched it, running his fingers gently over the tesserae.

'It's as if it was made yesterday,' he said in a hushed voice. 'As if the artist had walked away moments ago and is still in hailing distance. Look at the gold. The tiles are glass with gold foil behind. This was made in the middle of a desert.'

Max was still staring at the mosaic from a few feet away.

'It's the Temple,' he said.

'Temple?'

Max hesitated. He stepped closer to the mosaic and, like Gerald, ran his fingers over the gold and shining tesserae. He spoke in a quiet voice, but they all heard him clearly.

'"And now Herod, in the eighteenth year of his reign ... undertook a very great work, that is, to build of himself the temple of God, and make it larger in compass, and to raise it to a most magnificent altitude, as esteeming it to be the most glorious of all his actions to bring it to perfection; and that this would be sufficient for an everlasting memorial of him."'

'This is the second Temple, built over Solomon's Temple. The Romans burnt it to the ground when they destroyed Jerusalem in the year seventy – about thirty years before the inscription outside. The people who built this would have been Jews who

71

fled from the city. A great many wound up in Egypt and Cyrenaica. And if I remember correctly, they came south.'

'What's the cross about, then?' asked Donaldson.

'I think that's your answer,' Max said, and turned his torch to a nearby panel on the same wall. This mosaic showed a very different scene: a man bent beneath a Roman cross, stumbling as he carried it, with by-standers, some jeering, some running to help.

'This doesn't make any sense,' the doctor exclaimed. His Calvinist upbringing in Aberdeen had given him an allergy to icons. His father would have called the mosaic a 'work of the de'il', and his mother would have sat sucking her thumbs and muttering 'idol worship' beneath her breath. 'Why would Jews put a picture of the good Lord on the wall of their synagogue?'

'Ah!' said Max, trying to keep any hint of smugness out of his voice. 'But that's not Jesus Christ in the mosaic.'

'Who else could it be?'

'Haven't you read your Bible? "They compelled a passer-by, who was coming in from the country, to carry his cross; it was Simon of Cyrene, the father of Alexander and Rufus." There were Jews from Cyrene in Jerusalem at Pentecost, and some of the first Christians were converts from Libya, also from Cyrene. Simon and his sons were among them.'

'How do you know this is Simon?'

Max pointed to an inscription at the base of the picture.

'Because it says so. That's Jesus standing behind him.'

CHAPTER FOUR

Simon of Cyrene

As Max finished speaking, there was a sound behind them. It was Teddy Clark.

'Sir, the woman who came with us...'

Gerald turned, fearing A'isha had betrayed them after all.

'What about her?'

'She's back, sir. With a friend. They've brought lamps with them. I've told them to go in, but they won't budge, and I don't know what to do with them.'

They stepped outside. A'isha and a second woman stood some yards away, shivering like ghosts. Each carried a basket woven from palm fronds, and in the baskets were terracotta lamps filled with olive oil.

As Gerald approached them, his torch beam caught their eyes, and they flinched away. He lowered the torch and greeted A'isha.

'These are for you,' she said. 'They will help you see in that place.'

'Will you not come inside? There are beautiful things in there.'

'Is there treasure? The Old Ones used to say there is treasure, gold and jewels that belonged to the king and queen who are buried there.'

'I've seen nothing like that. If you come inside...'

The women thrust their baskets at him, but refused to be inveigled inside the structure.

They took the lamps inside and lit them one by one. They burnt steadily, revealing yet more mosaics on the floor and ceiling. Between the picture of the Temple and the portrait of St Simon stood a two-sided wooden door carved with finely chiselled images. Each register bore an elongated cross, and around it were fish swimming in deep waves, angels vanquishing demons, lions beneath palm trees, and lilies swaying in a breeze that had passed by long centuries ago.

Gerald pushed hard on the right-hand side, and the door opened to a shrill creaking and groaning of ancient hinges. He went inside, and the others followed, bringing some lamps with them, then returning for more. As the light grew in volume, they saw a world of long-forgotten shadows come to life, shadow by shadow, light by light, ghost by ghost. All around them, phantoms whispered, as if the dead of centuries were coming back to life.

On three sides, banks of seats, like the benches in a Roman amphitheatre, sloped back to mosaic-covered walls. Above, a dome of gold and glass twinkled as they let their torch beams play across it. Two angels held the dome, their pure white robes and golden wings occupying all but a tiny part of its glistening surface, vast and rimmed with flames.

'Whose appearance was as lightning, and their garments glistening and white...' said Max.

At the far end was a wooden desk, the bimah, where the Torah is read, and behind it the Ark, where the Torah scrolls are kept, and it seemed as though the congregation had just got up and left, and gone outside, back to the bright sun and the palm trees and the blue sky. Gerald fancied he could detect a faint smell as of incense, of myrrh, perhaps, or sandalwood or amber or opopanax of Solomon.

A synagogue, then. But above the Ark, where there should have been set the Tables of the Law, stood instead a golden cross whose beaten arms coruscated in the flickering light of the lamps.

'What does all this mean, Max?' Gerald asked, all sense of military hierarchy lost in this place beyond war. 'It's not a synagogue, it's not a church. I don't understand.'

Max was silent for a while, looking all round him, scarcely knowing where to start or where to stop.

'I find no contradictions here,' he said. 'The first Christians were all Jews. This place was built by Jews who believed in the Laws of Moses, but recognised Jesus as the last of the prophets, a miracle-worker sent by God, an archangel who rules over the angels. They regarded the family of Jesus as a sacred lineage. Don't forget that the church in Jerusalem was headed by James, the brother of Jesus. When the Romans destroyed Jerusalem, one of their leaders must have led a band of Ebionites out west, along with the other Jews who headed this way. I wouldn't think it at all unlikely that St Simon of Cyrene was one of them, maybe even their leader. If that's the case, this could be the most important archaeological find of the century, maybe of all time. It makes King Tut look pretty tame, don't you think? And we've only scratched the surface. Look there.'

He pointed towards the central area, an open rectangle flanked by pillars. Shadows had dimmed it, but as they looked closely they could see at its heart an opening in the ground, an opening that led onto steps.

'Whatever this place is about,' said Max, 'that's where we'll find it. Down those steps. Would any of you gentlemen like to go down with me?'

Max led the way, breaking through a net of fine cobwebs as he set his foot firmly on the first step. Things scuttled away from the light. The torch beam picked out about a dozen steps leading down into some sort of basement beneath the synagogue. Gerald followed, holding his breath, scared out of his wits, fearing what they might find, what secrets they had stumbled so inadvertently into.

The steps ended at another wooden door, each side of which was carved the embossed and gilded figure of an angel bearing a trumpet, and wearing on its head a crown. The crowns and robes of the two angels were studded with precious stones – rubies lay like cherries on the rims of the crowns; there were chrysoprase, turquoise, and sapphires on the horns of the trumpets; jasper and sapphires, emeralds and deep-blue gems of lapis lazuli lay along the hems of the robes.

Max laid his hand on an angel's shoulder and pushed. The door gave without murmur, sliding inwards. He shone his torch inside, revealing a silent open space that might have been as large as the building beneath which it stretched.

'Fetch as many lamps as you can,' he shouted.

While the others hurried to bring light, Max stepped inside, followed moments later by Gerald. The air felt stale, and both men found themselves yawning as they breathed in hard. Gerald slipped his Fairbairn Sykes dagger from its sheath and wedged it hard beneath the door, holding it in position. Max did the same with the other half, to let as much air inside as possible.

The first lights were carried in by Donaldson, the storm lanterns from the cars, flickering and sputtering from lack of oxygen. He laid them down and went back for more. Clark brought several of the palm oil lamps, and the light began to grow.

They had entered a crypt, a chamber of stone tombs and ossuaries set in niches cut in stone around the walls. Sarcophagi of differing sizes had been set on plinths. One wall had been honeycombed with semi-circular cells, each filled by a skull. On the foreheads of the skulls were written the names of the dead. Another wall had been painted with an inscription in Hebrew, Greek and Latin. Before the third wall, the one facing the door, stood a wooden structure very like the Ark in the room above. It consisted of a tall cupboard-like box some five feet tall and possessed of two doors. On either side of it stood the figures of two angels. These were cut from white marble and gilded, and each one held aloft a golden cross.

As if in a trance, Max made his way through the tombs, reading whatever inscriptions he could. He took a notebook from his pocket and began to note down details of what he found. No one spoke. Believer and unbeliever alike, they sensed a numinous presence here. The dead had slept in this place for close on two thousand years. Father and mother, husband and wife, son and daughter. Entire families interred in single tombs, or laid side by side in individual ossuaries, their bones unyielding to time or the end of time.

Several large sarcophagi stood together near the Ark. Max read the inscriptions and wrote them down, then stood without moving, one hand resting on the tallest. Gerald noticed that his face was ashen, and that he rested on the sarcophagus in order to stop his hand trembling. When he finally broke his silence, it was as though he had journeyed from a far country with news of war or a king's death, or as if he stood in their presence as a bride come to her husband in a moment of peace.

'Gentlemen,' he said, and his voice was shaking. He had always been considered the calm one among them, the least easily flustered, the most ready to counsel patience.

'Gentlemen,' he began again, 'we find ourselves in a place of ghosts. The phantoms here have names, and the names throw long shadows. The bones in these ossuaries are uncommon bones. This one, for example' – he indicated a large box to his right – 'contains the bones of Simon of Cyrene. Next to it are ossuaries holding the remains of his two sons, Alexander and Rufus. Alexander's box is clear: it says "Alexandros Simonos", Alexander, the son of Simon, on top, then "Alexandroi", belonging to Alexander, on the side. There are Hebrew inscriptions on each of the ossuaries. I'll make copies of those later. But this isn't all.'

He took them several feet further, closer to the Ark.

'There are five large ossuaries here. One is a double burial, probably a husband and wife. The man's name is Joseph, his wife is called Maryam. Mary. The Nazarene: from Nazareth. There are three other names: James, Jude, and Mary. You may remember that Jesus had brothers and a sister of those names. And that James was the head of the church in Jerusalem. There are longer Hebrew or Aramaic inscriptions on these boxes. I'll copy them as well.'

As his voice fell away, a silence settled around them by degrees, unlike any ordinary silence. It was not merely an absence of sound, or a quietude carried in from the desert; it was like nothing they had ever known. In the flickering of the lamps and the waving of the hesitant shadows, they saw each others' faces and were abashed. All that was military in them, all that had hardened them and taught them killing without remorse, fell suddenly away. They were held in the silence by a very different force, as though some compulsion had come to them across a great distance. They could do nothing but this, nothing but remain in that great stillness until one of them found words.

It was as though angels with wings as wide as the desert had dropped down into this narrow, airless space and folded their pinions behind their shoulders, silencing them in readiness for a new tumult and a fresh ordering of things, for a fresh ordering of things was coming.

Gerald was the first to speak after that.

'I don't … believe you. I don't see how…'

'They came here after the sack of Jerusalem. After the burning of the Temple. They must have carried their bones all the way, taken them from the family tombs outside the city, and brought them here to their new habitation. Alexander and Rufus may not have been very old, perhaps not old at all. They must have brought their father's bones here into exile, and when they reached this place, they must have had new ossuaries

81

made to inter them in. Who knows what other bones were carried here on mules or camels? How many of the second and third generations died and were interred here?'

'What about that?' Bill Donaldson asked, pointing to the great wooden Ark, guessing it had been put there for some purpose that would encompass all other purposes. In contrast to the gilded angels on either side, the doors bore nothing but a simple inscription in Hebrew. The letters had been incised neatly into the wood, then dressed with gold leaf. Though centuries had passed, there was still a flame in them, as though some divine fire had burnt in their creation.

The Ark had been built, as far as Max could tell, from cedar wood. As he ran the light across it, it became clear that, apart from the letters, it had been carved with fine ornamentation in the form of plants and flowers, by the hand of a great craftsman. A craftsman who had worked on the Temple in his youth, perhaps. It occurred to him that much of the work here might have been done by men like that: masons, mosaic makers, sculptors who had worked on the upkeep of Herod's great edifice, and whose fathers and grandfathers had, perhaps, built it.

There was no lock, but a metal clasp held the doors squarely together, and iron handles had been fixed to both sides. Bit by bit, he worked the clasp open. It had not rusted, but over the centuries it had grown awkward and stiff. Donaldson, the most practical among them, extinguished one of the palm oil lamps and poured the liquid onto the clasp. As the oil made its way between the hasp and post, they began to give. Suddenly, the clasp burst open, and the doors let out a creaking sound, as though something long suppressed had at last been released.

Max took a handle in each hand and pulled them towards himself. There was an initial reluctance, then the hinges groaned. The doors opened, and from the Ark came forth a deep perfume, and when Max looked inside the first thing he saw was a mass of dried rose petals that had been scattered everywhere across the contents.

It was as they had expected, and not as they had thought. In some deep part of him, each of the four soldiers knew there could be no turning back from this moment, that they had passed a point of no return.

The box on the floor of the Ark was white, and better carved at all points than any of the others. It bore an inscription on the front, the letters of which had been incised with care and precision, first in Greek, then in Hebrew or its sister tongue of Aramaic, none of them could guess.

Across the top of the box, which was some three feet long, someone had laid a wooden plank, rather like a shelf, and on this rested several objects, none of any great size, save for two long rods that stretched diagonally to the top of the Ark.

'What on earth are those?' asked Donaldson, curious now past measure, the cold scientist in him gone for good.

Max reached inside and, using both hands, gently lifted the rods out, one at a time. The first to be dislodged was a wooden shaft about four and a half feet in length, with what appeared to be a thick wooden handle at one end. The other was a metal spike with a barbed head, about the same length.

Max examined the two objects for a minute or so, then took the metal rod and pushed it down past the handle into the wooden shaft. It fitted perfectly, making a lance or javelin almost seven feet long.

'It's a *pilum*,' he said. 'A Roman lance. This lower half is probably made of cornel wood. There would have been nails to hold it together, here, and here.' He pointed to two holes through which nails might at one time have been driven.

'It's a fierce-looking thing,' the doctor said. 'You could do some damage with that.'

'It was used in battle by legionaries called *pilani*.'

'"One of the soldiers pierced his side with a lance, and immediately there came out blood and water."' Gerald spoke the words like someone in a vast cathedral, intoning verses for Easter, without force, knowing them lost in the vastness. 'St John's Gospel,' he said. 'He's the only one who mentioned the soldier.'

'Longinus,' said Max. 'That's supposed to have been his name. It's the stuff of legend. Like the lance. The Spear of Destiny.'

'You're having us on,' said Donaldson. 'You're not going to tell me–'

'Maybe I am, maybe I'm not. But I think you should see the rest of what's in here.'

One at a time, he started to take the other objects from the Ark, and laid them gently on the floor. They seemed fragile enough things, some of them, and heavy, not with substance, but with age and significance.

There were five items in all: the lance; an ochre-coloured pottery goblet shaped like a 'v', without decoration of any kind; a bowl into which someone had pressed what looked like a rounded cap of brambles; a finely carved ivory box whose lid came off easily, revealing inside three rough-cast metal spikes, each about seven inches long; and a large wooden rectangle that carried three inscriptions that had been painted hurriedly in Greek, Latin, and Hebrew, each on one line:

Ἰησους ‘ο Ναζωραιος ‘ο Βασιλευς των ‘Ιουδαιων
IESVS NAZARENVS REX IVDAEORVM.
עושי תרצנה רלמ סידוהיה

While Gerald held an oil lamp steady over his shoulder, Max deciphered the first two lines.

'They both say the same thing,' he said. 'I expect you can all guess. "Jesus the Nazerene, King of the Jews". This is the *titulus*, the wooden plaque that was nailed to the top of the cross.'

In the shadows, Clark's fingers flickered across his chest. Gerald, a run-of-the-mill Anglican, felt a fluttering at his heart. Even the two unbelievers, Chippendale and Donaldson, sensed the enormity of this object and the inscription it bore.

Max placed the *titulus* on the floor, and straightened.

'If this is the *titulus*,' he said, 'then the identity of these other objects is undeniable. The nails that held Christ to the cross, the Crown of Thorns, the Lance of Longinus, and the Holy Grail.'

'I thought the Grail–' began Donaldson.

'Was a jewel-encrusted goblet of gold?' Max shook his head. 'Jesus was a poor Jewish teacher born to a carpenter. This pottery cup is exactly the sort of thing the real Jesus would have drunk from at the Last Supper. I think this little trove is the real thing. Not even King Tut's tomb matches

86

this place. We've stumbled on the most important archaeological find in history. The question is, what do we do with it? We can leave everything here, just as we found it, and bring some archaeologists back here with us. Somebody who reads Hebrew and Aramaic for one thing. Or we can take some of it with us, to make sure it's kept safe.'

Gerald decided it was time he took back control of the situation, After all, he thought, he was in charge of the patrol.

'Gentlemen,' he said, 'we have to take everything back to Cairo. As much as will fit in the cars. We've already dumped a lot here, there's room for all this and more. If we leave them here, God knows what will become of them. We can bring Lieutenant Chippendale's precious archaeologists back later, and let them loose. The war will be over before they even make a start on it. But I don't have to tell you just how explosive this could be. Private Clark, get on back to the cars PDQ and fetch Leary and Skinner. Clear out some ammunition boxes and bring them here, as many as the three of you can carry.'

Max tried to protest.

'Sir, don't you think–?'

'I'm not here to think. I leave that to Johnnies like you. You've just done your thinking, but I'm in charge here, and I'm making the decisions. If the Tuareg lay their filthy hands on these, they'll probably chuck them in a bin somewhere, rip out anything that breaks off, and flog it all up in Ghadames for two bob apiece. They're Muslims, none of this would mean a thing to them.'

At that moment, a sound came from the direction of the stairs down which they had entered, and when they looked round they could see a wavering light growing in intensity among the shadows.

'I thought A'isha was scared of this place,' Donaldson said.

But it wasn't A'isha. Gerald let his torch beam play across the entrance to the crypt. A pair of feet came into view, followed by a dark-blue robe that came through the opening. A Tuareg man, fully veiled, appeared, hesitating as he tried to adjust to the flickering play of shadow and light, the whiteness of the sepulchres, and the figures of the four Englishmen standing among them.

It took a few seconds for Gerald to recognise the newcomer. Then he noticed the coarsely stitched leather wallets slung over his shoulder, containing a Qur'an and talismans. He lifted his left hand to shield his eyes from the light, and Gerald caught sight of the *masbaha*, the amber rosary hanging from his wrist. It was the Anislem, Shaykh Harun agg Da'ud, As he stepped forward, trying to escape the light, his right hand came forward, and Gerald saw he was carrying a gun, the service revolver he had given earlier to the headman.

'Shaykh Muhammad!' called Gerald. '*Al-salam 'alaykum.* You have found us in a very strange place. A holy place. The tomb of the Prophet Jesus.'

Gerald had thought quickly, referring to the fact that the Qur'an honours Jesus, not as the Son of God, but as a mortal prophet, lesser only to Muhammad himself. If Shaykh Harun recognised this and could be persuaded that this was a holy site connected to one of Islam's great prophetic figures, perhaps any looming trouble could be averted. He was to be disappointed

'This place does not belong to you. These are the tombs of our ancestors. This is the sacred city of Wardabaha; you have found the tombs of the king and queen of the city, but you have no right to be here. You have to leave this place and never return.'

'This place was built by my people,' declared Gerald impetuously. 'It is a Christian place. It is as I just said, it is the tomb of the Prophet Jesus.'

The Shaykh took several steps forward among the ossuaries. The light in his left hand shook, throwing shadows on the amber beads. In his dark robes, he was invisible unless light fell on him, and even then only his suspicious eyes were visible,

'Leave,' he said. 'Leave now or suffer the penalty.'

'I think we should talk. My friend here has healed the son of Musa agg Isa. We have shown our friendship towards the Kel Tamasheq. We have demonstrated our loyalty to the people of Ain Suleiman.'

The Anislem made a noise in the back of his throat, a light cough that seemed to sneer at what Gerald had just said.

'Musa agg Isa is dead. His wife, who helped you, is dead. They have been punished, and Allah will punish them in the next world. Si Musa allowed infidels to defile this place. His wife showed you to this sacred habitation belonging to our ancestors. A *kafir* defied the will of Allah when he saved the child from a certain death. I could not let so much go unpunished. I have taken charge of Ain Suleiman. If you leave now and swear on whatever you hold sacred never to return to this place, you may leave with your lives. Otherwise, not one of you will see his home again. Your bones will shine white in the sand for a little time before they return to dust.'

'I told Si Musa why we came here. You need our help. If the Germans come here, they will massacre everyone in this oasis. I swear by this holy place and the sacred objects it contains that the Germans will bring great evil on the Kel Tamasheq. They have no mercy. Even if Si Musa and his wife and son are dead, you still need our help.'

The Shaykh lifted his right hand and pointed the gun at Gerald.

'Put the gun down!' Gerald shouted. He had not re-armed, there was nothing he could do.

The Anislem fired, a single shot that echoed wildly through the enclosed space, as though a stone had cracked open, or a tomb.

As the sound died away, everyone looked round. Gerald realised he was still standing and seemed to be unhurt. He looked round to see Max on his right and Donaldson a few paces away to his left. But when he turned, Clark had disappeared. Looking down, he saw the soldier lying on his back, tossed awkwardly across one of the tombs.

Shaykh Harun started to aim the gun again, but as he did so another shot rang out, louder than the first, if that was possible, knocking him back as though a mule had kicked him hard in the chest. His body crashed to the ground. Gerald stepped across to him and bent down.

'He's dead,' he said.

Donaldson ran to Clark, but it was too late. The Anislem's bullet had taken the boy in the throat.

The gunshot hung in the air for what seemed an age. Its reverberations had invaded every inch of the crypt, and its ringing echoed in their ears for longer than it took for the air to grow still and silence to make its presence felt once more in the narrow chamber.

'I think it's time we made ourselves scarce,' said Max as he returned his pistol to its holster.

CHAPTER FIVE

In the Bleak Midwinter

Woodmancote Hall
Near Bishop's Cleeve
Gloucestershire
England
December 2008

The police had been and gone, two un-marked vans had taken the bodies away, the house party had been questioned, finger-printed, and sent home. Throughout the day, three teams had remained at the hall, carry-ing out further forensic work in the library, and on doors and windows in its vicinity. Uniformed police, plain-clothes detectives, forensic specialists, and pathologists had passed in and out in an unending stream.

Fingerprints had been lifted, everyone in the house had been fingerprinted, DNA samples had been taken from the room and the guests, everything in sight had been photographed and labelled, evidence bags had been filled with bits and pieces, and everyone above the age of three had been invited into the library to relate what they remembered of the night past.

Rather than hang around waiting to be questioned, several guests had taken on themselves the mournful task of taking down the Christmas decorations. The police had let them get on with it: the festive tree, the presents at its foot, the table laid for lunch, the lights, the candles, the nativity had all seemed the saddest things in the world, and no one could face them, not even the children. They'd questioned the parents first, so they could take their little ones off, along with their presents, to try to make some sort of Christmas for them, to find Father Christmas hidden somewhere at last, to forget the screams that had dragged them from their stocking-festooned beds in the bitter cold, greeted on the happiest morning of the year by adults weeping, and a sense of horror in a world of carols, angels, and midwinter lights.

The hall had been closed and sealed with police tape. The parish priest had come to pray at the door, as if his words and the tape together formed a ritual of closure. He too had gone on his sad way, wondering what to say to his evening congregation. Ethan and Sarah, barred from the hall, had taken themselves to the lodge, one hundred yards from the main building.

Outside, the snow continued to fall, and in the parish church, a diminished congregation bowed their heads and knelt and offered up thanks for the birth of God. In the darkling woods, birds shivered in their nests, foxes, badgers and squirrels huddled in their lairs, and silence clung to the trees. Smoke rose above the village, where wood fires crackled and spat, turkeys and geese roasted in hot ovens, puddings boiled, children played with new toys, and television screens flickered with inane shows beamed in from an array of satellites that, remote and unconcerned, circled a world of Christmases.

Ethan had sent Mrs Salgueiro off to stay with relatives. Her nerves had suffered a severe shaking, and the village doctor, who had been snatched with ill humour from his Christmas holiday, had given her a bottle of tranquillisers to ease them. She had not been the only one for whom he had prescribed that morning, but she had been Gerald's housekeeper for twenty years (and some thought rather more than his housekeeper for some time), and she took his death – and the manner of it – badly.

Ethan made a last tour of the grounds. While he could not be part of the murder investigation, Bob Forbes, who headed it, had made him responsible for keeping a general eye on things. He went back to the lodge and returned to the small library on the ground floor, where he had spent time earlier. He was surprised to find Sarah in an armchair, reading. A bright log fire was burning in the grate; the flames danced like sprites, their reflections painting patterns of light and shade across the young woman's face.

'Good book?'

She looked up.

'Not really,' she said. 'I picked it out at random. I just wanted to read something. After everything. I thought reading might help clear my head.'

'And has it?' he asked. 'Has it helped?'

She shook her head. He noticed that she hadn't fixed her hair or put on make-up since waking earlier. The smile he'd liked so much had vanished as if for good.

'It'll be dark soon,' he ventured. 'How long will it take you to get back to Oxford? To be honest, I thought you'd be gone by now. There's been a lot more snow through the day. The roads are hard going.'

The smile returned for a brief moment.

'I'm not driving back yet. I've got time on

my hands, so I thought I'd hang on here as long as necessary.'

'Necessary?' He sat down on the chair on the other side of the fireplace.

'Ethan, you're not very bright, are you? You've decided to stay on at the lodge because you're a policeman and can be trusted to look after the crime scene and see off any intruders. Haven't you given any thought to yourself?'

'Myself? I'm on leave till–'

'That is such a male response. "I'm on leave." I didn't ask about your working arrangements, I asked about you.'

He reached over for the poker, stirred it among the flames, and added several fresh logs. They spat fiercely, sending bright sparks up into the wide chimney.

'I'm fine,' he said. 'I can look after this place on my own till Mrs Salgueiro comes back.'

'You're still avoiding my question.' She closed her book and let it fall to the floor. 'Without Mrs Salgueiro, you are alone in this lodge. Your bedroom here is just a stone's throw from the room in which your grandfather and his friend were brutally murdered. Even though you have probably seen dozens of murder scenes in your time, and are probably inured to such things, you were badly shaken when you came out of the study this morning. Do you expect me to believe that staying here on your own will be a breeze, that you won't sit and brood about this from morning to night?'

'Sarah, I–'

'Whether or not you're willing to strain your emotions like that, I'm not going to let you. You have a companion for the duration. I will be your housekeeper. I will cook for you and eat with you, I will talk to you any time you feel like talking, I will go for long walks with you in the freezing cold, and I will read to you, play Scrabble with you, watch old movies on TV, or sit and listen to music. The only things I will not do are to wash your socks and underwear, put chocolates on your pillow last thing at night, or sleep with you. We might even get to know one another after all these years. Now, is this a deal or not?'

He sat for half a minute, totally bewildered. When he got his wits back, he ventured a smile.

'Actually,' he said, 'I'm not a bad cook. Really.'

She grinned.

'Really?'

The scepticism in her voice wakened memories of burnt toast and stringy scrambled eggs. He shook his head.

'If I take care, I can do a mean baked beans on toast.'

She winced at the thought.

'In that case, you should offer up a prayer of thanks, because I am a good cook. Cordon bleu is nothing to me. You were no doubt facing the prospect of beans on toast for breakfast, lunch, supper, and a late-night snack. The fact that you can't cook is reassuring. I don't like men who are cleverer than me. I may take pity on you and marry you after all. How come you never learnt–?'

She cut herself off, realising what she'd just said.

'I'm sorry,' she said. 'That was stupid of me. I should have thought before opening my big mouth.'

'That's OK. It's been eight years. You were only a teenager.'

'But I remember Aunt Abi well. She was lovely. We were devastated when...'

'We all were. It was devastating for everyone. The family. All her friends.'

'You found her, is that right?'

'Not exactly. But more or less. I identified her.'

Abi had been raped and murdered on a summer evening while jogging in a local park. Ethan had been the first detective on the scene, summoned by the patrol car that had gone to the secluded spot where she'd been found. He had gone there expecting to find a stranger, and looked down on the face of his dead wife, whom he'd last seen only two hours earlier, before he went on duty.

Finding his grandfather hanging in his study had brought the whole thing back again. Despite his first reaction to her suggestion, he was glad Sarah had decided to stay. The murder investigation was already under way, ruining Christmas for scores of policemen and policewomen throughout the county. He desperately wished he could be one of them, but getting involved in a family case was out of the question. For all he knew, he was the prime suspect.

'When do you want to eat?' she asked.

'How about now? I'm starving. I've only snatched a few handfuls of food all day. There were three families staying in the lodge, all with children, so the kitchen's still stuffed with food.'

'I'd forgotten about that.' She frowned. 'I hate to think of it all going to waste, especially today. Do you think some charity could make use of it? And what about the main kitchen in the hall?'

The armchair was too low and soft to leap out of, but Ethan struggled to his feet.

'The hall could be more difficult, but I could speak to someone on the force. This one's easier. I bet more than one charity could put all this to good use. As long as they can get here through the snow.'

A couple of phone calls later and a shelter for the homeless in Cheltenham had promised to get a van over that evening. A police van would take what they could from the hall kitchen and pass it on to the Salvation Army. Ethan and Sarah headed for the kitchen, where they sorted out the food they would need to keep for themselves, and put as much of the rest into boxes as they could.

Sarah raided the cupboards and the large fridge. She found a box of carnaroli rice, large prawns, cheese, and a bottle of Pino Grigio.

'Fancy a risotto?' she asked. 'I'll have to use stock cubes, but otherwise there's enough here to make something halfway decent.'

He nodded and offered to help.

'Ethan,' she said, 'there is a simple rule in every good home kitchen: one chef is enough. Go and sit down over there and talk to me.'

She grabbed an onion and began to peel it. He sat down at the kitchen table and looked at her. It was beyond him that someone so lovely should have emerged from his family, a tribe not well noted for the personal beauty of its members.

'Tell me more about yourself,' he said. 'I'm not even sure what you do exactly. You're a lecturer, I know that, and since you live in Oxford, I presume you teach there.'

'Mostly I do research,' she answered, her eyes watering in the fume from the onions. 'And I do some teaching from time to time.'

'Poor you. What's your subject?'

'Ethan, could you find a risotto pan? Something cast iron if there is one.'

He got to his feet again and started hunting through cupboards. Through wet eyes, she watched him. His movements relaxed her. He seemed at ease in his body, slow, capable, intent on what he was doing, yet clearly interested in what she had to say.

'Biblical Hebrew and Aramaic,' she said. 'I'm based in the Centre for Hebrew and Jewish Studies, out in Yarnton. Actually, my main field is documentary and epigraphic evidence for archaeology in the Holy Land. I go out on digs, and when anything turns up that needs to be deciphered, they whistle and I come running. I specialise in the Roman period. My thesis was about the destruction of the Temple. You'd be bored to tears. I'm really very dull, you know.'

With a flourish, he pulled out a heavy Le Creuset pan of exactly the right proportions.

'I find that hard to believe,' he said. 'But your studies do surprise me. How on earth did you get into something like that?'

'Can you find a match or something to light the gas?'

He remembered where he'd seen the matches earlier. A box was sitting on a biscuit box on the side opposite the cooker. He took out a match and lit a gas ring. He slipped the box into his pocket, and went off to look for candles.

Sarah took the pan, then filled a kettle with water. Ethan returned to his seat with two table candles and small glass holders to put them in. While the water heated, Sarah chopped the onion, her hand moving economically as the knife jumped up and down. The water boiled. She poured it into a large glass jug, and crumbled chicken stock cubes into it, then set it aside. Wiping her eyes, she sliced through a fennel bulb and several cloves of garlic. He noticed how her hands moved, how her fingers clasped the knife, how the sharp blade slid effortlessly through the flesh of the vegetables.

'You mean, what's a nice girl like me doing in a place like that? It all started with Great-Granddad. It was a great interest of his. Surely you knew that?'

'Well, yes. He mentioned it a couple of times, something about the Bible, ancient Israel, the life of Jesus. I can't really remember any detail. And he went to Israel several times, I know that. Jerusalem, mostly. All the same, I never knew it was any sort of big thing with him.'

'Have you never looked through his library?'

'I've glanced through it a couple of times.'

She gave him the sort of look a woman gives a man who is proving not quite with it.

102

She took the skillet and started to heat olive oil on top of the gas ring.

'And you're telling me you never noticed his books about biblical archaeology?'

'Maybe, I can't remember. I was only interested in fiction. I wanted ripping yarns to read on my hols, that's all. And when I was in my teens I sometimes wondered if the old dog had any ... well, off-colour stuff.'

The look again.

'Don't say anything more. I don't want to know about your taste in porn.'

'It wasn't exactly... I was a spotty teenager. Anyway, I never found any.'

'I shall have to keep a very close eye on you, Ethan. Perhaps I won't marry you after all. Now, as I was saying, Great-Granddad built up a remarkable collection of books on the subject. Taught himself some Hebrew and Greek, messed about with Latin. The collection isn't very systematic, but it's full of good things. I used to pop over here a lot when I was an undergraduate.'

The rice went in, along with the onions. A warm smell rose from the pan.

'I never bumped into you.'

'I kept away from you. I had a strong feeling you were a lecherous old man, and now I know I was right. Now, keep quiet and let me get on with this.' She paused. 'What was I saying? Yes, when I was in my teens, he talked to me about his interests and started

103

suggesting that I might study languages and maybe study Hebrew and some archaeology. He even paid for me to go on visits to the Holy Land. Took me with him once.'

'I knew about none of this. He never talked of it.'

She added some wine, then two ladles of the stock. As the rice started to absorb the liquid, the mixture began to look like a risotto.

She turned to him, a pensive look on her face.

'Never?'

'Not to me. Maybe my father, maybe someone else. But I've only heard about it now. I knew you had a degree from Oxford, and a PhD and so on, but that was the full extent of it. I'm sorry I wasn't more curious. You must think I've been negligent.'

She shook her head, and her expression changed, for her flippancy in finding him slow on the uptake had passed, and with it the little impatience she had felt. She had just started her degree eight years earlier, only a month or two after her aunt Abi had been killed. How on earth would he have found time or a space in his mind to enquire after the doings of a niece to whom he had never been particularly close? Their families had had a falling out years earlier, Ethan's father had argued with his brother James – Sarah's father – and things had festered.

'You weren't to blame,' she said. 'There was the feud, then ... what happened to Aunt Abi. Actually, if I'm to be honest, I didn't try to see you back then. I was just nineteen, and I was afraid of you. Because of what happened to Abi. What happened to her frightened me a great deal. I thought you might have taken it badly, that you might not be someone I could cope with. I heard of you from time to time, and I thought you might be bitter. I let a lot of time go by. We just have to make up for that.'

He nodded, but said nothing. Sarah had been right. He hadn't added things up until now, but his life since Abi's murder had been a blur, not quite a life in any real meaning of the term. He'd relearnt the basic skills of meeting and working with people, but for most of the time he'd been a recluse, leaving work for an empty flat and a takeaway, falling asleep in front of the television most nights, avoiding the constant temptation to drown his sorrows in drink. His colleagues regarded him as a loner, good at his job, but no use for a night out in the pub. Even after eight years, a dark depression could descend on him out of nowhere and cripple him for days. Last night and today were the first occasions he'd talked to anyone properly in all that time. Suddenly, the thought of Sarah leaving filled him with a puzzling dread.

'Apart from being brainy,' he went on, 'is there anything else in your life? Books, music, men?'

'You're trawling. All of them, if you must know. Well, not so many men, as it happens...'

'You must get plenty of offers.'

She frowned.

'Offers? Yes, I suppose so. I turn them all down.'

'Please don't tell me...'

Her frown deepened, but she shook her head.

'No, it's not that. I like men. I'd like to get married one day and have children and all that. It's just...'

She hesitated, and he sensed that she didn't want to be pushed, that he'd have to wait for her to say whatever it was she had difficulty in saying.

'After I graduated, one of my lecturers asked me out. Dr Gardner. Jeremy Gardner. We ... got involved. At first it was just sex, but as time went by it turned into a proper love affair. He was ten years older than me and married, but unhappily. It lasted over two years, and he was talking seriously about getting a divorce and marrying me. It turns out, he did file for divorce, but that...'

She stopped talking and took a slow breath.

'It's all right,' said Ethan, 'you don't have to go on.'

She looked directly at him, and he saw something troubled in her eyes. As if she was haunted, as if she could see ghosts.

'It's all right. I'd like to tell you. But keep it to yourself. Nobody else in the family even knows I had a lover, let alone... Something happened. Jeremy was a climber. He would go away for a month or more at a time, climbing one peak after another, each one higher and more difficult than the last. That year, the team he was with chose Nanga Parbat in Kashmir. He was about halfway up when a piton broke and he fell onto a ridge and broke his back. I didn't hear about it at first. He'd kept me secret. I didn't even get to go to the funeral.'

She came to a halt. All the time she'd been speaking, she'd been stirring the rice. Now she added the prawns in generous spoonfuls; they were large and pink. The cheese, which looked like cheddar, added a final touch of flavour. She grated it into thick yellow ribbons and spooned them into the risotto. As they melted, she stirred them softly until they vanished into the soupy mixture.

While the risotto settled, Ethan laid two places at the table, using Christmas plates that had already been set out for the lunch that had not taken place. He found a bottle of sparkling white wine and two fluted glasses to go with it. And he lit the candles.

When he finished setting the table, Sarah

had already conjured a light green salad from the fridge and sprinkled it with an Italian dressing. She put the bowl in the centre of the table, and Ethan hurried off to find servers. Finally, the risotto was lined up alongside the salad, and all was ready.

With one mouthful he was smitten.

'This is delicious. A pity I'm your uncle and you're my niece.'

She gave him a curious look, as if what he'd just said was not quite what it should have been. Then she smiled.

'You'll just have to live with it,' she said, and spooned more risotto into her own mouth.

She wondered privately if she should tell him the truth. They were both grown-ups now, after all. The truth wouldn't have hurt him, but she knew it would bring acute embarrassment to her relatives. Ethan was not her uncle, she was not his niece. To be exact, they weren't even remotely related. She and her mother were the only ones who knew that, and what her mother had told her on her deathbed had been said in strict confidence. In the end, she decided against telling him, for now at least. What harm could it do to let him go on believing they shared the same bloodline? The rest of the family thought so, and she did not relish the thought of disenchanting them.

About halfway through the meal, after Sarah had put second helpings on both their plates, she put her fork and spoon down and looked directly at Ethan.

'Ethan, what will happen to Great-Grand-dad's will? I mean, now there's this murder inquiry taking place.'

He frowned and put his implements down as well.

'I'm not quite sure,' he said. 'The study had been ransacked. Someone had spent time in there looking for something, maybe money, maybe something else. It's far too early to say. If the will was still in there, it's probably in the hands of the police. If not, it may have been among the things that were taken by the intruder. Or intruders, it's too early to know anything definite. It's not really important, though, not until the investigation's fully under way. I don't think anyone much wants to think about their inheritance at the moment.'

She blinked and picked up her fork, only to play with the food in front of her.

'It was just...' She paused, as if trying to put some thoughts together. 'Ethan, did he ever mention his will to you?'

He shook his head.

'Not that I remember. I wouldn't worry about it, though, Gerald was always pretty careful about that sort of thing. He had good lawyers, as I remember, some firm over in Gloucester.'

'Markham and Pritchett. They used to

handle stuff for my father.'

He smiled.

'Mine too. I think they were solicitors for the whole family. I'll get in touch with them after the break. They're bound to have at least one copy in their offices.'

'The thing is, Ethan, Great-Granddad said something to me about three years ago, when I was still working on my PhD. He said that if anything happened to him, I had to find his will, that there was another document with it, a letter to me. He showed it to me once, but it was folded up so I could only see the outside. He wouldn't say what was in it, but I gathered it wasn't to do with an inheritance. It was important, though, he made a point of stressing that. He said I had to get hold of this letter the moment anything happened, that it contained instructions.'

'Instructions? What about?'

'That's what I don't know. Look, I'm probably not even in the will, or if I am I must be pretty far down the pecking order. But I have a funny feeling about this.'

'Funny?'

'Funny peculiar. I didn't take it too seriously at the time, but when I think back, I'm pretty sure he wasn't referring to his inevitable death a few years down the line. There was something in his manner, in the tone of his voice: as if he was worried that something unnatural might happen to him. And ... well, it has done, hasn't it? I think we should look for it. I think we should do that right away.'

CHAPTER SIX

Voices from the Dead

Over the next hour, Ethan made several telephone calls. He spoke to his father, to his uncles, to Bob Forbes at police head-quarters, and to his grandfather's solicitors. A copy of the will was with the solicitors, but no letter for Sarah. The police had found neither a will nor a letter in Gerald's study.

Ethan found Sarah and explained that he'd drawn a blank.

'Then it has to be somewhere else,' she said. 'Any ideas?'

He shook his head.

'What about the library?' she asked.

'The library?'

'You know, the room with books in it. Along the walls. On shelves.'

'Oh, that room. Sounds more like your preserve than mine.'

'Exactly. All I want is an hour or two in there, Ethan. Half an hour. I think the letter may be important. Your police friends won't know what to look for, but I may be able to recognise it.'

It took an hour to persuade him to take her to the hall, help her slip beneath the yellow and black crime scene tape, and open the door with his personal key.

'This is very irregular,' he said. But she had piqued his curiosity. The letter just might hold something of relevance. So long as they kept away from the study, there was little risk of disturbing anything; the house had been filled with people for two days, and the crime scene officers had concentrated their efforts around the room where the murders had taken place.

They started with a stack of box files filled with journal articles, newspaper clippings, and an occasional letter. Ethan had to nudge Sarah every few minutes when, finding something of interest, she would stop searching and start reading. They moved on to two tall filing cabinets. The first contained records of book purchases, letters from antiquarian and modern booksellers, and correspondence with authors and editors. Ethan glanced through these, stunned to find his grandfather so assiduous in his studies. The second cabinet was stuffed with objects of an archaeological nature. Sarah's eyes opened wide as she took in the range of them. Ethan almost had to drag her away.

'Sarah, there's nothing here, nothing addressed to you anyway. Wait till the will is opened, it may say something in there about it.'

'Rubbish. You spoke to Markham from the solicitors, and he knew nothing about it. Either it's in the study or whoever killed Great-Granddad and his friend took it. By the way, has anything been done to contact his family? The other man, I mean.'

'Max Chippendale? Yes, I told Bob Forbes all I knew. He has Max's bags, and he's made enquiries. None of us knew anything about the man, except that he'd served in the war with Granddad. Tough old birds that lot. Desert Rats or something.'

'Long Range Desert Group. You should know that. Tougher than the Desert Rats. Harder than the SAS. No wonder the ones who got through lived long lives.'

It was cold, and they decided to go back to the lodge for coffee and a plate of Mrs Salgueiro's home-made cranberry short-bread. Ethan had lit a log fire earlier in the drawing room. While he tended it, Sarah made a coffee for him and a strong hot chocolate for herself. The shortbread was in an old tin with a tartan pattern. She remembered it from childhood visits.

'We're getting low on milk,' she said, putting down the tray. 'We'll have to get some in the village tomorrow. Or drive into Gloucester.'

They sat in front of the fire, watching the flames lick through the beech logs, their appetite unquenchable. They talked again, less animated now after their lack of success in the library, but more deeply, more intimately than before. He spoke of how he'd met his future wife Abigail, the shortness of their courtship and the brevity of their life together, of the sleepless nights and empty days, of blind dates organised by well-meaning friends, none of which had gone to a second innings, of his steady recovery of a life of sorts, a life without a soul.

And she spoke of loves lost, of a life lived through books and periodicals, of academic colleagues who had never become companions, of sexual adventures that had drifted into animosity in a matter of weeks, of a heart that longed for something more than parchment or ink or voices from the dead.

It seemed only right to speak of love, or the absence of it, or the longing for it in the face of wilful death, on a day of ruined festivity, on the verge of what might have been a great celebration of a great man's life. They spoke at length of Gerald Usherwood, his military service, his work for the government, his charities, and his passion for the Holy Land and the mysteries of its past. They laughed, they shed tears, they sat for long minutes in silence; Sarah decided it was time to explain how things really stood.

She said nothing right away, but shook her head gently, as if trying to dissuade herself. Once she crossed the line, there would be no turning back. She couldn't guess where it might lead. For several moments, she stared directly into the copper flames. The golden light was reflected off her face, gilding her like the goddess of some long-forgotten Greek cult. He was silent beside her. The moment might not come again, she thought, or, if it did, might be ruined by matters out of her control.

'Ethan,' she said, 'there's something I have to tell you. It has to be between us. No one else in the family must know.'

'This sounds serious,' he said.

'It is serious.' She bent down and used the long poker to push a log back into the flames. Sparks rose like fireflies, sudden and flame-forged.

'It's about my mother,' she said, still hesitating. 'About something she told me three years ago on her deathbed. Her long-kept secret. Her long-hidden love. She had an affair about thirty years ago, an affair that lasted up until her death. I'm the result, though my father knows nothing of it. She told me who my real father is. He's still alive, but I've never met him, though I've often thought of turning up on his doorstep:

Hello, Dad, it's your long-lost daughter. I knew his name long before she told me, though. He's an eminent academic, a historian.' She stumbled to a halt. 'I'm sorry, I should have told you before this.'

Ethan was shaken by the news. He remembered his Aunt Ann, a small woman with delicate features and an infectious laugh. And he thought of his Uncle James, a quiet man who had often spoken to him at difficult times in adolescence. Now, he had to adjust to Sarah being nothing but a friend, while pretending to the family she continued to be his niece.

They talked through the evening, gradually leaving behind the two pressing topics of the day, the murder and Sarah's unburdening of herself.

It was almost time for bed when something crossed Sarah's mind.

'Ethan, I've thought of another place.'

'I'm sorry... A place?' He was tired after a late night and early morning, followed by a stressful day.

'For the letter.'

'Oh, the letter. Why didn't he just post it to you? Or tell you where he'd put it?'

'I think he was going to do that at the birthday party. He said something a few weeks ago about having something to tell me on the day. As usual, that was all he said. But it has just occurred to me that he might have put it in

116

the library after all.'

'Sarah, we've been right through the library–'

'No, we haven't. I don't know what's in his will except for one thing: he was going to leave all his biblical studies books to me. Plus his papers. He knew I would get the books after he died, that they'd go straight to me. He might have left the letter in one of them.'

After an argument about going back to the crime scene in the freezing cold, Ethan shrugged his shoulders and they went across.

It took them ten minutes to find it. Ethan stumbled on it in a book entitled *The Earliest Christian Artefacts: Manuscripts and Christian Origins,* slipped between pages 50 and 51. Sarah smiled.

'I used to use this a lot when I was here. He knew I'd look at it before long. Now, let's see what this letter says.'

It wasn't just a letter. It was a thick handwritten memoir that began with Gerald's account of an LRDG expedition into the south-western Libyan desert in May 1942. Sarah read it aloud. It took a long time, but as the story unfolded, exhaustion lifted from them and they grew transfixed. A temple in the desert, a shimmering of mosaics, relics of the crucifixion, the tomb of Christ. It read like something from *Indiana Jones.*

A sheet of headed notepaper followed

those that recounted the discovery of Wardabaha, its tombs, and its relics.

My Dearest Sarah, it began, *If you are reading this, I shall have gone to meet the men I have killed and receive justice for any wrongs I have done to others. More likely, I have returned to oblivion, and perhaps that will be for the best. Of all men, I have been among the closest in life to Jesus. I have stood by his tomb and handled relics of his passion in my bare hands in a cold place while silence swallowed me alive. But I do not believe. Not in him, not in any god, not even, perhaps, in myself.*

No doubt you are asking yourself 'What happened?' To Wardabaha, to the relics we found, to the Tuaregs. The truth is, I'm not exactly sure, at least insofar as the city is concerned, and the Kel Ajjer. Some bad things happened after we left the oasis. Word got out somehow, and there was an attempt to steal the relics and to find the city. We destroyed our records of the trip, but it was too late. One of our number had boasted about the find to the wrong person, someone who was sent to the front the following day and made a prisoner of war. No one knows what happened exactly, but the story got into the hands of the Germans. No, not the Jerries as such, a queer bunch, dyed-in-the-wool Nazis. Or rather more than that. The Hungarian, Almásy, was mixed up in it somewhere. He wanted to get his hands on the things we brought back; two of our party

118

were killed as a result.

The war in North Africa moved west and ended less than a year later. Things seemed to go quiet after that. Chips and I hung on, then we were transferred to Palestine till the whole show ended in '45. I've devoted my time since then to finding out more about it all, the tombs, the relics, everything. I've come to the conclusion that it is all genuine, that we really did find the place where Jesus Christ and all those others were buried.

But it's not over. I chose you to take this thing on after me; you were the only one in the family to show a flicker of interest. Now it's up to you. To tell the world. To organise an expedition into the desert. You'll have to keep it low key until the university is ready to make an announcement. Chips has three of the relics, I have the other three; he knows all about you. I'll introduce you at my birthday bash next year, get you properly acquainted. We're both too old to take you out there, but I know the coordinates by heart: 20 4 1 N by 20 7 3. I've drawn a rough map on the next sheet. I can't tell you what you'll find there, or whether anyone will have got there before you; one thing we both know is that, if anyone did, they haven't said a word about it to anyone.

Take care of yourself, my dear. You've pleased me very much, above all by your intelligence and determination. Whatever you may think now, you are a beautiful young woman who deserves a good man and a happy marriage. I'm only sorry that I may not live long enough to see that happen, but I'm confident it will.

Speaking of wills, I've seen to it that you're quite well provided for in mine. Most of the older generation lack for little, so my money will go mainly to my grandchildren and their children. I know you will use the money well.

I know there's something I haven't mentioned, but I can't for the life of me remember what it is. Unless... Could it be the relics? I still have them here at Woodmancote. Where are they? In the safest hiding place I could think of. By the time you read this, my funeral will have come and gone. Perhaps then it will be time for you to visit the family mausoleum. It's a stuffy old place, and I've decided not to spend the rest of eternity dumped there. It would remind me too much of that other place, that place the sands have probably covered again. I'm to go up in smoke. The world I knew is long dead. You have your life ahead of you.

All my love,

Gerald

The next sheet was the map. And that was all.

Sarah put the letter down. Her hands were shaking, and her eyes were filled with tears. The full horror of Gerald's death had finally

120

struck her, and her wounded heart repined at the thought of its manner and its possible meaning.

Ethan put his arm round her, and she let herself be comforted, but not consoled. She leant into his body, her head pressed against his shoulder, her frame racked by cruel sobbing. He did all he could to ease her pain, but he felt clumsy and without the amplitude of feeling that might have attuned him better to the limits of her distress. He rubbed her back and spoke soothing words, all the time struggling not to let himself be stirred by her presence, by the physicality of her, the smell of her perfume, the softness of her hair, or his own need to give and receive comfort. She was an entrancing and beautiful woman, and he feared he already had feelings for her that had to be suppressed for both their sakes. Even if she wasn't his niece, the family didn't know that.

In time she grew still. He let her pull away from him, blinking and drying her eyes with her knuckles.

'I'm sorry,' she said.

'There's no need to be. I loved him too. He should have died in his bed with all the family round him. Not where we found him, not in that way.'

She nodded, sniffing as she did so. Then she glanced at the clock.

'Where are we going to sleep?' she asked.

'Can we stay here? The lodge is still cold, and all my stuff is here.'

'We're not really supposed to be here,' he said. 'We could be contaminating important evidence.'

'We don't have to go near the crime scene. And you've been in there already.'

He hesitated, then nodded. Bob should have posted someone in the house as a matter of routine. Perhaps it would be a good idea to stay.

'We'll have to get up early,' he said. 'Before Bob and his team arrive.'

'Ethan...' Sarah hesitated. 'Can I sleep with you tonight?'

He looked at her, astonishment vivid on his face.

'Come again?'

She reddened.

'Oh, not ... not like that, I don't mean... Oh, hell, you mustn't imagine I... What I meant was... I don't want to spend the night alone, not after what happened. Our bedrooms aren't exactly close together. What if something happened?'

'Sarah, I don't exactly think... I couldn't... If you slept in my bed, well ... you might be my niece and everything, but you're an attractive woman and...'

'Oh, I didn't mean in your bed, not that. Why would you think that? In your room. There's some sort of bunk bed in mine, we could just...'

He opened his mouth, then closed it again. She was talking sense. He had already brought a shotgun up from the gunroom in order to keep it next to him overnight.

'You promise not to prance about in anything too ... revealing or...'

'Ethan, it is about a million degrees below freezing outside, a freezing fog is on its way from the West Country, and I shall be wearing my thickest thermal undies beneath layers of the gear I wear when I'm mountaineering. Or would you actually prefer it if I – what did you say? – pranced around in a tiny thong and socks?'

He had rather hoped to avoid having such an image implanted in his already overcharged brain.

'I'm ... that's to say ... I'm perfectly sure we can contrive something. But I'll have the camp bed.'

'That's the first sensible thing you've said all day.'

'What about these relics, though – if that's what they are? Shouldn't we get them out of that miserable place? They may get rusty or something.'

'Ethan, they have waited for decades. If they are rusty, they are rusty. If God has need of them, He has infinite patience, or so I'm told. I'm sure another night in the vault won't do them any harm. We'll fetch them in the morning. Now, all I want is to put my head on a pillow and crash out.'

They left without thinking, leaving the letter and the map behind.

When he next saw her, she was wearing a heavy-duty dressing gown raided from Senhora Salgueiro's wardrobe. She kicked a leg to show him the flannelette pyjamas underneath.

Ethan did the rounds of the vast, almost empty house. He found the control panel for the burglar alarm, but could not locate the code number anywhere. It was too late to ring Senhora Salgueiro, but he thought it unlikely there would be any fresh break-ins over the next few hours. He headed back to his bedroom and slipped inside a sleeping bag on the narrow camp bed, mentally preparing himself for an uncomfortable night. He switched out the table lamp he'd placed on the floor next to him and wished Sarah goodnight.

'Goodnight, Sarah. Try not to think about what's happened. Get a good night's sleep.'

'I'm going to sleep for the next week,' she answered, her voice slurred with tiredness. Moments later, light snoring filled the air.

'Sarah? Sarah, are you still awake?'

Obviously not.

CHAPTER SEVEN

A Visit in the Night

Sleep came to Ethan at last, but it proved a troubled sleep, broken with dreams of the dead, nightmares in which every murder victim he had ever seen rose up from blood or water or earth to stalk him. They came to him, one followed by another, pallid remnants of human beings, some recognisable, others beyond all recognition. And they spoke to him of death and its suddenness, of the minute inflictions of pain that had brought them down, of the speed of a knife or the agony of a bullet crashing through the naked skull. Abi his wife stood among them, pointing and still, and his bleeding grandfather stood behind her, grinning and deathly pale.

He woke with a start. Images from the depths of sleep hung before his eyes, sounds from his dreams reverberated in his ears, and his brain struggled to break free. Then he heard a sound and knew it was in the room with him. Someone was moving in the darkness.

'Sarah?' he mumbled, thinking she must

be trying to find her way through the dark to the bathroom. 'Put the light on. Don't you bloody fall on me.'

There was a scream, then someone switched the light on. The glare was too harsh for his sleep-filled eyes. He blinked, his head filling with jagged fragments of light that hurt his pupils like shards of fine glass. The scream echoed a second time. Sarah. He forced himself to keep his eyes open.

Two men were standing over Sarah, who lay on her back in bed. One was just switching off a torch. The other reached down and grabbed Sarah's arm, pulling her out from the bedclothes, while she struggled to resist him. Her legs tangled with the covers, her assailant's grip tightened, and inch by inch he dragged her out.

Ethan wriggled out of his sleeping bag. It was freezing cold, but he pulled himself free and got to his feet.

The man who had been holding the torch turned and looked at him.

'Sit down,' he said. 'If your life means anything to you.'

When Ethan looked again, he saw that the man was holding a pistol and that it was pointing straight at him. Somewhere in his brain, he registered that the man had spoken with a foreign accent, German, perhaps, or Scandinavian.

'Who the fuck are you?' he asked. 'What's

going on?'

'I'm here to ask the questions,' the armed man replied. 'Do as I say and sit down.'

The other man had managed to pull Sarah free of the bedclothes, and to haul her to a standing position beside the bed. He remained silent throughout.

The man with the gun spoke.

'I told you to sit down. If you don't, my friend here will hurt her. Keep your hands in front of you, and forget any thoughts you may have of heroism. If you try to attack either of us, I will not hesitate to shoot you.'

The camp bed was too unstable to sit on, so Ethan crossed to the nearest chair and sat on it. He took care to commit the faces of the intruders to memory, singling out the most obvious features that would work well later in an e-fit or EigenFIT session at the station.

The man with the gun wore a black woollen cap from the edges of which strands of blond hair poked out. He looked to be in his mid-thirties, well fed, calm. His face was northern European, his eyes were deep cerulean, his lower jaw was set back half an inch from the upper, his ears stuck out slightly more than average, a long scar ran from high on his forehead almost to the point of a sharp nose. But while the region of Ethan's brain that was a policeman took all this in, the emotional centres focused, not on the disparate parts, but on the man himself; and the man sent a narrow blade of ice all the way along Ethan's spine. He had interviewed his share of killers in his time, and he knew at once that the man only a couple of yards away would be capable of anything, that murder would come to him as easily as blowing his nose.

The other man was, Ethan thought, quite probably eastern European or Russian. He was much bigger than the first man, well over six feet tall, and muscular. His face, like his partner's, showed neither emotion nor any sign of stress. Thick, startled eyebrows like giant hairy caterpillars loomed above heavy, wrinkled eyelids. Beneath the latter glared somnolent, dark olive-green eyes, and lower again pale thin lips framed yellowing teeth. Beauty and the Beast, thought Ethan. If Beauty was a killer, Beast would be the torturer who prepared his victims for the *coup de grâce*.

Beauty snapped an order to his companion in a language that sounded Slavic to Ethan's ears. The big man nodded, took tight hold of Sarah and twisted her round till she was facing him. Suddenly, he grabbed her clothes at the neck and started to rip them. His meaty hands tore the fabric apart like paper. He stripped her to the waist, then pushed down her trousers and pants before forcing her to step out of them.

Ethan looked away, but it was all he could do not to throw himself on one or other of the attackers.

Beauty walked across to Ethan and put the barrel of his gun under his chin, forcing him to raise his head.

'Mr Usherwood. Ethan. You bear a great resemblance to your photograph. Miss Usherwood too. She's a lovely young woman, is she not? Pretty, and with such a striking body. My companion is, as you can imagine, a lonely man. Not a great success with women, unless he has them by force or whatever small sums he can afford to pay the more desperate among them. His attitude to the sexual act is, if I may put it bluntly, much like that of an ape. I don't expect him to live long, but for the moment he is strong and devoted to me, and I find him useful.

'Now, I should add that I find Miss Usherwood most tantalising. If you would care to open your eyes, you would see that she has the most delectable of bodies: firm young breasts, a waist and hips that would make a man of stone desire her, long, slim legs... Imagine it all for yourself. And while you do so, let me tell you what Lukacs here is going to do with your precious niece. He is going to rape her. He is going to force himself on her, and it's very likely he will hurt her while he does so. He is not a gentle man; I'm sure you can see that. She is already shivering, so I imagine the ordeal will be worse for her than if she were warm, relaxed, and welcoming.

'When he has done, he will withdraw and take out his gun to point at you while I rape her as well. Of course, I am hardly as well endowed as my little friend Lukacs, but I shall be eager. And when I too have done, I see plenty of objects in this room that could be well employed to rape her as many times as Lukacs and I desire.'

'You may as well kill me,' shouted Sarah, fighting hard to stop herself quivering from cold and fear.

'We may do that in the end,' said Beauty. 'Once I have all I need from you, that's exactly what I may do.'

'What do you want?' asked Ethan, praying it was something he could give. He knew he would give anything to prevent everything the man had threatened. Even had Sarah been the remotest person to him, a passing stranger from any street or street corner, he would have offered her assailants whatever they wanted just to spare her the ordeal they threatened. And it dawned on him then, in that moment of crisis, that in the short time he'd known her, Sarah had, of all people, become the least remote to him.

'How touching of you to ask. Your grandfather asked the same thing of me last night.

When I answered him, he clammed up. No matter what inducements I offered him and his friend, they refused to part with the information I needed. Perhaps you will do better, you or your niece here.'

'Then get on with it,' spat out Ethan.

'What we came for last night, what we are here for tonight as well, are not things of any great significance to you. You have never seen them, they have no sentimental value to you, as they did for your grandfather. Perhaps you will find it easier to part with them. You already know that Lukacs and I have no compunctions. No morals, no ethical code. At least, none that either of you would recognise. You are a policeman, and you see the world with a policeman's eyes, all rules and regulations passed on to you by someone else. That's pitiful. Your sort will always lose. You lack the willpower, the inner strength, the natural hardness of mind and body that gives victory to the strong.'

Ethan opened his eyes. There was no shame in anything now. Sarah's nakedness was no reason for embarrassment, not for her, not for him. He could see nothing beautiful or desirable in her, not now, not in this bitter cold, with the threats of rape and death hanging in the unfeeling air. The only emotions he felt were pity and fear. For some reason – a true instinct, as he would later reckon it – he thought of photographs he had seen of women herded into concentration camps and stripped naked.

'Tell me what you want, take it, and get out of here,' said Ethan.

'Pray to whatever god you worship that you know where to find them. We're here to take what rightly belongs to us. The Spear of Destiny, the Grail, the Crown of Thorns, all the Christ relics. If you know where they are, you would do well to tell us. And if you don't know what I'm talking about, I find it hard to believe your niece will have any trouble.'

He looked round at Sarah, who was shivering badly now as the intense cold bit through her skin. The Beast was holding her firmly from behind, pinning her arms to her side. Her skin was showing signs of exposure, her lips had turned blue, and wave after wave of involuntary shudders passed through her. Ethan looked into her eyes and almost recoiled at the horror and helplessness he saw reflected in them.

'Tell him, Ethan. Whatever they are, they aren't worth this.'

'You promise you will let her go the moment you have the relics in your hands?'

'Of course. Why would I encumber myself with her? Lukacs and I will be out of your hair as soon as the relics are handed over. Believe me, you will never hear from us again. Your bumbling police will never track us down; perhaps you can warn them not to bother trying. Now, tell us where they are.'

He told them.

Beauty looked him up and down.

'How do you know this?' he asked.

'I ... told him,' said Sarah. 'The relics are still there. You can take them. I hope they make you happy. I hope they bring you close to God.'

The sarcasm was lost on the intruders.

'Take us there now,' said the blond man.

'I have to find the key to the mausoleum.'

'Then you'd better be quick before the little lady here dies of cold.'

The place to start was in the kitchen, in the old pantry, where a key box had been fastened to the wall for generations, and where every key that had ever passed through Woodmancote Hall hung from a hook or nestled among a tangled heap of its brass and iron companions. Ethan worked his way through them systematically. Behind him stood Beauty and the Beast, and with them Sarah. Ethan had insisted that they give her a blanket to cover her, and slippers for her feet, but that was the only concession they would make, and at every moment, it seemed likely they would take it away again.

The key to the family vault was on a hook at one side of the box, apart from the rest. A thin cardboard label in a copperplate hand had obviously hung from it for a very long time. It was a large brass key that had clearly not been used very often. The last but one death had been Gerald's wife Edith. She had been interred in one of the last vacant spaces, in the expectation that Gerald would join her there in due course. Ethan had been twenty-three when Edith died. He had never known her very well, and for most of that time as a child.

He had been a man at the time of the last interment, a man of thirty weeping uncontrollably, watched by friends and family, helpless to assuage his grief. Struggling against the tears, he had helped shoulder Abi's coffin to its final destination inside the vault. He had locked the door behind her with his own hand.

'Let's get this done,' he said, and led the way outside.

The snow had stopped falling, but a bitter frost lay in the air and, in the sky above, the moon hovered in silence, as though itself the origin of all this coldness, its white light lying undimmed on the unbroken passages of snow. Sarah thought she would die as the frost crept across her skin. This was the way they had gone the night before, on their way to midnight mass. She had slipped her arm through Ethan's, feeling great comfort in it.

But tonight there was no comfort in anything, no mood of celebration, no dimly remembered holiness. Just this: a killing cold and men who would rape and kill her as they would shoot a racehorse with a broken leg.

The mausoleum was set back at the end of a sloping lawn, beside the willow-bordered expanse of Beecham Water, a large pond that some called a small lake and others dismissed as an outsize puddle. Built from marble in the eighteenth century, the vault held the remains of generations of Usherwoods, husbands and wives, children and grandchildren. The earliest coffins had been removed and reburied in the churchyard at the end of the nineteenth century, to make way for another crop of the dead.

The lock turned reluctantly, aided by sprays of hot water and WD-40 brought for the purpose by Ethan. Beauty held a torch while he worked the lock.

An owl hooted mournfully somewhere close by. Bare willow branches moved against the sky, rattling in the light breeze. Across the surface of the frozen pond, moonlight lay like spilt milk. Suddenly, an animal screamed. There was movement among the trees on the other side of Beecham Water. The lock gave way, and the key turned fully. They were in.

The door swung back with a tearing sound, as if it was about to peel away from its hinges.

Ethan made a mental note to have the hinges oiled before they came to need replacing entirely. Beauty shone his torch inside. He said nothing and betrayed nothing of the excitement he felt at this moment.

The bright beam played across a central aisle flanked on both sides by deep niches filled with coffins. Not even the sudden influx of fresh air could dispel the musty odour of death and disuse that hung over the entire vault. Cobwebs festooned the interior, and spiders that had known nothing but darkness all their lives scurried away at the touch of light.

Ethan hesitated at the entrance, knowing how simple it would be for their attackers to kill him and Sarah here and leave their bodies until it was time for the next burial. Beauty shoved him inside, and Lukacs came after, dragging Sarah unwillingly behind.

Despite Beauty's torch, the tomb seemed a vast place of darkness, darkness that began with the eyes and ended in the very depths of the soul. From the ceiling above there hung banners of tattered spiders' webs, grown dirty after long, long years without light. Each niche and each coffin bore the name of its occupant, but Ethan preferred not to take note of them. Some of these were people he'd known in his youth and childhood, others bore the names of ancestors of whom

136

he'd heard stories told by his father and grandfather round the fireplace or in his bed late at night. And there, on his right, without need for a nameplate or other sign, lay Abi's coffin tight inside its niche, its metal ornamentation already rusted, cobwebs weaving their way into the gaps and interstices. He had to fight against the temptation to picture what lay inside.

At the far end, placed on a table and propped against the wall, were several objects whose identity was not at first obvious. They walked down in silence. Ethan heard a sharp intake of breath beside him as Beauty showed emotion for the first time. He heard the man mutter something in a language that was not German. In front of them stood a Roman lance, and at its foot a pottery cup, and what looked like a dome of thorns. The German – for Ethan was by now certain that was his nationality – played the torch beam everywhere, picking out yet more objects: a wooden board with writing in three languages, a short piece of wood, and a piece of fabric, folded several times and rusted with age.

'Is this everything?' the German demanded. 'If there's anything else and you don't tell me, you will both die.'

'This is all I know about. I've seen nothing like them anywhere else in the house.'

For several moments, their fate hung by a

thread. Ethan knew that if they were to die, it would be now. Then the German nodded. Lukacs stepped forward, still gripping Sarah tightly by one arm, while she fought to cover her half-naked body with the other. Her feet were filthy, and her skin was already grey with cobwebs. She stifled a cry as a large spider scuttled across her right foot. With his free hand, the big man reached inside his coat and brought out a large lump of fabric that opened moments later to become a holdall. He handed Sarah to the German, then placed the relics – the *pilum* in two halves – into the bag and zipped it tight.

'I hope you are telling me the truth,' said Beauty. 'If not, you will see me again.'

Ethan opened his mouth to protest, but at that moment the German lifted his hand and brought the gun down hard against his skull. Everything went black. Ethan fell in a heap to the floor.

CHAPTER EIGHT

The Charnel House

First there was darkness, then he opened his eyes and there was still darkness. His head was aching and spinning, and when he tried to move it, the pain grew instantly more intense and the spinning made him want to throw up. He took a deep breath and lay still. Blinking hurt, and it did nothing to dispel the darkness. He could hear voices, but something told him they were only in his head, echoes from the past, fading, then running back with renewed intensity. It took some time for it to sink in that he must still be in the mausoleum. That was when he realised just how cold he was. He'd no idea how long he'd been lying in that spot, he could barely remember the moment when he'd been struck. Hours might have passed, a whole day. He tried to stand up, but the dizziness took hold of him, and a crashing pain sliced through his skull. He fell back to the floor and lost consciousness again.

When he became lucid for a second time, the darkness was just as intense, the cold was more biting, but the pain in his skull had receded somewhat. His first thought this time was to ask himself what had happened to Sarah.

'Sarah?' he asked, then again, this time more loudly, 'Sarah? Are you there? Can you hear me?'

No one answered. He was stabbed by the thought that their assailants had killed Sarah and left him for dead. And that was when it sank in to him that he was lying on a stone floor surrounded by the bones of his family, and that if he didn't get out of there fast he'd freeze to death and remain there until someone brought a coffin and put him in it. Something unpleasant walked onto his face and began to creep across it, over his chin, then onto his mouth; but he was too far gone to do more than take notice of its presence.

Part of him – and not a small part – wanted to curl up and go back to sleep. He hadn't noticed the cold or the pain throughout his head and limbs when he'd been asleep, and at the moment sleep felt like the best thing in the world. Just another minute, maybe two, maybe half an hour; an incessant voice soaked through his brain, teasing and enticing him. 'What's the point of getting up?' the voice insinuated. 'Sarah's dead, Abi's dead, Granddad's dead, you'll be dead soon, better sleep it out, better give in, better let go, go with the flow, with the slow flow, with the so so slow flow, with...'

He snapped himself awake, sending a bolt of pain through the base of his skull, where it met his spine and travelled on down his body. It was the best thing he could have done. The pain brought him fully awake. He reached up and knocked the huge spider squatting on his mouth flying into the darkness.

It took most of his strength to struggle to his feet, and the moment he did, he pitched forwards onto the floor again. His legs, numb with cold and nerveless from hours of immobility, simply would not support him. Using his arms this time to push himself to a sitting position, he bent forwards to rub his legs in an attempt to force warmth and life back into them. He had come out dressed only in the thick pyjamas he'd been wearing in bed, over which he'd thrown on the tweed jacket he'd left over a chair. Flexing his legs and gritting his teeth against the jagged pains that shot up and down them, he took a deep breath, then thrust up from the floor, staggering for balance.

He thought he'd go down again and feared another fall might break a leg or an arm. But remembering where he was, he managed to lurch to one side, first one step, then a second, until he crashed into an obstruction and grabbed hold of it by both hands.

Running his hands over it, he recognised it as the end of a coffin.

That was the moment he realised that he didn't know which way he was facing. There wasn't a single chink of light in this place, not so much as a pinprick. It was eternal dark in here, interrupted only by the brief moments of death that brought men in dark suits carrying coffins.

The layout of the mausoleum was straightforward enough: a high-ceilinged space divided on each side into niches, like a wall of pigeonholes. Most of the niches were filled with coffins, leaving only a few to receive the next interments. It should be a simple matter to find the door, open it, and get out into the fresh air. Using the coffins to his left as a guide, he crept forward, aching in every joint as his legs moved across the granite floor.

It took him less than a minute to reach the far end. He ran a hand across it, and encountered nothing but cobwebs and stone. The stone wall ran right across the rear of the building, from one bank of niches to the next. The mausoleum had been well built, to withstand the ravages of rain, damp, and storm. It took less time to turn and walk to the other end, where his outstretched hand struck the door. Carefully, he ran his hands over the wood until he came to the line that separated the two halves. His fingers moved up and down on either side of the line, but even as they did so, his heart sank and he became absolutely still. He'd been looking for a handle, or two handles, two knobs, two ways of opening the door. But he knew it was a waste of time, that no one put handles on the inside of a mausoleum.

He pushed hard, now against one side, now against the other. The heavy door remained unmoving. Harder now, he pushed and pushed again. Surely his assailants would have run out, not taking time to lock him inside. Surely they would not have wished such a fate on him. But then he thought of what he had seen in his grandfather's study, the mutilations on the two bodies, the callous way the man called Lukacs had stripped Sarah and forced her half naked into the coldest night of the year.

As it sank in on him that he was trapped, that he would die here in the cold and dark, absolutely alone but for the uncaring dead, he felt panic rise in him. The door was solid wood built into the masonry on heavy-weight brass hinges, and he knew it was utterly beyond his strength to effect the slightest damage on it, or to move it even by a fraction. His legs, weakened by cold and hunger, went from under him, and he fell awkwardly and painfully on his right hip, knocking the breath from his lungs and jarring his elbow. In that moment, he knew himself defeated, and with that ghastly understanding, knew Sarah too would soon be dead, if they had not killed her already.

He dragged himself into a sitting position, with his back to the door, and waited until he had more control over his breathing, and the pains in his hip and elbow subsided to a more bearable level. He had no way of knowing whether or not he had broken anything, but he realised that it scarcely mattered. Where would he walk to, what would he use his arm for?

He had no idea how long it would be before the air became stale, but he was sure it would in time. His eyes had adjusted to the dark, but that meant nothing for there was no light in here at all. The only sense that meant anything in here was touch, and all he touched was the work of spiders, or the rotting masks of death ancient and renewed. Everything in this stone chamber would return to dust, and he would go down to dust with the rest.

It was hard to think, hard to bear the inevitability of what awaited him. He felt a tugging and tearing at his heart to think how, without blame, Sarah had been pulled into whatever plot lay behind this whole business. He thought hard to grasp what it could be about, but nothing fitted, nothing made sense, nothing satisfied his sense of justice and orderliness. Objects that might be relics of the crucifixion and might not, taken from a tomb in the Libyan desert, had ended up in a tomb in the English countryside, and had now been stolen by men whose motive Ethan could barely guess at. Could Christian relics drive men to murder, or to bury a stranger in a mausoleum, or to strip a woman naked and threaten to rape her?

His hip was still painful. Carefully, he transferred his weight to the other side, holding himself upright by his left hand. As he shifted, he felt something dig into his left thigh. He couldn't think what it was at first, but when he slipped a hand into his trouser pocket, he brought it out holding the box of cook's matches he'd put there the day before, when lighting the candles for dinner.

He put the matches down on the floor beside him, thinking that they would at least give him a little light before the darkness took him entirely. After a few minutes, however, it occurred to him that he might strike a couple of matches in order to take a closer look at the door, in case there was some mechanism he had missed with his bare hands.

He opened the box gingerly, fearful of spilling the contents across the floor, and took a match from inside. It was a long match designed to burn for some time. He struck it against the side of the container, and a bright light flared up. Holding the match carefully in order to get the maximum time from it, he used the little flame to orient himself.

The door was right in front of him, as he had known it would be, and on either side coffins stretched back into darkness. In some ways, seeing where he was proved more horrifying than imagining it in the dark. The light burnt for its short life, then flickered and went out.

He got to his feet and struck a second match, and this time he scrutinised one side of the door carefully. Using a third match, he did the same with the other side. When the flame died, his hope, slender though it had been, died with it. There was nothing but the flat wooden surface of the inside of a door through which it had never been intended that anyone should pass back to the light. No handle, no knob, no bolt, no fixture of any kind that would bypass the lock.

He sank back onto his haunches and contemplated suicide. Anything but stay here in the dark, starving, breathing in stale air, ripening to death like a decaying fruit in a sped-up video installation. He could try choking himself to death with his handkerchief rolled into a ball, but he knew that the vomit reflex in his throat would make him spit it out again. Death would come to him slowly and in delirium.

And then he thought of fire. He had it in his means to light a fire that might engulf him and kill him in due course. But where would he find enough kindling, and how could he create enough heat to burn himself without suffering cruel pain?

Perhaps he could find a cord somewhere, and a hook to tie it to, and strangle himself. Prisoners in cells managed it. As a young policeman, he'd once had to cut a man down in the cells beneath the magistrates' courts, too late to save his life. Some managed it with shoelaces, others with neckties. He had neither.

He went over it all again, thinking himself through all the ways to end a human life, and he declared himself bereft of ideas. It occurred to him that, if he could bring himself to it, he could open one of the older coffins and plunder the skeleton inside. A broken leg bone might be sharp enough to let him cut his wrists or his throat. But how to break a coffin open without tools?

That was when he thought of fire again. The coffins were covered in cloth, cloth that would burn like a dream, and beneath the cloth was wood that would catch fire, and beneath the lid lay a lining, and beneath that a shroud. If he could burn off a lid enough to let him break it, he could do the rest. But it would be a waste of time if he could not steel himself to dig through rotten flesh to find a suitable bone, or use a fragment of bone to cut his own flesh to the bone.

And then he realised he would not need to go so far. All he had to do was set a lighted coffin against the door, get it burning until the dry wooden door caught light and burnt. If he could ignite a fierce enough flame, the door would give way in time, and he could burst it open. If he didn't choke to death on the smoke first. But if he could punch a hole in the door early enough in the process, he could create a vent through which most of the smoke would escape.

Would it work? He shrugged. He'd thought of everything else and drawn a blank. If he didn't act soon, the cold would send him back to sleep, and he might not wake up. That would be a peaceful enough end, but he feared it more than all the others.

He put the box of matches back into his pocket, in case he crushed them while trying to set a fire. In the dark again, and fumbling, he walked back down the wide aisle, stopping halfway to select one of the older coffins. Older cloth, older wood, older bones; he hoped this combination would help create quicker flames and greater heat.

The coffin fitted tightly inside its niche, but there was just enough space on either side for him to push his hands through, grazing his knuckles on the rough stone. Pulling the dead weight out would not be easy, he thought. But he had no choice. He got what purchase he could on the outer wrapper of felt, hoping the cloth would hold long enough for him to get a foot or so of the box out of its hole. He pulled, but the coffin would not budge. Taking a deep breath, he exerted all his strength; the cloth ripped on both sides, and he fell backwards, winding himself as he crashed into the array of coffins on the other side.

Picking himself up, he chose another coffin at random, this time slipping his hands beneath the box, with his thumbs above. The felt cloth tore again, but this time it did so nearer the broad-headed nails that held it in place close to the foot of the coffin. This in turn formed a handle of sorts that held long enough for Ethan to pull the coffin a fair distance from its niche.

Bit by bit, inch by inch, he yanked and dragged the long wooden box out into the aisle. As the head finally came free and crashed onto the floor, Ethan felt his arms drained of strength. He sat again, waiting for the blood supply to return, fearing again that gentle lapse, that slip into unconsciousness that would imprison him here for ever.

Pushing now, he got the coffin to the door and laid it lengthways against it. He was so far weakened by his exertions that he knew he would have to make do with a single coffin. He knew he would never find the strength to drag another from its niche.

Bracing himself, he stood next to the coffin, raised his foot, and brought it down on the lid with all the strength he could muster. It was little enough. The wood splintered, but the lid did not seem to break through. Again, he stamped down, and this time the lid cracked beneath him, and his foot went down into something that gave way like ice on a pond. Something that must have been bone shattered like twigs breaking. Despite the dark, he shut his eyes, hating to think what else his foot had come into contact with. Gingerly, he removed it from the jagged hole he'd created, moved it a foot to one side, and stamped down hard again. Wood and bone gave way, and this time something sharp tore his ankle.

He did it twice again, then stood breathless and filled with revulsion by the broken coffin. Reaching inside his pocket, he drew out the matchbox and opened it. His hand shook as he removed the first match, but he clenched his jaw and forced himself to strike it.

Bright flame shot up again. Pausing only to look for the first hole, he held the match into the coffin. Instantly, the tiny flame caught something inside, and he withdrew it, using the last part to ignite the baize covering. A second match set alight more of the shroud and inner lining, and a third, and a fourth. Everything he touched was dry as tinder. He grabbed the coffin from beneath and tilted it, so that the blossoming flames burnt with growing strength against the door.

Though he covered his mouth and nostrils with a handkerchief, the smoke drifted up into his eyes, and slowly began to work its way through his nose into his lungs. As the blaze grew, so the smoke became thicker and more corrosive. He was finally forced to stagger back, coughing and choking.

Recovering his breath, he ran towards the door and kicked it hard low down, where the flames had taken hold. It gave slightly, but the smoke forced him back again. His eyes were stinging, and his throat burnt with the acrid fumes. He retreated again. The flames were bright enough now to illuminate more of the door and the burning coffin, but he could see that they had not taken hold sufficiently to ensure a constant blaze. The smoke was spreading persistently through the vault. If he could not create a vent, he would soon be overcome.

He ran back, and this time managed to tilt the coffin far enough for it to wedge itself against the door, allowing the flames to catch hold of the side and bottom. Something rattled and shook within the box as he moved it. Coughing deeply now, he pulled back again and waited as long as he could for the flames to bite more deeply into the wood.

Holding the handkerchief tightly against

his face, he ran forward again, kicking again and again at the charred door. Just as he was about to stagger away, he felt something give, and his foot went out, piercing through a hole that further lacerated his ankle. But as he looked down, he saw what seemed wholly miraculous to him, a broad lance of sunlight pouring into the mausoleum from outside. The smoke, granted a means of escape from the charnel house, rushed through the hole, blotting out the sunlight. Ethan went back as far as he could and watched as the flames took firm hold. Then forward again, kicking at the space around the hole, widening it, allowing more smoke to billow out.

Once the door was burning fiercely, Ethan waited. His lungs were still seared by the black smoke, his eyes were red and puffy, and he could barely open them. From time to time, he would open them a crack, to see how far the flames had advanced, and at last he saw them overcome the centre of the door. The spot where the lock was situated. Too soon, and he might yet fall foul of the fumes, too late and he would certainly succumb. He waited as long as seemed to him reasonable, then ran full tilt against the door; he took it in the centre with his right shoulder, crying out with pain as he struck it, but it gave, and he shoved again, harder now with desperation, and a third time, and the wood broke, the lock separated one half from the other, the door burst open, and he fell, head over heels, coughing and spluttering, bleeding and torn, tumbling onto the mausoleum steps, and down onto the thick snow, where he lay weeping in the sunlight, sucking in fresh air that tasted like the finest wine. Blackness started to come over him then, and sleep, a desperate, gnawing need for sleep; but he knew that the snow and the air would kill him as soon as smoke or famine. Pushed to the limit now, he got to his feet and stumbled across the curve of white field in the direction of the house.

CHAPTER NINE

Between Heaven and Hell

Thoughts of hell in high coffins filled Sarah's head at every moment. She could not clear that glimpse of the spider-haunted tomb from her mind, the stacks of coffins, the final darkness of that foul habitation. Nor could she dig deep enough into her thoughts to eradicate all memory of what had been done to Ethan. That blow on the head, the heavy crash of the doors shutting him inside, the clunk of the key as Beauty turned it in the lock. What had happened to her, what was happening to her, was nothing when set against that blow, that cruel consignment to a fate of unimaginable horror. Perhaps the blow had killed him, she thought, thinking that the best thing. But she could not rid herself of the image of him coming round in the darkness, of the slow realisation of where he was, of the slow death he would suffer, of the madness that might take him before the end.

She shuddered, and tried to ease the pain in her legs, but as she twisted, the pain worsened, forcing her to turn back to her original position. The German had injected her with something when they'd finished at the lodge, and everything had gone black. There had been dreams, terrible dreams, nightmares really – no, more than that, a sort of hell without flames, a kind of passage through some underworld of misery and fear. She'd come round to find herself strapped to some sort of narrow table, with leather straps across her legs and hips and chest, and as she'd grown more alert, pains had started all across her body, and with the pains memories she wanted to destroy but could not.

Whatever drug they'd given her was wearing off now, but its after-effects lingered. Her head was pounding, her brain felt as though a master chef had sliced it into thin pieces, her skin crawled as though ten thousand spiders from hell were dancing a tarantella across her flesh, her stomach heaved as though some dark poisoned wine had been poured down her throat.

But none of these pains and discomforts troubled her half as much as the bruising and burning she felt between her legs. She squeezed her eyes shut against tears, as vivid memories of the rape flashed through her mind. Her heart lurched again as the memories acquired detail, as if each loathsome moment had been stored in her body.

It was, of course, a mistake to speak of 'the rape', for they had raped her more than once, taking turns. How many times, she could not be entirely sure; but the agony of being taken by force, without response or will on her part, the stench of the big man's body, the mechanical thrusting, the tearing, the knowledge that this was done, not for anyone's pleasure, but as a token of humiliation and as a warning – all this had choked and bewildered her, cutting her off from her own feelings, turning what had once been an intensely pleasurable act into something monstrous.

The German (if that was what he was) had told her several times that the rapes were a prefiguration of what would happen to her later if she did not play ball. Where they were going, he said, other men were waiting, men who would gladly use her in the same way, carelessly, as the mood took them, or lust dictated. She would be left naked and bound for them, in a room open at all hours of the day. Sometimes they would visit her singly, sometimes in pairs, often in small groups.

Unless, he said, she cooperated fully.

'What do you want me to do?' she had asked. 'How can I cooperate?'

But he'd told her to wait, said that all would be made clear in time.

They had raped her in the lodge, in the main bedroom. They had gagged her to stop her screaming. She'd been tied to the bed, and all the time, if she turned her head, she could see through the bedroom window to Woodmancote, a shadow in the darkness. The screams had all erupted in her own head. She wondered if either of them had AIDS.

As she grew more aware, she realised she was strapped to a stretcher in what looked like an ambulance. There was no one inside the main compartment with her, but if she raised her head, she could see a curtained window in front of which lay the driver's cab. In an effort to relieve her physical distress, she succeeded in getting the lower part of her right hand free from the strap. From the size and design of the ambulance, she guessed it must be private. Were they taking her to a hospital or clinic somewhere? She felt cold at the thought. What would they intend to do with her in a place like that?

On her right, a venetian blind covered a side window. The cord was just out of her reach but, reinvigorated, she squirmed and twisted until her fingers gained a tight enough grip on it to pull. Slowly, the blind lifted, far enough for her to see out. As she turned her face to look out, the ambulance slowed down.

She saw part of a street with old cars parked by the kerb. A cart drawn by a donkey ambled past in the opposite direction, then they were passing a row of odd-looking shops. The sign above one read as *Macelarie*. She had no idea what language it was. As they neared the end of the row, the ambulance turned into a narrow track and the buildings were replaced by dark trees whose branches hung beneath the weight of snow.

She let the blind fall back into place. Much as she wanted to continue looking out, she knew it would mean running a risk should her captors know she'd seen through the window. Reluctantly, she slipped her forearm back under the strap and let her head drop down once more onto the stretcher.

At least she knew one thing: she was no

longer in England.

Ethan got to the house just as fresh snow clouds mounted the horizon and began to empty themselves across the frozen fields. He had no key, and for a long moment feared he might not get back inside. He had no idea what time of day it was, or even if hours had passed or a day or two days. And it occurred to him that Beauty and the Beast might still be in the hall.

But as he rounded the side of the house and came to the front, he saw cars parked in the drive, including several police cars. They were still doing the forensic work, he thought with relief. He went up to the young constable who'd been posted at the front door.

'I'm DCI Usherwood,' he said. 'I think you'd better let me in.'

It turned out to be the same day, early afternoon. Boxing Day. The snow showed no sign of abating. All things were frozen, the world was like folded paper. Apart from the cuts on his ankles and scrapes on his hands, Ethan had not suffered great injury. The police team all knew him, and were shocked by his appearance. He was filthy, and parts of his upper clothing had been charred in the fire.

The house was full of police. Bob Forbes

said the search for forensic evidence had been widened, and that his bedroom was currently under investigation. Someone took him to a spare room, where a fire was lit and fresh clothes brought from his suitcase. They asked if he needed a doctor, but he shook his head and said the first-aid box would be enough.

Hot water was drawn from the unreliable old boiler, and half a bath filled. While he luxuriated in the water, DCI Forbes, came to talk to him. Ethan explained what had happened, and insisted they start a hunt for Sarah right away. Forbes gave orders to a junior detective, who went off to alert headquarters.

'We'll need a photograph,' said Bob, 'details of what she was wearing, all the usual stuff.'

There was a good-quality photo in Gerald's bedroom, in a frame on the bedside table. Ethan added what details he could remember, then went down to the kitchen to fix himself something to eat. Sitting at the table brought back vivid memories of the previous evening. What had happened during that meal? he wondered. He'd never met anyone like Sarah before, and he cursed his bad luck everyone thought she was his niece. They weren't blood relations at all, but if they wound up together, it would certainly *look* like incest, and that would hardly go down well in the family or anywhere else. The awful thing was, he had only ever felt this way about one person in his life before. Abi. And the events of last night had intensified his feelings, made raw by fear and a desperate need to protect Sarah from the brutes who'd taken her. Or killed her. He shuddered, and realised there was something he'd forgotten.

He asked Mary Boyd, a detective he'd worked with on several important cases, if the forensic team was planning to go through the library.

'I don't think so, sir. Maybe later. Do you want something in there?'

'Just a book,' he said. 'There's something I want to check. I was reading it yesterday.'

'I'm sure that will be OK, sir. This is your house, isn't it?'

'It's the family house.'

'He was your uncle or something, wasn't he? One of the victims?'

'Grandfather. I was very close to him. It's a huge blow.'

She sympathised, then he went to the library. No one was there, and it took him only moments to find the book and put the letter and map in his pocket.

He was on edge, desperately wanting to know if there was any news of Sarah. He found Bob Forbes, who said he'd heard nothing yet, but assured him HQ had taken

Ethan's story seriously and had sent out a general alert.

'Who's in charge?'

'Not sure. I'll find out.'

'I want to be put on the search team. Bob, I'm just wasting my time here. The super doesn't want me on the murder case because I may be emotionally involved. I've been taken off my other case, and here I am standing around making coffee and fretting.'

'Actually, the super's on his way over. He was asking about you, wanted to know if you were here. There's been a bit of a delay on the A46, but he's past that now. Should be here any minute.'

Five minutes later, Superintendent Willis left his driver to find a parking space, and came trudging up the drive to the house. Watching him through a ground-floor window, Ethan thought he seemed tired and distracted. Snow already lay on his bare head and the shoulders of his black overcoat. Ethan did not think it was just the snow that hampered his footsteps. The policeman on the door let him in.

Willis spent several minutes talking in the hall with Forbes. Ethan waited in the morning room, which was unaffected by the investigation. Being there brought back memories of holidays with his parents, and of his mother in particular. Today, his heart misgave him. He awaited Willis's arrival without hope, or the expectation of hope. The super's face as he approached the door had told him all he needed to know. Ethan thought of his mother, of her hope for life and the sudden illness that had spent two years defeating her, turning all hope sour. He had spent so many hours with her in this room, playing while she read, and, much later, reading aloud to her as she sat wasting in the chair he sat in now.

The door opened and Brian Willis stepped into the room. The door clicked shut behind him. The dim afternoon light, pearl-coloured from the snow, gave him a translucence at once contradicted by the expression on his face.

He did not sit down. For several moments, he looked at Ethan, who got to his feet to greet him. Ethan thought he seemed uneasy, wanting to speak yet unable to frame the right words. Then the super spoke.

'DCI Usherwood, I know you were questioned along with the other guests' yesterday. I understand you were the one who found the two bodies?'

Ethan shook his head.

'Mrs Salgueiro found them, sir. She came out screaming, and I went in. I notified HQ right away.'

'That was very prompt of you. Tell me, did you do anything else while you were in the study? Did you touch anything?'

162

Ethan frowned.

'Sir, I was shocked by what I found, but I didn't panic. I've been on dozens of murder scenes. I closed the door and forbade entry, then I found the nearest phone and rang in.'

'Where was the phone you used?'

'In my own room. It was quite close, and I knew there was a phone there. Sir, is something wrong?'

There was a long pause, then Willis shook his head.

'I don't know. I'm sure there's an explanation, but... Just a tick.'

The super went to the door and opened it part way. Moments later, Bob Forbes came in. He was carrying something in his hand, a plastic evidence bag with something in it, something long.

Superintendent Willis took the bag and held it out towards Ethan.

'DCI Usherwood, have you ever seen this before?'

The object he held out was a knife. It was a folding knife of unusual design, with a brown horn handle and a long, slim blade. The blade was about five inches in length and seemed very sharp. Ethan noticed traces of blood on it.

He shook his head.

'No, sir. If it was in the study when I went in, I didn't notice it.'

'You're quite sure of that? You're sure

you've never seen it before?'

'It's quite distinctive, sir. I've seen plenty of knives in my time, but never one like that.'

'That's curious. Just a moment.'

The super turned to Forbes, who hadn't looked Ethan in the eye since entering the room, and handed the transparent envelope back to him. He muttered something which Ethan didn't catch, after which Forbes left the room.

'What's going on, sir? Are you suggesting I know something about that knife, that I'm holding back...?'

The super tutted, as though in disapproval.

'Just wait a moment,' he said.

Ethan wondered what was going on. The super had never been the friendliest of men, but he'd never been curt like this.

The door opened and Bob Forbes stepped back inside. This time he was holding several larger bags, all containing what looked like items of clothing. Again, DI Forbes avoided looking at Ethan.

One by one, the DI handed the evidence bags across.

'Have you seen this before?' asked Willis, holding up a bag containing a woman's thong, a pretty thing with a pink see-through panel in front. There were darker marks on the panel, random blotches that might have been blood.

Ethan shook his head.

'I no longer have a wife, and I haven't had a girlfriend in several months, sir. No, I've never seen this before.'

'How about this?'

This time, the super held up a bag containing a bra that matched the thong.

'No, sir. Not that either.'

Forbes handed a third bag across. Willis let it open out. It held a white woman's dress on a hanger. The front of the dress had been slashed in several places, and was covered in blood.

'And this?'

Ethan wanted to throw up. He moved back a couple of steps, then collapsed onto the chair he'd been sitting on earlier. The food he'd eaten forced itself back up his throat, and he vomited onto the carpet. Shutting his eyes, he wiped his mouth and tried to concentrate. No one said a word. When he opened his eyes, the others were still looking at him.

'Well?' asked the super. 'Do you recognise this dress?'

Ethan nodded. His head was spinning. He felt something trickle from his nose and put his finger to it. He was bleeding. Staunching the nosebleed with a handkerchief, he nodded again.

'It belongs to Sarah. She was wearing it on Christmas Eve, at the party.' He bit his lower lip and repressed a sob. 'Where did you find her? What ... did they do?'

'We were hoping you'd tell us where she is,' Willis said, his voice hardening now, his manner honed in years of conversations with suspects.

'I have no idea. I told you, they must have driven off with her.'

'We found the dress in your bedroom, hidden underneath your mattress. The bra and knickers too. The knife had been shoved behind the radiator.'

Ethan felt suddenly like a butterfly pinned to cork while still alive. For several seconds, he stared at the clothing. His old colleagues looked back at him, unsmiling. Ethan felt his heart go out of him. He'd been standing where they were standing many times. He knew what they were thinking. Like them, he'd used an accusing silence to intimidate a suspect into confessing.

'You think this was my work?' he said. 'You think I killed her?'

The bra and thong, the dress had all been bloodied and planted. He had no doubt of it.

'DCI Usherwood, I think you should know that fingerprints were lifted from the knife several hours ago, and that they match samples of your fingerprints we hold on record. You should also know that the blood found on the dress and underwear is from two individuals. When DNA tests have been completed, we expect to confirm that the smaller patches of blood belong to you.'

'This is insane. She was my niece. Why would I harm her? And why the hell would I murder my grandfather? Or his friend?'

Willis breathed in sharply through his nostrils and held his breath tightly for some seconds before letting it escape again.

'I spoke with your family lawyers an hour ago. Apparently, the bulk of your grandfather's estate has been left to you, apart from a large sum bequeathed to your niece Sarah, and smaller amounts to other members of your family. Woodmancote Hall passes to you, along with its contents, apart from specific bequests listed in the will. You have a motive for the murders, and I have to act according to the evidence. I leave the rest of this to DI Forbes, who remains in charge of this investigation.'

Saying which, Willis turned and strode out of the room, leaving the door to swing closed behind him.

Bob Forbes stepped up to Ethan.

'DCI Usherwood, I am arresting you on suspicion of the murders of Gerald Usherwood and Max Chippendale. You are not obliged to say anything but anything you do say may be taken down and used in evidence against you.'

There was a knock on the door, then two

uniformed officers stepped into the room.

Ethan said nothing. He knew the score, knew what to say, what not to say.

'I'd like to make a phone call,' he said.

Forbes nodded, and he took the mobile from his jacket pocket. He tapped in a number and waited for someone to answer at the other end.

CHAPTER TEN

On the Loose

Adam Markham turned out to be exactly as Ethan had imagined him. He was what people call a 'safe hand'. Some said he was that rare thing, a man of the law you could trust. The moment Ethan set eyes on him, he had the same impression. Middle-aged, conventionally dressed, slightly plump, with a kind face, wise eyes, and frameless spectacles. In all probability, he would turn out to be a dull sort, a man for whom life pretty much began and ended with the law, with a little church attendance and sherry drinking to add spice. That, of course, was the impression he sought to convey, and the impression Ethan took.

But Mr Markham was not a criminal

lawyer, nor was anyone else in the much-esteemed family firm of Markham and Pritchett. When he met Ethan in the police cell where he was being held before an appearance before the magistrates' court the next day, he pointed this out to him, and added that good defence lawyers with experience in murder cases were thin on the ground in Gloucestershire.

'But I'll sort something out,' he said, his little eyes twinkling, as though Ethan was being pulled up before the beaks for an infringement of some forgotten by-law.

'I need to get out,' said Ethan.

'Out? You can't get out. Not before the magistrates' hearing.'

'I want to get bail. I need to get bail.'

'Ethan – if I may call you that – everyone wants bail. Ordinarily, there is little difficulty in obtaining it, as I'm sure you know. But these charges... They are, if I may say so, monstrous. Of course, I am your legal advisor, and I have every confidence in your lack of guilt in the matter. Unfortunately, the magistrates may not see it that way.'

'I was set up,' said Ethan. 'If I'm locked up, there's nothing I can do to prove myself innocent. I know Willis and Forbes and the rest, and I know what they do when they think they have a watertight case. They close down all other lines of inquiry and focus on getting a conviction.'

'There's time to deal with that once this goes to the Crown Court. You'll have a barrister, probably a silk, you can afford the best counsel.'

All Markham's clients were well heeled, and Ethan detected in him a carelessness to the risk he was running, a perception of things rooted in a preening assumption that money and status brought innocence in their train.

'If I'm right,' Ethan said. 'Sarah hasn't been killed at all. She's out there some-where, kidnapped probably.'

'But I can't see–'

'They took it too far, can't you see that? If they had killed her, why strip the body? If she'd been stabbed in the heart, why would her thong be bloodstained? It doesn't add up. If I were in charge of the investigation, I'd have a team of officers out there now, hunting for her.'

'Very well,' said the solicitor, 'I'll see what I can do.'

The following morning, he surprised Ethan. The heir to Woodmancote Hall had spent a miserable night in the cells, where he'd been treated with a mixture of em-barrassment and contempt. He'd been a popular officer, but now the shine had been taken off his image by the stories passing from mouth to mouth, stories that told of more than mere murder, that painted a gruesome portrait of a multiple killer who tortured his victims before despatching them in a bizarre and blasphemous fashion.

The chief constable had issued instructions that as little as possible be said to the press about the arrest. Ethan was hurried in to Gloucester Magistrates' Court through a back entrance used by the magistrates, and taken to a small court normally used for smaller cases. On his arrival, he was met by Brenda Pritchett, Markham's partner. She introduced herself to Ethan, then brought forward a tall, dark-haired man in an expensive-looking suit and soft silk tie.

'Ethan, this is Myles Clavering. Myles is a barrister with a long experience of criminal cases, including homicide.'

Ethan shook hands.

'I've not seen you in court before,' he said.

Clavering smiled. It was a rich smile, warm rather than polite. For some reason, Ethan took to him at once. Or was it because he desperately needed to put his faith in someone, anyone? He could not be sure.

'Actually, I'm not local. My patch is London.'

'And you've handled homicide cases before?'

'Fifteen, to be precise. Some manslaughter too.'

'And the outcomes?'

'Fifteen acquittals for the homicides.'

Ethan paused and thought hard.

'That's a good record,' he said. 'Bloody good, in fact. You'll be representing me at the Crown Court as well, I take it?'

Clavering nodded.

'That's the plan. I should mention that your father picked me out. His people employed me on a number of occasions in the past. He'll be in the public gallery.'

'Do you think I can get bail?'

Clavering did not answer right away. Ethan had the impression he had not thought about it before.

'Tricky, to be honest. The charges are serious, there are three counts of murder. But you're a policeman with a perfect record. I'll point out that you, of all people, would know exactly how to cover up your tracks. Leaving your fingerprints or your DNA behind would be such an elementary slip-up, you'd have to be suicidal.'

Ethan told him about the underwear, and he nodded and seemed thoughtful. Then an usher came and escorted the barrister to the courtroom, while Ethan was taken to a different door, through which he could access the dock.

The hearing took ten minutes. In court, Clavering could have won Oscars. He dominated the room. He did not stumble in his address, he did not fumble with papers, nor even look down at them. His mastery of the slim evidence available was complete and devastating. This was not a trial, but had it been, Ethan might well have been acquitted by all but the most obtuse jurymen and women. By contrast, Bob Forbes came across as uncertain and hampered by the knowledge that a colleague and superior stood in the dock.

But what swung the hearing in Ethan's favour were two fortuitous matters. The chairman of the bench had just completed his chairmanship training, and had arrived that morning expecting to sharpen his teeth on motoring offences. To compound this, the senior clerk who should have been sitting in front of the bench had been snowed in at home, leaving her place to be taken by a junior who seemed dwarfed by the rows of legal books on her desk. Clavering knew act and statute by heart, and while she fumbled, he took the magistrates through the complexities of bail legislation.

Ethan walked from the courthouse with an agreement to appear at the Crown Court in one month's time, and bail set at a figure of fifty thousand pounds. His father met him outside, and shook his hand.

'I know you didn't do this, Ethan. Clavering will get you off, don't worry.'

'It's not that simple, Dad. If the CPS field somebody first class, even Clavering could be out of his league. But the first thing is to find Sarah.'

'Sarah? I thought she was back in Oxford.'
Ethan explained.

'What are you planning to do?' his father
asked.

'I'm not sure yet. But if she's alive, somebody has to do something. Even if I can just
persuade someone to get a search under
way it would be something.'

They had a late breakfast at a little cafe
near the courthouse. The heavy snow was
keeping people out of the city centre, and
the place was almost empty. They sat in
overcoats, their hands hugging mugs of hot
coffee, snacking on crumpets smeared with
butter and Marmite.

'Dad, they're going to appeal the bail.
Once this gets into the press, which it will
by this evening, everybody and his dog will
start bawling about why a mass murderer
was released.

The Home Office will panic, MPs will get
up in Parliament, the tabloids will scream
for my blood, and I'll be back in clink before
you can ring Clavering's mobile.'

'What was the point of getting out, then?'

'I've been thinking this over all night, Dad.
Here's what I'd like you to do.'

A forensic team had already gone into his
flat in the town centre and spirited away
everything of interest, including his com-

puter. They made him sign all sorts of papers and warned him of the consequences of leaving Gloucester. He took it all in his stride. The entire thing felt more like an exercise at work, and once or twice he'd had to explain the procedure to the young officers who'd gone back to his flat with him. He'd felt more worried about them than about himself, and he spoke to them reassuringly, promising he would report at the station every day. They asked for his passport, and he handed it over without a word of protest. It would not, he knew, be long before someone more senior was in touch, Willis perhaps, or someone from the CPS, to say the bail decision had been overruled. He had to move quickly.

Leaving the forensic team to continue their work, he drove straight to the bank. His father had already paid a large sum into his account, and he drew out most of it in cash. After that, he bought himself a travel bag, fresh clothing, a pay-as-you-go mobile phone, and an Apple laptop. His final stop was the cathedral, where the coffee shop offered a quiet environment away from prying eyes.

With a coffee on one side and a plate with chocolate cake on the other, he opened the laptop and got to work. He prayed that no one had yet thought of shutting down his access to the police computer, and his heart was beating fast when he keyed in his username and password. Moments later, the remote access system let him in.

His first stop was in the files where his own arrests were listed. Slowly, he scrolled down until he came to the name he wanted. He went in, retrieved a telephone number, and came out again. After this, he opened thirty more files, selecting the names at random; if his visit was being tracked and recorded, this would help throw them off the scent.

He took the phone from the bag, dialled the number he had just noted, and spoke briefly to someone at the other end. Ending the call, he went back to the computer.

He had logged on to the main Interpol system numerous times in the past; he clicked his way through to the European section of the Wanted database, and put in the keywords 'German/Austrian, Antiquities Theft/Fraud'. His screen filled rapidly with records. He sighed and started on what he knew would be the most tedious part of the task he'd set himself.

Moving to Advanced Search, he added fresh keywords: blond, blue eyes, 1.8 to 1.9 metres, nasal/frontal scar.

Three names and three photographs came up on the screen. He clicked on the second thumbnail, and it expanded in size to reveal the man who had attacked him and killed or kidnapped Sarah. His name was Egon Aehrenthal, he was forty-four years old (born February 1964 in the Austrian town of Bernstein in Burgenland). His profession was given as antiquarian, with a special interest in biblical, Byzantine, and Umayyad antiquities from the Middle East. He had convictions for smuggling in Israel and Egypt, and for forgery in Lebanon, and had spent time in jail in each country.

Ethan smiled. Like a Mountie, he had found his man. But finding him in police files was not the same as finding him in the real world. He went on reading. Long accustomed to filling in the gaps of bland police records, he began to construct a picture that might provide the leads he hoped would take him to his target and, if his hunch was right, to Sarah.

Aehrenthal had been born Egon Armin Dietmar Hilarius Oktav Werner von Aehrenthal on the day the Austrian ski champion Egon Zimmerman had carried off a gold for the men's downhill at the 1964 Winter Olympics in Innsbruck. His jubilant father, who had watched the skier race to glory, flew that same night from one end of Austria to the other in order to be with his wife in Bernstein, bestowed Zimmerman's Christian name on his newborn son, and prophesied a golden future for him.

Gold would certainly have proved useful

for the von Aehrenthals. Egon belonged to an aristocratic family that had risen to the nobility in the last days of the Austro-Hungarian Empire. Egon's father never ceased to tell his golden-haired son that they had once been rich, and fervently expressed his belief that they would be rich again. He told Egon how they had intermarried with the Zvolen line of the perturbingly magnificent Eszterházys, the greatest family in the empire, the *ne plus ultra* of nobility, the embodiments of refinement and wit and elegance, who had amassed the greatest fortunes and built the most beautiful palaces. Young Egon, brought up to a life of genteel pretension and a slightly shabby existence, was a frequent visitor at Burg Bernstein, the magnificent if somewhat run-down castle at the other end of the village. The castle, now a hotel, dated in one form or another back to the ninth century. Its fame in modern times lay in the fact that the controversial desert explorer, Laszlo Almásy, had been born and brought up there. Almásy, Ethan remembered, had been the English patient in the film of the same name.

Egon's father had stimulated an interest in the baroque palaces of the Austro-Hungarian Empire, and from this beginning Egon had built himself a career as a dealer in antiquities. At some point, he had moved away from the gilded rococo grandeurs of the European baroque to the antiquities of the Jewish and Roman Middle East. Ethan made a note to check on what had led him into this new interest.

Egon opened an office on Jerusalem's David Street, and travelled widely through the surrounding Arab states, with regular visits back to Austria. His early travels were not well documented; but it was not long after embarking on this fresh enterprise that Aehrenthal (still in his late twenties) began to go crooked. Or perhaps that had been his intention all along. He spent three months in an Israeli prison for the illegal export of coins from the Bar Kochva Revolt era. A year later, the Israel Antiquities Authority's Theft Prevention Unit pursued him about the purchase of items stolen from tombs in the Judaean foothills.

Under surveillance in Israel, he travelled through the Levant as far as Anatolia, then down to Egypt and Libya, where he spent over a year. The Turkish authorities sent him to jail for six months following the break-up of a forgery ring in Antakya, the ancient Antioch. He was later deported.

He had continued like this for several years, moving from place to place, making and losing money, locating and selling genuine artefacts, acting as a front for smuggling and forgery operations.

Ethan made note of dates and places,

looking for a pattern, something that might hint where Aehrenthal had gone. Could he have taken Sarah out of the country? he wondered. It would have been difficult, he knew, but not altogether impossible, especially for someone with experience in smuggling.

At the end of the record was a notation Ethan did not recognise: RE. A brief search revealed that this was an abbreviation for the German *Rechtsextremismus:* Right-wing extremism. The entry indicated that Aehrenthal had had or still had connections with at least one German or Austrian political grouping of that description. When he clicked on the link, however, a message came onto the screen: *Access Prohibited.*

CHAPTER ELEVEN

'Evil shall hunt the violent man to overthrow him...'

He knew who he was hunting, but not where. Given his international links, Aehrenthal could be almost anywhere. Sarah might be dead, dumped by the roadside after an interrogation that had given up none of the information the Austrian wanted. Or she could be with him even now, beaten, raped, kept by for a sunny day. Was it possible she did know the things Aehrenthal wanted to drag from her? She was an expert, after all. Maybe she could help him authenticate the relics. That must be what he was after, some sort of certificate of authenticity so he could sell the objects on the black market. Once he had Sarah's name on a piece of paper, perhaps he'd go higher, find someone at the British Museum, or someone in Jerusalem. The relics could be worth millions to the right people. If he had the nerve, he might even go to the Vatican, ask for money, threaten to destroy the relics if he didn't get what he asked.

Sarah would have to die at some point, that was obvious. Aehrenthal couldn't afford to have her on the loose, telling everyone what he'd done. With Ethan taking the rap for the killings, Aehrenthal could probably polish his image with a little cash and start an auction that would end up making him rich for life.

Ethan put 'Aehrenthal' into Google and came up with dozens of references to Alois Lexa Graf von Aehrenthal, the ruthless Austro-Hungarian foreign minister who had presided over the annexation of Bosnia-Herzegovina and thus helped plunge Europe into the First World War. Ethan wondered if this Count Aehrenthal had been one of Egon's ancestors, to whom he owed his fascination with the Austro-Hungarian aristocracy and their lavish palaces.

Narrowing the search by adding 'Egon', he came across random references to the antiques trade, to biblical archaeology, and to a football club in Bernstein to which he'd belonged in his teens. Oddest of all was a site for the international Air Sports Federation, which listed Egon as one of many Austrian fliers who had been awarded the Paul Tissandier Diploma for services to the sport. When had Egon learnt to fly? Did he still have a licence? Did he have access to a plane, either one he owned or one he hired?

Ethan went on searching. If Aehrenthal did have a current licence it was most likely to be a JAA-PPL issued by the Austrian Civil Aviation Authority. He started at the Joint Aviation Authority website, then a site for the Aircraft Owners and Pilots Association of Austria. There were no member lists he could access, no licence records to check. If only...

He sat back from the table. His coffee had gone cold, his cake was half eaten. He looked at the clock. Two hours had already passed. He couldn't stay here much longer. If he had to leave the country, he'd have to be ready by the evening.

For hours he'd been racking his brains. Aehrenthal had not kidnapped Sarah on a whim. For the moment, she was useful to him. He might have settled on a hotel or a rented flat to work from, some place he could invite potential buyers. Only a full-scale police manhunt had any hope of tracking him down if he was still in the UK.

But he might just as easily have planned to get her out of the country. The question had been how. And now he thought he knew. They would dope her, bandage her face, put her in an air ambulance, and fly her somewhere. Somewhere Aehrenthal would feel comfortable working out of. A place in Austria, perhaps. Not Jerusalem: Israeli security was too tight, he'd never take her there.

He took the mobile from his pocket and dialled directory enquiries.

Her name was Lindita. Lindita Cobaj. She hurried into the cafe wearing a dark green anorak trimmed with rabbit fur. Her green and pink hair stood up in spikes, and her ears, lips and nose would never have allowed her through a security barrier armed with a metal detector. If he remembered rightly, she was an average of thirty-two years old, though he'd seen her down as young as twenty-five and as old as forty. She had one of those faces, one of those bodies that transcended age and pain. Neither pretty nor plain, neither skinny nor fat, neither a child nor an adult, she traversed all his preconceptions, all categories, all expectations. He had arrested her six or seven times, borne witness against her in court, grown impatient with her, grown to like and loathe her with equal vigour. She grinned broadly as she caught sight of him.

'Not see you is ages, Usherwood, man. Lose some weights, eh?'

He shrugged. She shrugged back. A half-smoked fag dangled from the corner of her mouth. Catching the eye of the barista, she took the cigarette from her lips, extinguished it, and put the unsmoked half behind her left ear.

'No waste, no want.'

Ethan grimaced. Her English hadn't got any better.

'Take a seat, Lindita.' He invited her to sit beside him. 'What would you like?'

She asked for a caffè mocha with cream and a double slice of chocolate cake. He looked her over: size ten or twelve. How did she do it? He could believe she was some kind of supernatural being. In fact, he was counting on it, counting on her supernatural powers to find and rescue Sarah. And maybe, just maybe, she could explain to him why he was so intent on this, why saving Sarah had become more than a rung on the ladder back to self-preservation and professional integrity. Much more.

The barista brought her coffee and cake,

and a second coffee for Ethan. Going back to the bar, he ejected a CD and put in another. Antony and the Johnsons burst into ripe song, charged with emotion and dread, the half-human vibrato rising and plunging through lyrics as dark as treacle.

Lindita dug her fork into the first slice of cake and popped a large tranche into her bright mouth. It disappeared and her eyes widened as her mouth moved in a slow grinding motion. Ethan waited for her to finish. Her tongue came out at last and licked her full, purple-lipsticked lips.

'You not try arrest me, then?' she asked, turning her big green eyes on him.

'Have you been doing anything I should arrest you for?'

She grinned and drank deeply from her coffee cup. Her eyes were filled with defiance and mischief.

He explained what he wanted, the hunt and the means for his own escape.

She played at the laptop for several minutes, then sat back and finished the cake – both slices – and the coffee.

'Thank you,' she said, words he'd never heard from her lips before. 'Now we goes my place, yes?'

From many other women it might have sounded like an invitation to romantic intrigue. From Lindita Cobaj, it could as easily have been a threat. He didn't hesitate.

He wasn't in a position to go against her.

He drove her home to Barton, the dodgiest part of Gloucester, keeping a close watch in the mirror to make sure he wasn't being trailed. He knew he'd recognise any car belonging to the local CID. Then it occurred to him that the police might not be the only ones looking for him. There were boys and young men in the street. Ethan recognised some of them, and he guessed they knew him too. He locked his car, then stood looking at it and the boys. Lindita walked over to the watchers, spoke quietly to them, and came back.

'No need worry. Car very safe. More safe here than front police station.'

Her flat – she called it *apartament im*, my apartment, to give it the only cachet it was ever likely to get – was in the basement of a building whose peeling walls seemed to suffer from a notifiable skin disease. She ushered him inside, like a new lover introducing her beau to the outer chambers of hell.

Lindita was an Albanian, a *Shqiptare*, from Vlorë on the Adriatic coast, seventy miles from Brindisi and the Italian mainland. Like the city she hailed from, Lindita had more than one name, more than one face, more than one identity.

She belonged to the Solejmani crime syndicate operating out of Vlorë. The Solejmanis had started life smuggling illegal migrants out of Albania to the Puglia coast, then moved into heroin, sex slavery, and illegal gambling. The people-smuggling racket took them eventually to England, where Lindita put her startling abilities as a graphic designer to work forging documents in every imaginable language. She'd moved from London to Gloucester, where she worked her wizardry with an Apple computer and half a dozen printers that chirruped away all day long, supplying IDs for gangsters and slaves like a machine that feeds Chupa Chups lollies to greedy children.

Along the way, she had learnt to use her computer for hacking. It had become a hobby and a source of extra income. She'd always been careful to limit her scams and to keep her tracks well covered. Once in a while, though, there'd been slips that had led to her being picked up for questioning, and more than once the questioning had led to conviction and short prison terms. Ethan had come to know her that way, and grown to admire her strength, a single woman among ruthless men.

She led him to the kitchen, where gleaming new appliances rubbed shoulders with damp patches on the walls and windows that looked as though they hadn't been washed in twenty years. She made strong Turkish coffee in a long-handled metal pot, poured it into two small glasses, and added a generous splash of Albanian brandy from a slim green bottle labelled Konjak Gjergj Kastrioti Skenderbeu. She put the cork back in the bottle and set it down.

'Skenderbeu,' she said. 'Great fucking Albanian hero man. Fight many fight, kill many Turk. Is big hero for Albanian. His flag, flag to Albania.'

She pointed to the winged eagle on the label and grinned. One of her teeth had fallen out. She took a pack of cigarettes from her pocket and lit up. Ethan recognised the brand: Priluky Osoblivi, made in the Ukraine and smuggled from Albania. She probably had cases out in the back.

He downed the contents of his glass in one gulp. Two seconds later, he regretted it. He coughed and spluttered. Lindita took a long drag on her cigarette, blew out a plume of smoke, and knocked back her cognac without blinking.

'In Albania,' she said, 'you would not be man. Only child cough.'

He recovered his breath and set about explaining to her what he was trying to do in more detail. She fetched a pad and pen, and wrote down everything. He told her about Sarah, about himself, about Aehrenthal.

'I think he may have taken her out of this country,' he said. 'Do you think that's possible?'

She nodded and lit another cigarette.

'Maybe. Yes, maybe possible.'

'But if he has taken her somewhere, can you track him?'

She shrugged. Her mouth curved, not in a smile, not in a frown. A gesture of possibility. Ethan had no time for possibilities.

'What this worth to you, Inspector of Detectives?' she asked. 'You got any money?'

They agreed a price for the hacking job, then a price for a passport. If he succeeded in tracking Sarah down, he'd have to leave the country at once.

She used her own computer – an iMac G5 with an 18-inch screen – to search through the records of a dozen Austrian flying organisations, and each time she narrowed the search down. She had moved plenty of people across the Alps from Italy into Austria, and her German was much better than Ethan's GCSE version. As she hunched over the table, her tobacco-stained fingers flickered across the keyboard like seagulls darting over waves. Bit by bit, the facts started coming in.

Aehrenthal learnt to fly with Motorfiug Union Wien, at their flight training centre in Vienna and at the little airfield at Bad Vöslau. He was a member of the Wiener Luftfahrer Verband club at Bad Vöslau, where he'd once kept a rare 1940 Bücker Bü 131 Jungmann. A further search revealed

that he also belonged to the Punitz Flug-
betrieb, a flying club operating out of a
smaller airfield further south, Punitz Gus-
sing. The only other landing site in the
vicinity of Bernstein was a short grass strip
at Pinkafeld. Lindita shook her head. She
knew a lot about landing small planes in
hidden locations. A grass strip might have
been doable, but at some risk.

Selecting Bad Vöslau as the more likely
destination, she hacked into a closed-access
system, the Aeronautical Fixed Telecommu-
nications Network, through which flight plan
details are sent between air traffic control
units. If Aehrenthal had logged flight plans
from any UK airport, they would have gone
to Eurocontrol in Brussels. Confirmation
would have gone to the departure airport and
the details forwarded to the area control
centres. This gave several portals through
which the information could be found. It
took ten minutes from start to finish.

At 06.15 hours that morning, a Beechcraft
King Air B200 air ambulance registered to a
company in Eisenstadt, Austria, had taken
off from Oxford's Kidlington airport with a
destination of Bad Vöslau. It had touched
down about three hours later. It had been
piloted by Egon Aehrenthal and co-piloted
by someone called Dietmar Koubek. There
had been a single passenger.

CHAPTER TWELVE

The Blue Danube

As the 19.30 Austrian Airlines jet lifted from the tarmac at Heathrow, Ethan relaxed for the first time since discovering the bodies in his grandfather's study. In his inside jacket pocket nestled the doctored passport that had seen him through passport control and would take him into Austria and beyond if necessary.

He'd paid Lindita three thousand pounds for it. Passports were her speciality. She'd cloned an ePassport for him, using RFdump software to download data from an original, before loading it onto a blank chip. Once that was done, she'd added some visa stamps from her stock and asked Ethan to add a false signature. She'd restyled his hair, added a fake moustache (she had a box of them, all different sizes, shapes and colours) and coloured contact lenses, taken a digital photo of Ethan, tipped it into the clone, and covered the ID page with a hologrammed plastic sheet.

And the original passport? Still safe and snug in its owner's pocket or a hotel safe. Ten days earlier, its RFID chip had been read from a short distance away by a Solejmani gang member in London, using a reader he'd bought on eBay for two hundred euros.

Ethan was travelling as Dafydd Williams, a teacher from Swansea. Apart from their age, the two men had nothing in common. Passport control wouldn't be able to compare the photo in Ethan's version with the one in Williams's original.

He passed through Austrian passports and customs, then out into the main concourse. As he did so, a wave of overwhelming tiredness swept over him, almost dragging him down all the way into dark waters. He'd planned to hire a car and drive straight to Bad Vöslau, desperate to get on Aehrenthal's track. But lack of sleep over the past few days had left him limp and uncoordinated, and he knew he couldn't risk making mistakes.

Deciding on sleep, he walked to the NH Airport Hotel and checked in to a single room. Here again Lindita saved his bacon. She had created an online bank account for Dafydd Williams, into which Ethan had transferred a large balance. Once this had been done, it was a simple matter for her to encode all the necessary details onto the magnetic strip on the back of a blank Amex Centurion black card.

'It's real thing,' she'd said.

'Real?' He'd picked it up. It was in his

wallet now. And he remembered how strange it had felt. Heavy, even though it was light.

'Is titanium,' she'd said. 'Is not plastic. Is only maybe ten thousand made in whole world. Cost two and half thousand dollar from year. You only get from invitation. Is only for very rich.'

'Won't it make me stand out?'

She'd shaken her head.

'You carry this in hand, you buy almost anythings you wants. Is no limit.'

He'd nodded. He still had no idea how much this was going to cost him, what the final bill would look like. He'd spend all he had and more to rescue Sarah, to see her safe and well again.

After checking in (and learning the true meaning of the word 'fawning'), he went straight to his room and made a telephone call. There was something vital to do before he could risk putting his head on a pillow. The number had been given to him by Lindita. Half an hour later, there was a knock on his door. Ethan didn't know the name of the man who stepped inside, nor did the man know his. Money was passed over, and Ethan took a small parcel in return. Not a word was exchanged during the brief transaction.

He slept badly that night. Not even tiredness

granted him sweet dreams. The places he entered were uncanny realms of nightmare, where words and images combined to tarnish his soul. Sometimes he would wake with the taste of ashes in his mouth, or a vision of death before his unseeing eyes. More than once, he was returned to the tomb and its humid, musty smells, and more than once he saw his grandfather pinned to the wall and watched as Sarah was stripped and threatened.

When he woke at last, the nightmare still lay on him like a fog. He felt a terrible fear mixed with guilt. He was, after all, on the run from a murder charge, and if he couldn't find and save Sarah, he would never be able to prove his innocence. His greatest fear was not prison, or what he would face inside as an ex-cop; it was for Sarah, whose face was as clear to him as his own face in the mirror while he shaved.

He rented a four-wheel drive, a Mercedes ML, and headed south. The urban landscape began to open out to the east after Wiener Neudorf. He picked up speed on the Süd Autobahn as it swept like a sword between fields on his left and a cluster of small towns on his right that formed an almost unbroken chain between Vienna and Wiener Neustadt. As the traffic thinned, he rammed his accelerator down hard, taking the car smoothly up to just below the speed limit of one hundred and thirty kilometres per hour.

Sometimes the buildings would open, revealing high forested hills that ran back westwards to the Alps. Snow covered the fields, as white as lilies; it lay like sifted flour on the forests, it covered the roofs of passing houses as if laid there to provide insulation. Outside, it was minus three celsius. The air was crisp and pure beneath a dark blue sky. He drove with his eyes fixed on the road. His thoughts were dark and bitter, constrained by memory and anger. The dream had not quite left him, and though the white fields and the lambent air did their best to lighten his spirits, his mood remained low. Anxiety gnawed at his thoughts like a rat, filling him with the fear that he'd done the wrong thing, headed in the wrong direction. Sarah could still be in England, he had no way of knowing. Aehrenthal could have killed her, dumped her body somewhere, and headed back to some sort of hiding place here in Austria.

On his hip, in a concealed holster, he wore the gun Lindita's man had brought him before he slept, a Beretta 93R. The 93R had two unusual features for a handgun: a front grip that could fold down beneath the barrel to permit two-handed action, and a shoulder stock, now tucked away in Ethan's bag. The man had left him with a box of 20-

round magazines carrying 9mm Parabellum rounds, and shown Ethan how to set it for single-fire, burst-fire, or semi-automatic modes. The gun gave Ethan some comfort, but the last thing he wanted was to get caught up in a gunfight.

He left the autobahn just after Baden, got himself onto the ERS9, and drove a short distance along side roads to Bad Vöslau airport.

Aehrenthal had touched down in the Beechcraft at 09.30 hours on the morning of the previous day. He'd piloted the plane along with a co-pilot. The Beechcraft had been configured as an air ambulance, and there had been a passenger in the rear, a woman called Ileana Paulescu.

Hearing this, Ethan frowned.

'Did you see the woman?'

He'd found a representative of the airport management agency, Flughafen Wien AG. The man wasn't sure that the details of Herr Aehrenthal's journey should be made available to a stranger. But Ethan had brought the police warrant card he'd pretended had been stolen. He flashed it, knowing he wouldn't be asked to compare it with his passport.

'*Kriminaloberkommissar?*'

Ethan nodded, hoping that was right.

'Can you tell me, Herr ... Kriminaloberkommissar Ushingwood...'

'Usherwood.'

'Yes, so sorry. Why do you want to find this man?'

'That's restricted information. But it is urgent.' Ethan prayed the man would not contact the local bobbies.

'Very well. I understand.'

It was then Ethan realised the man would not call the police. He would be hoping no local law enforcement officials would be called to his airport.

The representative, Herr Veit Schiegl, nodded sagely.

'You have not mentioned this to our local *polizei*, to the *kriminalpolizei*?'

'They've been informed, naturally, but they don't want to be involved. It's a purely British matter. And I would prefer not to cause any fuss here. Especially not for you or the airport.'

Herr Schiegl nodded again.

'The woman was bandaged,' he said. 'They were taking her to Romania, to a spa. She has a skin condition.'

'Romania? Where?'

'Herr Aehrenthal refuelled, then made arrangements with air traffic control to fly on to Oradea. He did not give the name of the spa. They have many spas in Transylvania. My wife wants to go to one. She is always pestering me, she says she wants to visit Dracula's castle and stay in a spa. Rheumatism. It is a big problem for her.'

Ethan arranged a private flight with one of the companies operating out of Bad Vöslau. It took half an hour to arrange things. The plane was a Cessna 208 Caravan. It would fly the nearly 600 miles to Oradea in well under two hours. What would happen after that, Ethan had no idea.

CHAPTER THIRTEEN

Transylvania

They flew across the great Hungarian plain, and all the way there was little cloud. But as they came near to Romania the weather darkened and winds buffeted the little plane. As they dropped from the clouds, Ethan, who was flying up front in the co-pilot's seat, saw mountains rise up ahead. The Carpathians formed a circle of sullen snow-enchanted peaks, carpeted with trees. The pilot turned and grinned.

'Transylvania,' he said, baring his teeth to make a vampire smile. He turned back and started the descent into Oradea.

Ethan was waved through customs, his pistol tucked deep inside his overnight bag, a tourist come at the wrong time of year, without skis or a snowboard. He found a taxi and told the driver to take him to a good hotel. With luck, he wouldn't have to stay for long; but for now he needed a base to work from.

The driver, whose English was far from good, deposited him at the Hotel Vulturul Negru. The name, to Ethan's surprise, meant The Black Eagle. It formed an art nouveau building, refurbished and restyled for the upmarket tourism its owners hoped to draw to what was still Europe's poorest country. The receptionist was goggle-eyed at the sight of Ethan's Centurion card; the influx had clearly begun. Ethan realised he could have asked for women, drugs, caviar flown direct from the Caspian, and they would have been sent up to him without a murmur or a raised eyebrow.

His room was smart if eccentric, with a tall four-poster bed. He'd have slept in the bath so long as there was somewhere to plug in his laptop and get Internet access. The boy who showed him to the room did it all for him. Ethan handed him fifty new lei, about ten pounds, and told him he didn't want to be disturbed.

He was still tired after his ordeal and the journey that had followed. By now, the police in Gloucester would be looking for him. Lindita had created an untraceable email address for him, and so far only she knew it existed. She'd promised to let him know as soon as his escape appeared in the papers or on the radio and telly.

He was at a loss. All he had to go on was that Aehrenthal had chosen to fly Sarah all the way from Oxford to this place. Not to Bucharest, not to Bernstein, not to Budapest or anywhere else along the way. What was so important about Transylvania or, for that matter, this particular neck of the woods? Was there a connection with the relics, with scholarship on Libya or the early Church? Was there a collector living out there, Ethan wondered, someone from whom Egon Aehrenthal could expect a large sum of money just on Sarah's say-so? Or another expert, a scholar who could be relied on to echo Sarah's conclusions. It would have to be someone willing to overlook any signs of physical or mental abuse, to ignore anything she might say about her kidnap.

He started hunting. Piecing together a rough and ready knowledge of Romania and Transylvania, he read the country's history, from Vlad the Impaler, the original for Dracula, to Queen Marie, a granddaughter of Victoria given to grand gestures and displays of patriotism matched only by her assiduous promotion of her own image. He discovered spa towns everywhere: Baile Felix, Baile Herculana, Covasna, Sovata – enough mineral water to cure the ailments of the continent. There were Saxon fortified churches to visit, a bison reserve in Hateg, castles everywhere. If he travelled further afield, near Bramov, he could have visited Bran Castle, once owned by Queen Marie and more famous as the model for Dracula's castle in Bram Stoker's novel.

He googled for antique dealers, for societies of archaeologists and biblical scholars, using an online dictionary, but turned up only Romanian websites he could not translate. He discovered that Transylvania had once been part of the Kingdom of Hungary, then Austro-Hungary, and that there was still a sizeable Hungarian population there.

He decided that it was time to fetch an interpreter who might help him, someone who might even know the answers to some of his questions. He went to a general tourist website to see if he could find someone, and as he did so noticed something out of the corner of his eye.

It was a thumbnail of a castle, a dark-looking place surrounded by forest. The caption read *Castel Almásy*. That was all. Ethan might easily have missed it or ignored it. But he remembered Burg Bernstein, another Almásy castle, and one closely linked to the man he was hunting.

Feeling a knot tighten in his stomach, he clicked on the thumbnail picture. It opened to reveal a web page about the castle, with a larger version of the thumbnail photograph. He noticed a little Union Jack at the top of the page, and when he clicked on it the text turned to English. Not very good English, but enough to guide him through the basic facts.

Almásy Castle had been built between 1270 and 1275 by Zoltán Erdoelue, the first voivod of Transylvania, and had remained in the hands of the Erdoelue family until the country became part of the Hungarian Kingdom, when it fell into the hands of a branch of the Báthorys, princes of Transylvania for many generations. In the nineteenth century, it became the property of the Almásys. The short article did not make clear who the present owners might be. But it did go to some trouble to say that it was closed to the public at all times of the year. It had an evil reputation, the writer said, though that had nothing to do with vampires or any other superstition. It was more to do with the politics of the castle's owners in the 1930s and 40s, though this was not explained in any detail.

Several phone calls and a rented car later, he was on his way. The little Dacia 10 hardtop was a four-by-four, though Ethan found it hard to believe it would have the strength to tackle any seriously rough country.

The castle was located in the Vladeasa

Mountains, east of Oradea. At the hotel, they'd warned him that the castle could be cut off. It was midwinter, they said, and the place was remote enough in summer. A guide at the local tourist bureau said he might not be able to do the entire journey in the Dacia.

'Is no good roads in this area,' the interpreter told him.

'But this is a four-by-four, an off-road vehicle.'

She looked at him as if she'd just eaten sliced lemons.

'Is Dacia, not Land Rover. One big mistake, is axle broken.' She sold him a hiking map and pointed to the rough area where the castle should be.

'Is not on maps,' she said, shaking her head. 'For one things, is not called Castel Almásy. Before was Castel Lup. Local peoples, they call it Castel Lup. Always Castel Lup on old maps.'

'Meaning?'

She raised her eyebrows, as though the name should have been obvious.

'Wolf Castle,' she said.

Ethan thought she was about to sell him a string of garlic and some wooden stakes before making the sign of the cross and running off. But she stood her ground, and if she was trembling inside, she gave no sign of it.

'You have to ask local peoples,' she said. 'They know tracks. But is very hard to find in winter because is snows. Look...' and she ran her hand across a vast expanse of the map, '...all this is Apuseni Mountains. Is all forest from Mount Vladeasa in west' – she pointed – 'to here' – she stabbed her finger further east. 'It is Trascau Mountains here. All forests, all mountains, all caves. You find wolfs, you find bears. Maybe sleeping, maybe not. Seasons changing, some animals is waking in winter. Wolfs is hungry, sleepy, angry.'

He drove out of Oradea on the E60, in an effort to get into the Vladeasa Mountains from the north. These were not high mountains. The highest – Vladeasa itself – was around six thousand feet, much lower than any of the peaks in the Alps. But Ethan was not going mountaineering.

A drive of over forty miles took him through a long defile between mountains. Mist had formed on their lower slopes and, above it, clouds lay battening on the peaks. The countryside was white with snow, and dark green where the branches of tall trees peaked through. There was little sign of habitation anywhere. Roadside shrines added colour to the winter gloom, their frescoes bright in the still air. Twice he caught sight of a tall church steeple. Some cars and a bus passed him, headed for Oradea. And he passed a number of carts drawn by horses or donkeys, trotting in the opposite direction.

The Dacia's heating struggled to spread a little comfort through the interior. He'd bought a padded jacket and heavy trousers at a shop near the tourist office, but sitting still allowed the frost outside to work its way inside him.

He came to Huedin, a small town on a crossroads. This was the gateway to the Apusenis. It was a grim place, its buildings mainly erected in the communist era under the rule of the dictator, Ceaucescu. Gaunt and forbidding, they belied the rural character of the place, making ugly the countryside into which they seemed to have been set down by a malign hand.

He took a right turn, heading south towards Sancraiu, a Székely village. This was hilly country, but everywhere Ethan looked he could see the forest-covered mountains climbing and soaring to greater heights.

Entering Sancraiu, he imagined he was driving through a carefully contrived theme park, 'Hungarian World' (for this was little Hungary) or 'Medieval Transylvania'. Had it not been for the straggling telephone wires and the infrequent but more blatant satellite dishes on the sides of houses on both sides of the narrow road, he might have thought himself lost, not in space, but in time. The village had changed little in centuries, and the people wore an ancient air, their rustic clothing crying out, not merely poverty, but tenacity.

The houses, many of them painted blue, huddled among trees, thin wisps of smoke rising from their chimneys, grey merging with the grey sky above. There were two churches, one with a white steeple, the other with a white tower topped by a steep red steeple. Romanian orthodoxy swamped in a sea of Hungarian Reform, holding on in spite of everything. Ethan shuddered. He knew next to nothing about these people, beyond what little he'd read in a tourist brochure at the hotel. He pulled in to the kerb and stopped the car. As he did so, he saw their eyes on him, old men and women, young men in black leather jackets, young women in headscarves, their eyes bright and questioning.

He got out, feeling like someone who has landed in the Spice Islands after long journeying, knowing he is exotic, the object of fear or hatred or scorn, perhaps all these and more. No one smiled, no one welcomed him. It was not the tourist season, he had not brought skis; in short, he was an anomaly, an intrusion, a man from behind the glistening veil that lay between these people and the world outside.

It had started to snow minutes before he

got to the village, and now heavy flakes were shimmering from the slate-coloured sky. On the hills and on the mountain peaks, the clouds pressed down like cushions of damp wool.

The woman in the tourist office had told him he'd have to leave the Dacia here in Sancraiu and hire a cart with a horse or two horses to take him into the mountains, all the way to Castel Lup, or as near as he could get. Looking round, he saw indifference on the faces of the villagers. He couldn't even be sure of finding someone who spoke English. He'd been told they spoke Hungarian here.

There were no shops, at least not in any sense he recognised. Some of the houses had carved wooden fences and elaborate gateways. People passed in and out of the gates, but no one approached him. He saw two women standing watching him, then whispering to one another. He thought it might not be advisable to approach them.

Then, from a house opposite appeared a young woman, maybe between eighteen and twenty years old, dressed in brighter clothes than the crones staring at him. She came straight to him, a smile on her face, and stood on the road about three feet off.

'*Megszentségteleníthetetlenségeskedéseitekér?*' she asked.

Ethan just stared at her.

She giggled and put a hand to her mouth. Then, lowering it, she spoke again.

'*Bészel romanul?*'

He still had no idea what she'd said, but he rather thought she'd been teasing him with the long expression she'd tried him with at first. She was quite pretty, but there was a mischievous look in her eyes that made her prettiness positively dangerous. He thought she might be making fun of him.

'Do you speak English?' he asked.

'Of course,' she said, without the slightest surprise. 'I would have tried English next, but first I wanted to know if you speak Hungarian, and if not, Romanian. English would have been my third choice. I also speak a little German, some Ukrainian, and of course my father teaches me a little Russian. I thought you looked lost. Tourists don't come to Sancraiu much at this time of year. There are ski parties, but they aren't expected for some weeks yet. Perhaps you are not a tourist.'

He shook his head.

'And you need help. You have probably taken the wrong road. But this isn't a good place to talk. It's very cold, and it's going to get colder. It's four hours to sunset. Let's get inside.'

CHAPTER FOURTEEN

Ilona

She led him to a little house that served the village as a bar, a public meeting place, and a general goods store. The shelves were stacked with bags of flour, bottles of oil, loaves of white bread, and other basics. A group of old men stood at the bar, their chins unshaven, their eyes rheumy as they glided over Ethan, labelling him as another outsider they all had to put up with to earn someone in the village welcome foreign currency.

She sat him at a table and fetched two glasses of red wine. She took off the thick jacket she'd been wearing outside. In the bar, it was very hot.

'How come you speak such good English?' he asked.

'University of Bucharest. I'm in my final year. I've been studying English for four years now. I stayed in England last year, in Brighton. I'm on vacation now, until just after the New Year.'

He reached a hand across the table.

'Ethan,' he said. 'My name's Ethan Usherwood.'

She took his hand, gripping it firmly.

'Horváth Ilona,' she said.

'I'm pleased to meet you, Horváth.'

She burst out laughing.

'I'm sorry,' she said. 'I forgot. In Hungarian, the family name comes first, the personal name last. You can call me Ilona.'

'Which means?'

This time she blushed and mumbled something he could not make out.

'What did you say?'

'It's a very embarrassing name, but very popular. It means "beautiful". It's a silly name. Don't pay it any attention.'

He looked at her more closely. In fact, the name did her justice. She had wavy shoulder-length brown hair, her eyes reminded him of the cat he'd had when he was seven, and when she smiled she was captivating. But seeing a pretty girl sitting opposite him only brought back memories of Sarah and a realisation that he might be within an hour or two of learning whether she was alive or dead.

They drank wine and talked, mainly about Ilona and the plans she'd made for her life after graduation later that year. What they boiled down to was her longing to be free of Sancraiu, either to stay in the big city in Bucharest or to travel abroad. Since she was fluent in Hungarian and Romanian and had a confident grasp of English; she had hopes of a career in translation or interpreting.

As she spoke, he wondered just how much he should tell her. He could hardly pretend he'd just turned up in the region as an independent.

'I'm an architectural historian,' he said in the end. 'My current project is to study castles in Transylvania.'

'Of course,' she said. 'How interesting. There are so many of them. Bran, Huniazi – have you been to Huniazi yet? – Sighisoara, Peles. And Margau, of course. What a fabulous castle that is.'

'Absolutely. Fascinating, all of them.'

'Especially Margau. It has always been my favourite.'

'Mine too. Best of a great bunch. But I'm not headed there now. I want to visit a castle much closer.'

He saw her lips close, her eyes narrow.

'Really? What castle would that be? I don't know any castles round here. Perhaps you really are lost after all.'

He shook his head.

'It's called Castel Almásy. Or perhaps you know it as Castel Lup,' he said. 'Wolf Castle. Is that right?'

This time her facial expression changed completely. The friendliness went out of her eyes. She pushed back her chair and got to her feet.

'Ilona? What's up? What did I say?'

'Nothing. You said nothing. But now it's time for me to go.'

She picked up her jacket and shrugged it on.

'Won't you...?' he began, but she was already on her way to the door.

He took some notes from his pocket and slapped them on the table, hoping they would cover the bill, then rushed after her. She was out in the street, headed across the road, her jacket bright against the pearly afternoon light. He rushed after her, passed her and blocked her way.

'What's going on, Ilona? One moment we're talking, next thing you run off as though something's biting you. What the hell is up?'

She looked as if she was furious about something.

'First you lie to me,' she said, 'then you say you plan to head for Castel Lup, of all places. And you're surprised to find me running away? Now, please, I want to go home. I think I've talked with you enough.'

'I just need an explanation. You say I lied to you. What made you think that?'

'You said you're an architectural historian, but you know nothing about castles in Transylvania.'

'Of course I do, I–'

'There is no castle in Margau. I made that up, just to see how you would react. I thought you would say "I've never heard of such a place, tell me more." But instead you said, "this my favourite castle, this is the best of them all".'

He'd fallen right into her little trap.

'And Castel Lup?'

'You don't need me to tell you. If you plan to visit it, you know more than I do. But it's enough for me to know you're headed there, that you know people there. Now, please let me get past.'

'Ilona, I don't want to make trouble, and I don't want to upset you, but there are some things I think you should know.'

'Such as?'

'Well, to start with, I'm not an architectural historian, I'm a policeman.'

Ignoring the weather, they walked up and down the street several times. He told her as much as he thought she could stand: his grandfather's death, Sarah's abduction, the Austrian and his companion with what sounded like a Hungarian name.

She began to relax. The anger left her eyes and was replaced by puzzlement. When he finished, she walked him back to the bar. As they came in, eyes opened wide again, and the murmuring recommenced.

'Why should I believe this version?' she demanded.

He took the warrant card from his pocket. She read it, nodded, and handed it back.

'I know what a detective is,' she said. 'But what is a detective chief inspector?'

He tried to explain, but grew hopelessly lost in the complexities of police ranks. Seeing his confusion, she smiled for the first time since her walkout.

'And you think this woman, what is her name...?'

'Sarah.'

'Yes, this Sarah, you think she's in Vár Farkasnak?'

'Where?'

'That's what we call your castle. In Hungarian. Castle of the Wolf. Castel Lup.'

'I can't be sure she's there. It's a guess. Why does this place make you so angry?'

'No one here knows much about it. You call it Almásy Castle, but that was a long time ago, sixty, seventy years, perhaps much more. After the Second World War, when Transylvania finally became part of Romania, a lot of Hungarians left. Most went to Hungary, and some others went to Austria. I think that was when the Almásy family left. Maybe they still make visits here, I don't know. But the castle belongs to new owners. They don't like to come here to the town. And they don't like any of the townspeople to go there. Some people from Oradea, from the tourist office, went to the castle. They wanted to explain that it would make a great location for a hotel, that tourists would flock

214

there and pay a lot of money to stay. Or maybe just to visit.'

'What happened?'

'Something bad. They never went there again. I heard this from a friend, but that's all she knew. The castle is guarded behind some sort of fence. There are wolves in the forest around it. There are guards who carry guns and have big dogs. We hear stories, but nothing definite. Some say they sacrifice children there, that they belong to a sinister cult, that they bring women and hold orgies, that they are Nazis, that the castle is a very strict monastery. No one knows. Not here, anyway.'

She stopped and drummed on the table gently for a moment, then snapped her fingers shut.

'You should go to Bucharest,' she suggested. 'Maybe the government knows about the castle. You could go to the Serviciul Român de Informatii – the intelligence services. Or the police.'

'Ilona, I don't have time. If she's here, she arrived early this morning. These men are ruthless. If she's still alive, it may not be for long. All I want is a set of directions so I can find the place. The rest is up to me.'

'Do you have a gun?'

'I don't think that's–'

'Ethan, you're not in the land of the famous British bobby now. I won't help you

215

if you want to go up there without a gun. You'd just be... What is the word?'

'Impediment?'

'No. Liability. Is that right?'

He nodded. And he agreed.

'Yes,' he said. 'I'm armed. Will you please put me on the right track? How long will it take to drive there?'

She laughed, a light silvery laugh that danced through the room, bringing frowns and stares in its wake.

'You can't drive there. This is a country for walking. There's no road from here to the castle.'

'I'm driving a four-by-four. As long as I can get close...'

She gave him a pitying look.

'Chief Inspector, please listen to me. You're a novice here. I already told you, this isn't Blake's green and pleasant land.' She seemed pleased with herself for making this reference. Ethan smiled to encourage her.

'This is mountain country. There are many cliffs, places where the rock has sheared off, and there are caves everywhere. Big caves. Some of biggest caves you can find in whole world. If you fall into one or even if you just wander into one, you won't find your way out again. Someone will find what's left of you in the spring, or perhaps a few years from now. You need a guide. Not your own instinct, not a detective's guesswork. If I go with you, you must behave yourself. You must do what I say.'

Ethan spluttered.

'Ilona, I can't take you. This isn't a job for–'

'A slip of a girl? A woman? A pitiful, weak-minded, bird-brained woman?'

'I didn't mean–'

'That's exactly what you mean. But let me explain something about Sancraiu. If you expect one of these fine people at the bar to go with you, or if you plan to knock on every door, then you'll be here all tonight and all tomorrow, but no one will answer your appeal. If you give in and go up there alone, you will die. It's winter. This is country that can kill even the best prepared. The woman you're looking for, Sarah, she will die too.'

'How much do you want?'

'Nothing. No money, that is. But later, I want you to get me a job in England. And a visa to work there. Can you do that?'

Ethan thought he'd be the last person the authorities would want to hear from. But he had plenty of contacts, and his father had even more.

'Very well,' he said. 'When do we leave?'

CHAPTER FIFTEEN

The Wolf's Lair

A short bituminised road led to an opening in dense undergrowth, bare branches painted with frost-edged snow. Here a track started upwards, heading for the mountains. It was some four feet wide, and its floor of packed earth had been made iron with ice, as though they walked on permafrost. On all sides lay snow and hoar frost, spiky and crystalline in the cold air. The snow had stopped falling as night drew close.

Ilona had changed into a dark green outfit better suited to mountain hiking than the fleece jacket she'd worn earlier. She had brought a small pony to carry equipment she considered necessary. Ethan didn't know it, but she'd left home without a word to her family, knowing they would have banned her from taking part in what they would have considered a doomed expedition. To any villager who asked, she said she was taking the stranger to a little cabana higher up, where he was to carry out a survey for the government. She had loaded the pony with a spade, an axe, a pair of

218

Nieto hunting knives, food, a small tent ('If we get stuck, we will not survive without it. But I will not sleep with you, not even if you beg or offer me large sums of money'), a pickaxe, sleeping bags, two head torches, and things Ethan did not even recognise.

She put the longer of the two knives, an eight-inch blade, into a pocket on her trousers. Ethan took one look at it and whistled.

'Have you ever used a knife like that before?' he asked. 'It's an ugly-looking thing. You could spit an ox with it...'

'I have used a knife like this since I was ten years old,' she replied cheerily, snapping the pocket shut on a strip of Velcro.

'Won't we need ropes?'

'This isn't a mountaineering expedition,' Ilona told him witheringly. 'We won't need to do any rope climbing. The mountain we're going up is covered in trees as far as the castle and beyond.'

They climbed beneath the branches of dark trees, and if Ethan had thought Sancraiu quiet, or Woodmancote on Christmas Day a silent place, he revised his opinion with every step he took on the mountain trail. They walked in single file now, Ilona followed by Ethan, the horse coming in the rear. For all he knew, she might be leading him on a wild goose chase. It was hard to believe there was really a building, an entire castle up there.

Suddenly, something howled. Then a second time. There was an answering howl not far away. Ilona stopped the horse, stroking its head, whispering to it softly.

'*Farkas*,' she said. 'Wolf.'

Ethan shivered, but covered his fear with a quip.

'*Children of the Night,*' he said.

'Sorry? Why do you call it a child?'

He tried to explain, but the joke didn't travel very well. Maybe they didn't watch Dracula movies in Transylvania.

'They aren't always dangerous to human beings,' Ilona pointed out. 'But it has been a cold winter. There are no sheep on the pastures, so wolves sneak down to the farms to find what food they can. And if they can't find a sheep or a goat, and they come across a man or woman or child instead, someone walking outside... This year, several men and a boy have died that way.'

They went on climbing. And as they climbed, night came down, imperceptibly at first, but suddenly at last, as the sun dropped below the horizon, hanging fire on the mountains, beyond their reach. No moon appeared, no stars twinkled between the branches of the trees. They had left behind the skeletons of oaks and beeches. Now, thick branches of fir and spruce hung over them like a canopy of disquiet, boxing them in. The lamps on their foreheads spilt out on a tunnel of snow and scintillating frost, the light carving out the path ahead. They moved on, talking in soft voices.

Ilona spoke of her life in Sancraiu, of the changes that had taken place in her on travelling to Bucharest, of the horizons that had started to open when she lived in Brighton, and her frustration at the lack of opportunity in Romania, even in the capital. She was serious about asking him to help her get a visa so she could enter Britain legally, find a job, perhaps marry, obtain citizenship. She had ambitions, she had hopes. Ethan could prove the gateway through which she could reach them. He'd had brushes with immigration control and wondered whether his word would count for anything.

The track went through twists and bends, always moving up. The higher they went, the colder it got. Their breath hung in the air ahead of them like a mist. Not once did the horse snicker or protest.

He told her about Abi, he didn't know why. The words came unbidden, the memories made sharp by the frozen air or the concentration of light or Ilona's youthfulness. He talked and she listened. It was as if her being his guide had placed him in a relationship to her of pupil to teacher, supplicant to advisor. The wolves howled again, and he shivered at the thought of sudden death. He could not begin to guess what he was going to find at the castle. Sarah dead? Or his own death waiting for him? A bullet? A sharp knife? Something blunt and heavy to cave in his skull?

'This path will take us to the castle,' Ilona said. 'We must tie the horse.'

He saw a path leaving the track at an angle.

'I'll go ahead,' he said. 'You'll have to stay here.'

She shook her head.

'I agree to take you to the castle. I stick to that, if you not mind.'

He wasn't up to arguing, and he'd already seen what she was capable of. He nodded, and off they set.

The cold did strange things in their lungs. It was painful to breathe. Ethan felt as though he'd swallowed tiny splinters of glass. They wrapped strips of cloth across their mouths, but the fabric quickly grew wet as droplets of their breath mixed with the sub-zero temperatures. In the narrow path, there seemed to be no way out. Ethan remembered the woods near Woodmancote as a child. He'd gone there hunting for rabbits. It had seemed an adventure.

Suddenly, the trees fell away and they were standing on the verge of a white place. During the time they'd been in the forest, the clouds had broken up and dissipated, leaving a moon almost at the full, high up in a sky splintered with stars. Ethan had never set eyes on such a sky. The light pollution of western Europe did not reach this far. If there were lights anywhere, they were of little consequence. The stars were folded into one another, galaxy into galaxy, like egg white spooned into a bowl for meringue.

It was as if a grand theatrical designer had mounted lights on ramps to set off the centrepiece of his set.

'Vár Farkasnak,' Ilona said. '"The Wolf's Lair".' She lifted her right hand and pointed across the banked and drifted snow to a tall building that rose up like a ship cresting high white waves. On top, steep roofs were piled upon one another, their sharp angles gliding and pitching, and among them towers rose dramatically, topped by lanterns from which thin spires pierced the night sky like lances. Lower down, the body of the castle was lost in shadows. Trees stepped down from the forest almost to the rear of the building, and others stood in pairs or singly at the front and sides. A single light burnt in a window, high up on the second floor, close by a steep buttress towards the northern corner.

Ethan would have stepped directly from the trees onto the snow meadow in front of him, but Ilona grabbed his arm, shaking her head.

'If anyone is watching, they'll see you at once. We need to skirt round the trees and make our way to the castle from the rear.'

They crept along the treeline, shadows among shadows. Walking was harder here: the trees were set too close to let them easily work a way through them, and the snow was deep and soft from the most recent fall; at times they sank into it up to their knees.

It took about twenty minutes to reach the rear. No lights burnt here, not even an external lamp set for security or as a beacon. The moonlight stencilled the doors and windows in sharp outline. There were only three doors, one at each end and one in the middle. Ethan headed straight for the end door nearest him, and reached into a pocket for a set of lock picks he'd borrowed from Lindita, guessing he might have to break into a building or a room at some point. He'd learnt how to pick a lock years before, from burglars he'd arrested.

Before attempting the lock, he scrutinised the rear of the building carefully, to be sure there wasn't an alarm of any sort. Ilona followed suit. There was nothing visible to the naked eye. The lock was old-fashioned and rusty, but it took Ethan less than a minute to spring it open. He turned the knob slowly, his gloved hand finding it hard to find purchase on the icy metal.

He pushed the door open and stepped

inside. The pick was back in his pocket, and the gun already in his hand. Ilona came behind him. She closed the door and silence descended. Inside, all was darkness; fat, swelling, suffocating darkness. Ilona took one of the torches out of her pocket and switched it on.

They were in a short corridor at the far end of which stood another door of solid wood. Beyond it might be another dark room or a brightly lit chamber filled with castle staff. Ethan listened for a while and decided in the end that there was no one next door. Probably. Ilona switched off her torch. He turned the knob and thrust the second door open.

Darkness, as before. Silence, as before. Ilona sent another beam of light into the darkness, revealing some sort of games room. There was a dartboard on one wall, and table football in a corner next to a half-size billiard table. The room was spacious, low-ceilinged, and cold. Did someone come here to play billiards with frozen fingers? Was the room left unused during the winter? Ethan wondered if the answers would offer a clue as to how inhabited the castle was.

Through the next door they found a corridor. Low-watt bulbs burnt in wire cages all the way down a long whitewashed ceiling. Doors opened off it at intervals. It was obviously a service corridor, bereft of ornaments or pictures, the floor bare wood, its walls painted in light green paint that showed signs of damp in many places.

How to decide on a door? Ethan was reminded of the old dilemma in fairy tales: which of the three doors will our hero pass through? There's a beautiful princess behind one, and demons behind the other two. There must be at least a dozen in the corridor, he thought.

They walked on slowly, inspecting each door in turn. Some had inscriptions on small panels. *Bucatarie. Câmarâ. Furnituri.*

'This is all kitchens and storerooms – things like that,' said Ilona as they passed, her torch picking out the handwritten letters in old Romanian script, their outlines fading against blistered card.

Right at the other end, they came to a battered, red-painted door, above which a small sign read *Scar*â.

'Stairs!' said Ilona.

Beyond the door, a steep flight led upwards.

'I think we have to head for the second floor,' said Ethan. 'To find the room with the light.'

At the top of the stairs, another red door, likewise dented by who could tell how many years of servants pushing it open with heavy trays in their hands. It opened onto a narrow, unlit corridor, a more integral part of the castle proper. On the walls hung oil portraits of children dressed in fine clothes, their faces dimming and shining in the harsh light of the torches. They wore the clothes of little aristocrats, furs and velvets and silks, the girls with their hair plaited, the boys in boots and leather trousers. Their faces were the faces of ghosts, their eyes straining to see what living man or woman passed. Ethan wanted to ignore them, but they stared so arrogantly, at once children and the adults they were destined to become.

The end of the corridor gave directly onto a dark place that seemed at first to be without walls. They swung their torch beams through the blackness, like search-lights in a war zone, and slowly they formed a picture of an open space, some sort of hall bisected by a massive wooden staircase. The sides of the banisters facing them were studded with small heraldic shields on which were painted the devices of ancient families and the symbols of nearby towns and counties, painted in bright colours once, but dulled and faded now.

They picked out an armoured hand holding a long sword, and next to it a bunch of grapes. Further up, a white shield surmounted by a crown carried the image of a wolf suckling her cubs, and above that again a quartered shield portraying a church and a castle with high towers. Ilona noticed that several shields showed an angel and a lion passant with a cross between them, and a sun and crescent above their heads. Just beyond that was a stranger thing, a sable shield divided in half per pale, with small white swastikas on the sinister or left-hand side, and a single golden crucifix across the dexter. It seemed brighter and probably newer than the shields with which it kept company. They could not guess at its meaning. Ethan knew that the swastika originally had a benign meaning in Buddhism or Hinduism, he wasn't sure which.

They stepped further into the hall, knowing that, at any moment, their lights might be seen, and someone might come out to challenge them. Ethan led Ilona to the stairs, and they began to climb. They shone their torches on the walls, revealing a gallery of large paintings, portraits once more, but not of children. These showed men and women in all the finery of aristocrats. *Voivodes, boiers, dregators* and *serdars* in sable coats and chains of office, their hands on the hilts of battle swords, rings twinkling on their fingers, their inner jackets embroidered in thread of gold. Beside them their wives shimmered like walking tapestries, no expense spared on their finery, their earrings of pearl, their emerald necklaces, their delicate hands enriched with rubies, sapphires, and amethysts.

The stillness was palpable. High up, ancient tapestries hung on the walls, and flags, tattered and torn, moth-eaten or snatched from old battlefields, swung limply from their poles.

They reached the main landing and turned left, heading for the next staircase that would take them to the floor above. As they climbed, they listened for sounds, for any token of a human presence. No one stirred. But Ethan could not rid himself of the feeling that someone unseen was watching them, that someone was stalking them even as they climbed.

It soon became apparent that, from the second floor upwards, the castle broke up into its separate sections – a tower here, a turret behind it, a bartizan perched on its flank. A full investigation would leave them hopelessly lost in a maze of corridors, staircases, and hidden passages. They oriented themselves by a mixture of guesswork and calculation, and finally started down a corridor that would, they hoped, bring them to the lit room and whatever was waiting for them in it. Ethan chose the third room along and switched off his torch. Ilona followed suit. Controlling his breathing, he took out his pistol in readiness before he turned the knob and pushed the door open.

They stepped into darkness, like birds flying into sudden night. Of course, it was always possible that, if this had been the room in which the light had been burning, someone had turned it off. Ethan switched his torch on again, and behind him Ilona did the same. He had not known what to expect, and it took several moments before a meaningful picture emerged: a leather sofa, two leather armchairs, a fireplace, and a desk covered with papers and sundry items, including an old-fashioned bakelite telephone. There was something old about the room and its furnishings. It wasn't just that the room was part of an ancient structure. What struck Ethan was the atmosphere. The room did not seem to have been left disused, for there wasn't a trace of dust anywhere; but it had nothing of the truly modern about it. The air held more than a trace of warmth, as though someone had sat in here before an open fire not long ago. Ethan stepped across to the fireplace; yes, there were fresh embers in the grate, and when he used a poker to stir them, they glowed cheerily for half a minute.

Ilona went to the desk. It was scattered with the usual equipment: a tub filled with pens and pencils, a couple of glass paper-weights, a blotting pad. Next to these nestled a pair of embroidered shoes from Persia or India, she could not be sure: old trophies from the days Transylvania was part of the Ottoman Empire. She moved the torch to the other side and, moments later, she hissed at Ethan, calling him across.

'Look,' she said, pointing to some photographs in silver frames.

They were not family photographs. One showed a tall man sitting next to Adolf Hitler. Another showed a man and woman standing, one on either side of Heinrich Himmler. There were other photographs of the same three people with what Ethan took to be other representatives of the Third Reich. One showed a man in a fez wound with white cloth in conversation with Hitler.

Drawing back from the desk, they let their torches play across the walls, and here they picked out more portraits and photographs of places: two castles, one of which Ethan recognised as the Burg Almásy in Burgenland; several churches, not all of them Romanian; and landscapes of what looked like oases in a desert, possibly the Sahara.

'The Sahara...' he whispered.

'A holiday, perhaps?'

He shook his head.

'My grandfather,' he said, more to himself than to Ilona. 'We're on the right track,' he said, raising his voice. 'We're in the right place.'

CHAPTER SIXTEEN

Dracula's Bride

The corridor rolled away, its further end always out of reach of their torches. Alerted by the pictures in the first room they had entered, Ethan and Ilona paid more attention to the corridor walls. There were no portraits up here. Instead, a series of pictures in black and gilded frames depicted an assortment of themes. One showed a dove with golden rays fanning out from its wings and body, like the Holy Spirit in a religious painting; another a chalice from which a dove's wings emerged, and a cross where the bird's head would have been, and above it a second dove descending. A heavy black frame held what might have been an eighteenth-century print of a sphinx crowned by a five-pointed star. Next to it hung a framed flag about two feet by one, a red swastika flanked by four red fleurs-de-lis, all on a yellow background. Under the flag was a handwritten caption, 'Burg Werfenstein, 1907. Liebenfels'. Religious and occult subject matter predominated.

They opened door after door, finding cold

rooms in darkness. There was no need to investigate each one. Time was running out. It would not be long before someone noticed their presence and came to see what was going on.

The seventh door opened onto a very different scene. An oil lamp burnt on a table near the window. A dull fire glimmered in the grate, shedding a modicum of warmth into the chilly air. Bar a low truckle bed, the room was bare of furniture. A woman lay on the bed, huddled beneath a blanket.

It took slow moments before Ethan recognised her. Matted short black hair, frightened green eyes, pale cheeks turned green. She was staring at him, all the time cringing away from him, and it was plain to see that she was terrified and that she did not recognise him.

'Sarah,' he said, his voice soft, to avoid alarming her. 'It's me, Ethan. I've come to take you out of here.'

The terror did not wholly leave her, but her first reaction was simply a blank stare, as though worlds and ages had come between them, not the short time that had passed since her abduction or the brief passage from England to Romania.

He turned to Ilona.

'Ilona, will you take off your heavy jacket and your scarf, and let your hair down? Let her see you're a woman, show you mean her no harm.'

Ilona did as he asked, and approached Sarah slowly, smiling and speaking in a reassuring voice. At one point, she thought Sarah was about to scream, but she went on smiling and holding out her hands.

'I've not come to hurt you,' she said.

Sarah flinched as Ilona came to her and put out one hand to touch her cheek.

'It's all right, Sarah,' she said. Ilona had to fight back her own sense of unease, having no idea what had reduced this young Englishwoman to her present state.

Suddenly, a hand darted out from beneath the thin blanket, and Sarah clutched Ilona by the wrist.

'Don't let them hurt me,' she said. 'Keep Lukacs off me, don't let him do that to me again.' She dragged the words from her throat, then her voice died away and she was convulsed by sobs.

Ilona sucked her breath in hard. She scarcely dared ask who had done this to this woman. She moved in close and got an arm round Sarah, pulling her tightly to herself. It was a sort of bonding. Ilona had never been raped, but more than one of her friends had been, and she knew what it did.

'Sarah,' she said, 'we've come to take you away from this place. We won't let anyone hurt you again. Ethan's here... Your friend.'

Ethan ventured closer. He could not imagine what they'd done to her. Was Aehrenthal still here? Or his ugly sidekick Lukacs? Could they sneak Sarah out without alerting her kidnappers?

'Sarah, love,' he whispered. 'It's Ethan. I've come to take you home.'

Her eyes fluttered, and for the first time Ethan saw light in them.

'Ethan?'

Her voice was almost inaudible.

'Yes, dear, I've come to get you out of here.'

She shook her head.

'He said ... he'd kill me if I tried to leave. Someone ... took away my clothes... He said the cold...'

'The cold will kill you if you go out without clothes,' said Ilona. 'It will take some time before we can get you to warmth.'

'What can we do?' Ethan asked.

Ilona looked at Sarah, then at Ethan and herself.

'Ethan,' she said, 'you and I, we have good quality clothes on the outside, and I think we have some warm clothing underneath. I suggest I give Sarah my jacket, and you can give her your trousers. If we're fast...'

Ethan removed his thick outer trousers and handed them to Ilona. She flapped her hands in the air until he cottoned on and turned his back. Ilona drew the blanket away, wincing as she saw the bruises that covered Sarah's naked body. She helped her

235

into the trousers and the jacket. They fitted her well enough.

'What about her head?' asked Ethan. 'She'll lose a lot of heat if she goes out there bareheaded.'

Ilona frowned, then pounced on the blanket, which she proceeded to tear in half.

'Here,' she said, 'let me make a turban for you.' She twisted the cloth round Sarah's head, pulling it tight and tucking the loose end inside the fabric. It was bizarre, but a passable head covering.

'What about feet?' asked Ilona.

Ethan realised that, without some sort of footwear, Sarah would end up with severe frostbite.

'We could use the blanket,' he said. 'Tear it into strips...'

'No, I have a better idea. We saw a pair of slippers in the first room. If they fit her, we can tie them with half the blanket to give more warmth.'

'Sarah,' asked Ethan, 'how many people are in the castle? Do you have any idea?'

In the short time that had passed since they found her, Sarah had started to come alive. The deadness had gone out of her eyes. She looked directly at Ethan and shrugged.

'The one called Egon. The beast called Lukacs, who hurt me every time he raped me.' She screwed up her eyes, fighting back tears. 'Some others, maybe four. There was a woman who brought me a little food. An old woman, she won't stop you.'

But she could let out a yell and alert the others, thought Ethan.

'Let's get moving,' he said. 'The longer we hang about here, the higher the chances of someone coming.'

They left the lamp burning and got Sarah into the corridor. She moved painfully, each step a reminder of what had been done to her.

Re-entering the room they'd been in first, Ilona retrieved the slippers from the desk. They were fairly large, and as Ilona ran her hand over them, she realised they were leather, embroidered with a paisley motif. Sarah's feet went inside them well enough, though they would hardly do to walk any great distance in. Ethan tore half the blanket into strips as Ilona had suggested and, as Sarah sat in the armchair, he bound her feet. She would not be comfortable, but if they could get her as far as the pony, she could ride the rest of the way.

Moving as silently as possible, they headed back to the stairs, conscious that every moment that passed brought them closer to discovery. Ethan paused to replace the batteries in his torch, fumbling as Ilona gave him light from hers. Sarah was shaking, as if breaking out of the false security of the little room had exposed her to greater danger.

Suddenly, as though it came from within the castle, a wolf howled and howled again. Ethan felt his scalp go cold. Beside him Ilona, who had taken Sarah's arm and was helping her balance in her awkward shoes, shuddered. She had known wolves all her life, but had never come to love them.

'Where am I?' Sarah asked. Freed from the room, she was starting to come to her senses. 'I know I'm not in England. But where is this?'

Ethan told her, adding as much detail as he deemed suitable. Sarah listened, understanding his words, but finding no meaning in them. How could she be in Romania, in Transylvania? She had been at Woodmancote, there had been a fireplace with burning logs, Ethan had been locked in a dark place, a place that smelt of putrefaction. On the wall, Ilona's torch caught a picture showing a skeleton with a long scythe. Ilona looked at it and caught Sarah's gaze.

'*Tarokk*,' she said. 'What's that in English?'

'Tarot,' said Ethan. 'It's the thirteenth card of the Major Arcana. Death.'

'How do you know that, Ethan?' Sarah asked. There was something in her voice this time that sounded more normal. Almost as if she were teasing him.

'An old girlfriend,' he said. 'She made all her decisions with the cards. We weren't together long.'

'I'm not surprised.'

They made their way down to the principal landing at the top of the main staircase. Without warning, a light went on just above them, then another, then several at once, until the great hallway was flooded by electric light. Powered by a generator, the light was not particularly strong, and for several moments it flickered. But it was more than enough to capture them, as if spotlights held them pinned to a stage.

For half a minute, nothing else happened. Then the wolf howled again, very close, and Ethan heard footsteps from the ground floor. Sarah pulled away from Ilona and shrank against Ethan's side. He took his pistol from the holster and held it behind his back. Knowing what had been done to Sarah and what might equally be done to Ilona, he knew he wouldn't hesitate to use it.

Three men appeared from the side corridor Ethan and Ilona had come through. As they did so, another man started down the stairs they had just come down, and a fifth emerged from the other side. They were big men, dressed in some sort of uniform, all in black, with short hair. Ethan looked round quickly. The men were grim-faced; tough guys, men with powerful bodies built, not in gyms, but probably on the mountains surrounding the castle.

Near the foot of the stairs, he recognised the man who'd come with Aehrenthal to Woodmancote, Lukacs. But it wasn't Lukacs who grabbed his attention. It was the grey wolf straining at the end of a leash held in Lukacs' hand and snarling at the intruders.

Lukacs shouted something; whether a command or challenge, Ethan had no idea. Ilona translated.

'He says his wolf has not been fed all day. He says it will tear your throat out and dine on the rest of you.'

'Tell him to fuck off. And ask him where Aehrenthal is.'

She did as he asked, but Lukacs' only response was to laugh loudly, setting off the other men, who all seemed to find the whole thing amusing.

Lukacs spoke again. On all sides, the portraits stared down, fully illuminated now. The flags seemed to drift in a world of their own, in a time distinct and proper to themselves. Ethan watched how the eyes of the castle's ancestors followed them, showing neither alarm nor the rapt attention of a crowd intent on the shedding of blood. If the wolf attacked, these would be the Romans, inured to bloodshed, indifferent to death.

'He wants you to send us down alone, Sarah and me,' said Ilona. She was doing her best to put on a brave front, but this wasn't what she'd expected when she agreed

240

to take Ethan to the castle. Beside her, Sarah was quivering and hunching down, as if by shrinking she might avoid detection.

'Tell him it's finished,' Ethan said. 'Tell him there will be no more rapes. Tell him that if he presses me, someone will die, that I have no time for him, that I consider beating and raping a woman a capital offence. We walk out of this castle, we go back to Sancraiu, and we all live happily ever after. Make sure he understands that.'

Stumbling, Ilona conveyed Ethan's message as best she could. Lukacs grinned all the time she was speaking, his eyes fastened on Ilona's face, as though he was sizing her up. Then the grin vanished and was replaced by a look that might have turned sugar sour.

In the next second, he whispered something to the wolf and let slip its leash. It bayed as it bounded forward, and in two leaps it was on Ethan, its jaws open, its fangs exposed ready to shear through his neck.

Ethan shot it once through the head and a second time as its body reared up, striking it through the chest. Still moving, it crashed to a halt on the stairs directly in front of Ethan, its eyes lifeless now, its tongue lolling, red and wet, from the corner of its dripping mouth.

Ethan had never learnt how to fight a wolf. But during police training he'd been given a day's instruction on what to do when a fighting dog attacked, or how to handle a man with a pit bull terrier on a leash. There had been a simple rule: don't look at the owner, keep your eye on the hand holding the leash. And that's what Ethan had done.

Calmly, he turned to Ilona.

'Tell him the next bullet is for him. If he lets us go, the only victim here will be the wolf. If not, he can only blame himself.'

Killing the wolf went to Ethan's head. He had come within half a second of having his throat torn out, and here he was, alive and holding a gun in his right hand. He almost grinned at the absurdity and thrill of it. Without thinking, he started down the steps, keeping the Beretta pointed at Lukacs. The cartridge still held eighteen bullets. Knowing that gave added edge to his confidence.

He was halfway down when he heard a cry behind him, followed by a second. He swivelled and saw that the two men who'd been standing on the stairs above them had hurried down and grabbed Sarah and Ilona. They had knives in their hands, and were holding them to their captives' throats. Lukacs shouted something from below, his voice angry.

'Put the gun down, Ethan, or he says they will kill me and hurt Sarah.'

Ilona's voice was weak with fear. Next to her, Sarah had passed out. Ethan looked round desperately. They were trapped. Even if Ilona could break free and make a run for it with him, Sarah would still be here.

'Ilona,' he started. 'Tell him I'll drop the gun if he lets you go first. You're only a guide, you have no other connection to this.'

She shook her head.

'They will rape me first. And after that...?'

He saw her slump, as though she too had passed out. The man holding her grabbed her more tightly, trying to redistribute her weight. His knife dangled in front of her throat. A light bounced back from its blade. The knife moved.

Ethan saw the blood before the movement, or at least that was how it seemed to him afterwards. Suddenly, there was a lot of blood. An artery pumped a bright red stream into the air. Blood splashed on the floor and on a heraldic shield. Flecks streaked the face of an ancestral portrait. There was no sound, as if this was a silent film suddenly brought into a world of colour.

After the spurt of blood, he saw the man's hands loosen their hold, then saw him jerk back, leaving Ilona upright, her bloodied hunting knife still clutched in her right hand.

Have you ever used a knife like that before? It's an ugly-looking thing. You could spit an ox with it...

She had taken it from the long pocket on the outside of her trousers, the knife with the eight-inch blade, and she had slumped, making her attacker move off balance, before striking up into his groin, and again up and up until she met bone, then sideways. Ilona had hunted from the age of seven, she'd last been in the forest two weeks before. This was the first time she'd killed a human being. As yet, she felt no pang of conscience.

A couple of feet away, the other man kept a tight hold on Sarah. He had a knife like his brother, the first man, and he'd killed several human beings with it, including a child and two women. Despite this, he was nervous. He was under strict instructions not to harm the woman he was holding; she was important to Egon, she could be stripped and played with, but she was never to be hurt. Only Egon could do that, by himself or with Lukacs' help. He decided she was too feeble now to run away, so he dropped her and turned, intending to take revenge for his brother, who was bleeding his life out across the stairs.

He unsheathed his knife, a World War One bayonet, and faced up to Ilona. He was much bigger than her, but not that much older. His feet were braced for a quick lunge that would disable her knife hand and throw her off balance. He felt agitated by his brother's death, but counted slowly, rocking now on the balls of his feet, narrowing his eyes, letting his breath come slowly, calming himself, easing himself into the first move, getting ready to spring and thrust. Ilona held her ground, but she knew he would overpower her the moment he jumped. She had hunted, but she had never been a fighter.

He bent his knees for the leap. Ethan shot him, two taps in the temple. More blood on the stairs, red streams of it on Sarah, her hair flecked with it, his great bulk swaying, twisting, crashing to the ground.

'Ask him where Aehrenthal is,' Ethan told Ilona. She was still shaking. Ethan was grim. His voice showed no pity. Something about Sarah had lit a fire in him: her condition, the way Aehrenthal and his men had taken a beautiful, intelligent woman and reduced her to a cowering shadow of herself. He'd dealt with rape victims many times in his career, women of all ages, even children; but something had been done to Sarah that seemed singular to him, and forlorn, as though she had lost herself in the process, or had become another thing, a used thing.

Ilona could not deny him. Controlling her voice, she put the question to Lukacs. He did not laugh this time. He bided his time, as though a less flippant answer was called for. At last, he grunted out several sentences. Ilona nodded.

'He says this man Aehrenthal's not here, that you're wasting your time. He also says that if you want to leave here alive, you have

245

to drop your gun, and I have to put my knife down. He says you have stepped into deep waters. Waters you will drown in. He says you must leave Sarah here with him, if he lets you go. She knows too much, he says.'

'Tell him he must understand that I didn't come this far just to leave Sarah behind. I will use the gun again, tell him that.'

Ethan wondered how many more staff Aehrenthal kept at the castle, and asked himself how long it would be before someone else came running, drawn by the gunfire.

Calling his remaining companions to his side, Lukacs started up the stairway. He snarled and said something clipped in Hungarian.

'He says he has raped your woman a dozen times before, and now he intends to rape her in front of your eyes before he kills you.'

Ethan kept a close eye on Lukacs. Was he hoping that he and his friends would intimidate Ethan and the two women, that they would just back off?

Lukacs had other thoughts in his mind. The last thing Ethan expected was for a man of his bulk and slow-wittedness to move so quickly. Before Ethan had a chance to react, Lukacs threw himself up the stairs, tearing past Ethan, who fired late and wide, and hurling himself onto Sarah. He grabbed her round the neck, leaving her arms free, turning her to face Ethan and serve as a shield. She seemed like a child next to him. As he held her, he shouted at Ilona, and she translated rapidly in a broken voice.

'He says he will kill her, that he'll break her neck. If you don't put the gun down he won't hesitate to do it. He means it, Ethan – he'll kill her if you don't throw the gun away.'

But Lukacs didn't kill her. He didn't get the chance. Sarah killed him instead, easily and almost instantly. The long bayonet had been dropped right next to her hand, and she had taken it into her possession, weighing it against death. As Lukacs took hold of her, and while he was barking out threats to Ilona, Sarah grasped the knife in two hands and rammed it upwards into his naked throat, and harder again past his chin, and again in a gesture of utter contempt so that the blade pierced through his brain and exited at the back of his skull. Like an ox at slaughter, his legs gave way and he fell to the steps an inhuman thing, past all cruelty. The two men who'd entered with Lukacs hadn't the stomach to attack, but fled precipitately back into the castle.

Ethan went to Sarah now. She let the blade fall from her hand. She was done with it now, done with it and the men who'd brought her here and raped her.

'Take me out of here, Ethan,' she said. 'Take me home.'

CHAPTER SEVENTEEN

Dracula

Sancraiu
Early morning

Ilona guided them back through the cold night. Without her jacket, she shivered beside Sarah in the darkness. The forest was devoid of light. Barely visible, tall trees stretched their arms together to blot out the light of the moon and stars. Behind them, near enough to make it seem possible they would catch up any moment, came the howling of wolves.

Sarah had grown weak, and her fear was turning to panic as they struggled through the forest. Her legs buckled under her several times. Ethan and Ilona took it in turns to hold her upright and move her along as quickly as they could.

'Let me stay here,' she said, again and again. 'I'll be all right. I'll just lie down and sleep. I think it's better, don't you?'

Ethan explained that if she slept she would die, and she answered as if that was just what she wanted.

They used their torches to pick out a path,

and bit by bit the howling faded. At one point, Ilona veered from the path, leading them across the slope. It was harder for everyone to walk, but she kept them to it. Ethan lost track of time, and he knew Sarah knew nothing of where she was or how much time had passed since her capture.

By and by they came to a little cabana, a hunter's lodge. The door was open, and it was as cold inside as out.

'We'll be safe here,' said Ilona. 'No one will come here.'

'What about our friends up at the castle?' asked Ethan.

'Not at first,' she said. 'Perhaps later, if they find you haven't gone through Sancraiu. Don't worry about that. I'll speak to some people in the town; if anyone comes asking questions, they'll all swear that you and a strange young woman were in Sancraiu this morning, and they'll say you drove on to Bucharest.'

With the windows shuttered and the door firmly fastened, Ilona lit several oil lamps before putting logs on a large open grate and lighting them with dried moss. The pine logs sputtered and spat for a time, then the flames began to work their way into the wood. The spitting sounds continued, but now they were matched by a more satisfying sound, of flames gaining strength.

While Ethan helped Sarah huddle on a

stool by the fire, rubbing her hands in his and covering her with blankets he found in the little sleeping room, Ilona busied herself preparing food. There was a little metal stove, and it was quickly stuffed with logs and set ablaze.

'I'm afraid there's only tinned food here, and some dry things,' she pronounced. 'Everybody contributes something. It's kept here in case of emergencies. We all know these shelters will be fully stocked.'

Tinned or dried, it scarcely mattered. The food cupboard was full. Ilona put water in a pan and set it on the hob. She lifted out packets of Knorr soup labelled as Bors Magic. After that, she found a joint of *ciolan afumat,* which she described as 'smoked ham on the bone', several jars of beans with ham, a jar of beef goulash, and two jars of sausages with beans – *fasole boabe cu carnati.* It was all hearty food, just the sort of thing Ethan could imagine big Transylvanian hunters shovelling down their craws after shooting a bear and hauling its carcass back to headquarters. They would find it hard to starve here.

An hour later, Ethan and Ilona had eaten their fill; but Sarah remained motionless in front of the fire. She needed help, but Ethan doubted he had the capacity to give the sort of help she needed.

There were four bunks in the sleeping

room. With Ilona's help, Ethan managed to get Sarah into bed. She was still shivering, despite the heat she'd taken from the fire, and they covered her in blankets, leaving one each for themselves.

'I'll talk in the morning, Ethan,' Ilona said. 'Then I'll go in to Sancraiu. I don't think we should move Sarah yet.'

So it began. Ilona's visits to Sancraiu for news and supplies became regular. While she was away, Ethan would remain with Sarah in the hut, talking to her, stimulating her return to the real world. She had suffered something vicious, and her mind's efforts were focused on the act of forgetting. She had been taken away from all her realities, and if it had been for only a short time, the trauma had been intense. All that seemed between her and a breakdown was her inner resilience. Ethan wished he had known her better, that his had been a familiar voice. Ilona brought English books from home, and Ethan read to Sarah at every opportunity: Dickens, Austen, long stretches of PG Wodehouse. Sometimes, when he read the Wodehouse, she would laugh.

Time passed like water slipping beneath ice. There seemed to be no movement in things – in the forest, the sky, the frostbitten ground. They thought of the castle every day, and wanted to be as far from it as possible, but there was no chance of escape until Sarah recovered from her ordeal. Someone was seen in Sancraiu asking questions about outsiders, a man and a woman. He received no honest answers. But Ilona said it was only a matter of time.

In the meantime, Ethan made a call on Ilona's mobile phone. He asked Lindita to send another false passport made out in Sarah's name, and complete with Romanian entry stamps. Lindita promised to post it in a day or two. Ethan took a photograph of Sarah, using Ilona's digital camera; the picture showed a woman suddenly older, unsmiling, torn somehow, almost broken. Ilona used her home computer to transmit the image directly to Lindita in Gloucester.

Time passed like snow drifting down from unspent clouds, through darkness and light. Ethan spent each day with Sarah, talking or reading, and at times watching in silence. When she slept, which was often, she had nightmares. He would stay by her side, holding her hands and whispering.

Slowly, she came round. She would always be scarred, he could see that, but day by day she was recovering her wits. He began to wish he was her lover, not her friend, so intense had his feelings become for her. But he recoiled from the temptation of love so long as she was traumatised, even as he stroked the back of her hand or drew a lock of hair away from her forehead.

A week passed, then a second. Ilona brought back news that Egon Aehrenthal had turned up in Sancraiu with a group of his men, asking questions. No one had given him the answers he was looking for. Ilona may have spent time in the big city, but back in Sancraiu, she was still one of the towns-people.

'We must get you away from here,' she said. 'It's only a matter of time before he stumbles on you both. There are some people who distill illegal whiskey out here in the forest. They sometimes head over to a cabana when it gets very cold, or if supplies run out. If they find you and they know Aehrenthal is looking for you, they'll be up at Castel Lup before you've had breakfast.'

By then, Sarah had started to make a fair recovery, though Ethan didn't think she was ready to be moved. Her mood was labile, shifting by the hour, sometimes by the minute. She had panic attacks, reliving the terror of being snatched, then anger at having been raped, then general despon-dency, then elation at her rescue. She spoke with Ethan often, though not in her blackest moments. When she was silent and would give nothing up, he talked to her. He spoke of anything and nothing, old family stories that once in a while would make her laugh, or anecdotes of his police work. He steered clear of serious crime, of murder and rape and muggings, but found plenty to entertain. He told her of the man he'd stopped when he was still in uniform, a man of about forty, on the edge of the city, singing to a horse. She laughed at that one, and he held her hand. She looked at him, and there was a smile on her face. But it took only moments before she reverted to her troubled self.

One day, coming out of an uneasy sleep during which she had whimpered more than usual, Sarah opened her eyes wide and, catching sight of Ethan, she spoke quite clearly, but in a low voice.

'There's great danger. All of us, great danger. Must stop him. Stop all of them.'

Within seconds, she fell asleep again. Later, when she woke and grew fully conscious, she remembered nothing of what she'd said, and Ethan did not press her. But her eyes were troubled, and Ethan sensed that a fragment of memory remained behind them. She knew something, he was sure of it, something that posed a threat to 'all of us', whoever that included.

It happened again some days later. Great danger, great harm, an ancient evil, marchers on a high place, banners, boots polished to perfection. This time she spoke at greater length, only to fall asleep again.

Perhaps, thought Ethan, it was nothing more than words out of delirium. But he sensed her fear, and it seemed real to him.

That night, he heard her call loudly from her bed, and dashed across to help. She was calling in a tremulous voice, as if beset by wolves or stinging insects. He caught her right hand and held it tightly, wishing her asleep again; but this time she stayed awake.

'Put the light on, Ethan.'

He found an oil lamp and fumbled with matches until the wick caught. As he replaced the glass, a pale whitewash of light brought the little wooden room into view. Sarah was sitting up in bed now. Her forehead was covered in sweat, her hair lay bedraggled and lifeless across her cheeks. He pulled it back and sat down on the edge of the bed. Her hands were shaking. Again, he took one hand in his and held it until she began to grow calm. How he wished he could take her in his arms and hold her until the terrors died.

'We have to talk, Ethan.' She seemed suddenly more clear-eyed than he was. There was real consciousness in her gaze, not the blur he'd been looking at all this time.

'Go on. I'm listening.'

And in the immeasurable stillness of the forest her soft voice spelt out to him the outlines of a horror she could only dimly see.

'Don't underestimate Aehrenthal,' she said. 'He may surround himself with thugs, but he's not a thug. When he thought I'd been softened up enough, he came to visit me. He didn't rape me or hit me or threaten me in any way. He just talked. Mostly, he talked about himself. He's a clever man, but he never went to university, so he seems to think I'm some sort of marvel. He knows a lot about me, he's done his homework. And he told me why he kidnapped me.'

She took a deep breath. He could feel the tremor in her hand, and squeezed more tightly.

'He's convinced I know how to find this place in Libya where Great-Granddad found the relics. It seems he's not content with getting hold of them, but wants to see where they were found. I think he knows there's something else there, something more valuable than the relics.'

'The tombs.'

She nodded.

'He asked about tombs, but I just said I knew nothing.'

'It would be the greatest antiquities find in history. He probably doesn't even guess just how much is out there. It would certainly make his name if he could lead an expedition to Wardabaha.'

Her eyes widened and she shook her head.

'Oh, no,' she said. 'It's not about that. He's

not doing this to make his name or even to make the kind of money he guesses he could make. It's the other way round: he became an antiquarian because he thought it might lead him to all this.'

'To make a lot of money.'

She said nothing for several moments. He thought she was growing tired and decided to leave her to fall asleep.

'Ethan, he's the head of some sort of Nazi organisation. They have followers here in Romania, in Hungary, in Austria and Germany. A lot of followers. And a lot of allies, mostly right-wing Christian groups. He told me about them, said the relics would be in safe hands, and that I could trust the place in Libya with them too.'

He looked at her blankly.

'I don't get it. What has any of this to do with Nazis?' But even as he asked the question, he remembered the photographs he'd seen at the Wolf's Lair.

'I don't really know,' she said. 'But they've been hunting for the relics for years, he told me.'

In Ethan's mind, a memory stirred. He stared into the flames. Something about Himmler and the Lance of Longinus. The Nazis had been tracking it down. The Lance of Power. The Spear of Destiny. All occult nonsense, of course, he thought. But occult nonsense could inspire men to great deeds.

Great deeds and evil deeds.

When he looked round, Sarah had fallen asleep again.

CHAPTER EIGHTEEN

Children of the Night

Afterwards, he could not say how it happened. He had done his best not to encourage it.

Some sort of change came over her, overnight, or so it seemed. Since her rescue, Sarah had been overcome by a sort of lassitude. She had stayed in bed relentlessly, as though driving herself inwards, searching for some complete escape, to run to a place where neither men nor wolves could reach her. But now, the tiredness began to lift. She went to sleep one night in that mood of withdrawal, and woke in the morning ready to pull herself from bed.

Her legs were still weak. Ethan helped her to walk the few yards from the bedroom to the fireplace in the larger room. As he made to lower her into a chair, she kissed him lightly on the forehead, hesitated momentarily, then pulled his head down and placed her lips full on his.

Shocked and entranced, he drew back, letting her drop onto the chair.

She laughed.

'It's all right, Ethan, I won't eat you. Unless, of course, you're the sort of man who panics when a woman kisses him.'

'But why...?'

'To thank you for coming all the way out here to rescue me. Knight in shining armour stuff. And to say I think I'm making progress. It may take me years to put this all behind me, perhaps I'll never recover properly, but I'm starting to feel a bit more confident. And because I like you.'

He was about to ask her more about how she felt, when the door was flung open. A rapid gust of cold wind rushed in, followed by a frantic-looking Ilona. She slammed the door behind her.

'We've got to get out of here!' she gasped. She'd been running, and was out of breath. 'Get your things on, we must be out of here in the next two minutes.'

'What's going on?' Ethan was already looking for the coat Ilona had brought for Sarah. Ilona was helping Sarah to her feet.

'Not now. Move.'

At that moment, a sound echoed behind her voice: the baying call of a wolf. The cry was answered from far off by a second howl, then a third. For half a minute, their voices joined together, creating a moaning, pulsating chorus that rose and dipped in that uncanny music wolves intone.

They stumbled out, hurried along by Ilona. Ethan could sense her fear. The wolves? Or something else?

They quickened their pace, always conscious of how little strength there was in Sarah. Ethan held her tightly, taking her weight, guiding her path. They stumbled through snow, then withered undergrowth, then entered the trees, dodging between their trunks, their steps taking them further and further down the mountainside. Ilona led the way, at once urgent and careful, knowing Sarah might not have the strength to make it through the thickets of brambles that crisscrossed the forest floor.

After they had made some progress, Ilona looked back to see Sarah sitting on the ground while Ethan tried to pick her up.

'Hold back,' he said to Ilona. 'She can't go a step further. Look at her. She's still very ill.'

'If she stays here, Ethan, she will die. Take my word for it. She's got to make it down to Sancraiu. I have a car waiting, she can stay inside after that. But she can't stay here.'

'Why the sudden panic?'

'Because Egon Aehrenthal has come back. He has found a bunch of local hunters and paid them well. They need money in winter, and most of them are the sort of men who will do anything, whether they are paid or not. Some have trained wolves that they use to hunt for bears or wild boar. Of course, sometimes they are paid to hunt for wolves.

'They're out there now, scouring the forest. They started this morning, some beating from top down, others from bottom up. We have to find a way out past them. If we can get to my car, I'll take you out of here. There's someone I want you to meet.'

Ethan bent down to help Sarah back on her feet.

'Sarah, I know this is hard, but we can't let Aehrenthal get his hands on you again. He'll kill you this time. He'll have his wolves tear you to pieces. You have to try.'

He made her stand up, less gentle now, knowing the need for speed. He let her weight fall on him again, but less fully, lest she impede his progress. She cried out in pain, and at that moment another wolf howled. A harsh man's voice rang out among the trees and was answered by a second man somewhere off to their right. Ilona knew the men would carry guns, and the wolves had teeth, teeth that could crush bone.

They came to a small clearing. Here, the ground was covered in a thick counterpane of perfect snow. As they entered the open space, the trees on the other side parted and a man in the clothes of a hunter stepped through. He was followed by a second man who led a wolf on a short chain. The wolf snarled as it caught sight of strangers.

Ethan thought quickly, then turned to Ilona.

'Tell them that I will pay them ten times as much as Aehrenthal is paying.'

Ilona translated this for the hunters. As she did so, she slipped the glove from her right hand and slipped the hand into her pocket.

The men did not react. They were thickset men with heavy moustaches and long hair tied back in ponytails. On their backs, they wore thick sheepskin coats, and in their hands they carried hunting guns, old guns polished to a fine blue patina and loaded with quarter-inch-diameter steel shot.

The man with the wolf brought the animal forward and spoke curtly to Ilona. She translated for Ethan.

'He wants me to leave, to go back San-craiu. Either that or he says he will kill me and you.'

'Then leave,' said Ethan. 'You've done your part and more. The rest has nothing to do with you. It's my business.'

Ilona sighed.

'Take a close look at the two men,' she said.

He didn't know what she meant at first, but glanced nevertheless at the man nearest him. It took moments to see what she was referring to. He turned his eyes on the second man. The same thing. Each man had a long scar on his left cheek. The scars were whiter than the white cheeks of the men.

'They belong to the Arrow Cross,' she whispered. 'It's an old Hungarian fascist society. Aehrenthal is the head of the Transylvanian chapter. He initiates them by giving them a sabre scar. These are his men.'

'But if they...'

She shook her head fiercely.

'Not now.'

She turned back to the man who had offered her a way out. 'They're yours,' she said in Romanian. 'Do what you like with them. Take your time.'

She walked towards them, as though to pass that way out of the clearing and so on to Sancraiu. But as she reached the man with the wolf, she took her hand from her pocket. It held a tiny canister. She aimed at the wolf, spraying it in the eyes, then, before its handler could react, sprayed him too. The effect was instantaneous. The wolf howled in pain, the man screamed and dropped the leash, whereupon the wolf ran howling out of the clearing. Two more steps brought Ilona to the second hunter, who was standing as if rooted to the spot, unable to understand what had just happened to his companion and the animal. She sprayed him as well. Ethan went across to where the two men were crouching in agony. He took their guns and slung them over his shoulder.

'What the hell was that?' he asked.

'Pepper spray,' Ilona said. 'Now we get out of here.'

CHAPTER NINETEEN

The Falling of Snow and the Shimmering of the Sun

Putna
Bucovina

They reached the monastery between compline and vespers, in a time of silence. The monks had returned to their cells, the priests were preparing for the artokiasia service that would follow vespers that evening. Ilona led them through darkness to the candlelit church where it stood at the heart of a great complex made up of turreted buildings sheltering behind the high monastery wall. This was Putna, the gem in the crown of Romania's monastic foundations. For long centuries, the voices of the monks had intoned the liturgy from hour to hour throughout the day, in summer and winter alike, beneath the falling of snow and the shimmering of the sun.

The monk priest was waiting for them in an archway near the great iconostasis. Most of the candles had been extinguished, and the priest, dressed from head to foot in black, was hidden in shadow at first, while the clouds of incense that still filled the church swirled like the breath of dragons all about him. He watched them coming and, though they were expected, he felt his heart shake. He knew why they had come. For so many years he had anticipated this moment and feared it. So much depended on what happened now. More lives than he dared think of, innocent and guilty alike; Christian churches everywhere, perhaps all religions. How could he really know? He stepped from the shadows.

He held out his hand, and Ilona went forward and bent her head to kiss it. When she looked up, she saw again the kindly features that had struck her at their first meeting one week earlier. The long white beard gave him something of the appearance of a western Santa Claus, but there was, she noticed, a look on his face that might have provoked tears in susceptible children.

'Ethan,' she said, 'let me introduce Archimandrite Iustin Dumitreasa. Father Iustin is a hieromonk. That's to say, he is a priest. But when his wife died, he entered the monastery here and now he serves as a monk as well.'

'His wife?' Ethan wasn't sure he'd heard properly.

Ilona was about to answer, but the priest stepped forward and took Ethan's hand.

'Your Anglican priests marry, do they not?' he said. 'Well, so do Orthodox priests. We are part of the world. How can a man without a wife or family hope to understand the concerns of his parishioners? Ilona tells me your name is Ethan.'

Ethan nodded. He felt in awe of this strange priest. As he shook his hand he looked at his sunken cheeks and slow-burning eyes. This was not an ordinary man. He seemed driven, almost prophetic, a modern-day Isaiah or soothsayer who might perform miracles or utter forebodings of things to come.

Ethan broke away and brought Sarah forward. She would never understand her action later, but as she reached him, she got down on her knees. Father Iustin placed his gnarled and wrinkled hands on the crown of her head and whispered the words of a short prayer.

It was the Jesus Prayer, on the lips of Orthodox Christians at all times. 'Lord Jesus Christ, Son of God, have mercy on me, a sinner.' Sarah didn't know what it was or what it meant, but something in the priest's touch or in the timbre of his voice settled her. The gestures were alien to her. She was not a religious woman and had not been a particularly religious child. But whether it was the posture she had adopted or the laying on of hands that her kneeling had inspired, it was as if a shudder passed through her, and after it a stillness had followed. She got to her feet, still a little unsteady, like someone rising from her sickbed ready to walk. All around her the shadows stirred, and to her the lights of candles shimmered across the rich colours of the iconostasis, with its portraits of Jesus, Mary, and a high host of saints.

'Let me take you to a place where we can talk without being overheard.'

The archimandrite led them out of the church. The building, which in some ways resembled a French chateau, was set in the centre of a square whose sides were made up of the defensive outer walls. They left through the south door, then went on to a doorway set in the southern wall. A half moon hung in a cradle of light, as though suspended directly over the monastery. Father Iustin took a large key from his pocket. It fitted a lock that had not been changed since the seventeenth century.

Once inside, the priest pressed a switch and the ceiling flickered and blazed with electric light.

'I'm sorry about the lights,' he said, 'they're a little harsh. This is our conference room. Putna is one of the country's chief monasteries, so we end up hosting conferences for just about everybody. Let's go to the table over there.'

They followed him to a large octagonal table and sat round four sides. The priest looked at Sarah with concern.

'After this,' he said, 'I will take you to the refectory for food. There is always a table for guests. Until then, I want to talk to you. Later, you can ask me any questions you want. When we are with the other monks, say nothing about what I have told you. It is vital you say not a word.'

'You speak very good English,' Ethan said. 'Where did you...?'

'From my wife,' he said. 'She was English, from Canterbury. We lived for many years in London.'

Ethan raised his eyebrows.

'You were in London?'

Father Iustin smiled and shook his head.

'Romania may not be the centre of civilisation,' he said, 'but some of us have travelled. I used to be the senior priest at the Romanian church in Fleet Street, St Dunstan-in-the-West.'

He looked at Ethan as though he expected him to be familiar with the church.

'I'm sorry,' Ethan said, 'I don't ... I don't

know London all that well. I don't think I–'

'St Dunstan's is the oddest church in London. One half is an Anglican church, the rest is Romanian Orthodox. There's an Anglican altar with icons in front of it, and to its right a large iconostasis. It's a very special place. I have very fond memories of it. My wife was English, as I said. Her name was Jacqueline. She lived most of her life in Romania, with me. When she reached the age of fifty, she expressed a wish to go back home, and the Metropolitan kindly posted me to St Dunstan's. And now I am an old man and a widower. My wife is buried in London and I am seeing out my last years here in Putna, singing the divine service morning noon and night, praying for a vision, listening for the voice of God, waiting to be reunited with the soul of my dear wife. I have become a man of sorrows. And now you are here, you and your sister. You have found me in my last refuge.'

'You sound as if you've been waiting for us,' said Ethan. He was feeling bemused by the monastery and the old man. The priest's words tangled him in brambles.

'I have waited for you for many years. Perhaps not you in person. But I knew someone would come in the end. Someone who would bring me news of Egon Aehrenthal.'

'How do you know–?'

'Ilona here told me, of course.'

Ilona leant across the table.

'I spoke to the minister in my church. My church is Hungarian Reform, of course, which is normal for most Hungarians; but my minister knows many Orthodox people, naturally, because he is very ecumenical. I told him about the relics. He sent me here and gave me Father Iustin's name. When I got here, I explained as much as I could. The good father listened to me and told me to bring both of you here as soon possible. I think we got here a bit faster than expected!'

The priest leant forward. Ethan noticed that the lids of his eyes were red, as though he suffered from an eye condition, blepharitis or conjunctivitis.

'Ethan,' he said, 'I need to know everything you can tell me. In return, I will tell you things you ought to know. Ilona tells me that you have seen some relics, that Egon Aehrenthal has tried to steal them. Can you explain them, please?'

Haltingly at first, Ethan explained. He started with the discovery of his grandfather's body and repeated some of what he could remember from Gerald's letter to Sarah. As he told their story, an hour passed, then a second hour. The old priest fixed his eyes on Ethan and did not take them off him once. Despite the bright lights, the room shrank to the confines of their table. On the walls, the photographs of long-dead priests and monks looked down on them, as though listening to Ethan's narrative.

When he finished, Sarah took over, relaying what she knew and what she guessed, bringing her expertise to bear on Gerald's story.

It was late by the time she finished. At first Father Iustin said nothing. The only movement he made was to rub his eyes with his knuckles, then cup them for a few moments beneath his palms.

'I'm sorry,' he said. 'My eyes are painful. I have sat up every night praying ever since Ilona came to visit me. All things have their time. Now our time has come, and I pray for it to pass well, for if it does not, this beginning will have a bad ending.'

He breathed deeply several times, then murmured the Jesus Prayer for as many times again.

'You must all be very hungry,' he said. 'You have travelled far today. I am sorry, I should have fed you when you first arrived, but I felt a great urgency to learn what you had to tell me. After we eat, I will tell you what I have to tell you.'

They ate together in an empty refectory, by candlelight. The food was plain, a mushroom stew and stuffed cabbage washed down with a weak red wine and followed by apricot dumplings. They ate with keen appetites, and the plain food tasted like dishes

271

from a banquet. Sarah avoided the wine, and by the end of the meal she was too tired to go on. Ilona took her to a little house just outside the walls, where nuns looked after female guests. The long journey had worn Ilona out: she'd driven all the way, through harsh weather and sometimes difficult terrain. From Bistrita, they'd crossed the Carpathians, reaching high altitudes on icy roads. She needed sleep more than anything now. A smiling nun took her to her room and gave her nightclothes to wear. Before she even had a chance to undress, sleep took her and threw her sideways on the bed.

CHAPTER TWENTY

A Man for All Seasons

The ring of hunters that had been closing in on the little hut had been broken. A wolf was missing, and the two men leading it disabled by pepper spray. From deep in the forest, the screams had been muffled, impossible to trace. None of the hunters had carried a mobile phone. Aehrenthal himself had gone away for the day, and would only return that evening. A senior member of the Arrow Cross was in charge of the hunt, and as the day passed without result, he grew more and more worried that his prey might have slipped the net.

Just before dusk a pair of hunters came across a dreadful sight. In a clearing not far from the hunting lodge lay the bodies of two of their companions, their throats ripped open and their faces gnawed to bloody pulp. The wolf that had gone out with them that morning was nowhere to be seen, but when it was found two days later it was still maddened by something in its eyes and had to be put down.

The Arrow Cross man – a Hungarian from Debrecen called Ágoston Fodor – was furious. He punished the man who brought him the news with a series of heavy blows to the face, followed by a whacking with the stick he always carried. Desperate to do something before Aehrenthal returned, Fodor knew he had to find help. Leaving the hunter moaning and writhing on the ground, he headed back to the castle.

Castel Lup was currently being made ready for a council of leading members of the Ordo Novi Templi. Some fifty luminaries had arrived already. It was their presence that had prompted the hunt for Sarah, for Aehrenthal wanted desperately to parade her before his peers and to use more pressing methods to extract from her the coordinates of Wardabaha.

Fodor scurried up to the castle, which he knew as Vár Farkasnak. When he arrived, preparations were already under way for that evening's meal. Already designated Aehrenthal's deputy in Hungary, he was in charge of the castle during his leader's absence. He explained the situation to a small group of his fellows, dressing the tale to cover up his own incompetence in not guaranteeing better communications between the hunters and himself.

By the time Aehrenthal arrived, over an hour later, the meal was ready and Fodor had laid out a plan that would lead them to Sarah and Ethan. He met the Austrian in the entrance hall and helped him out of his coat. With a shaking voice, he explained what had happened.

'It may even be to the good that they escaped,' he explained, fearing the snarling insult or the driving fist that might relegate him to the lowest ranks or worse.

'I'm listening to you, Ágoston. You did wrong to let this happen. I may have you punished. But for the moment I'm listening to you. Why is it good that they escaped?'

There was a sound of knives and forks on plates. Aehrenthal, though exceedingly hungry, paid no attention. Cringing inwardly, Fodor tried to keep an upbeat tone in his voice.

'They may lead us to the monk, wherever

he is. And he may lead us to the others you told me about.'

'What makes you think they know of this monk? Even I don't know his name.'

'Sir, the girl who helped them escape, she's considered clever. She attended Bucharest University, studying English. But she took a course in Romanian architecture, specifically ecclesiastical architecture. She wrote a dissertation on the painted monasteries. It's a popular subject with students.'

'And from this, you think she may know the monk, may know the man who sniffs around us like a dog sniffing another dog on heat, may perhaps know whatever it is he knows about us?'

'Not so much, perhaps–'

'Not so much. The girl knows nothing, but she may still lead us to something. You, follow me.'

Aehrenthal led the Hungarian into the great dining room. It was a high-ceilinged chamber that dated from the earliest days of the castle. A fireplace the size of a small dwelling stood to one side, its two-storey chimney piece built from great slabs of Usak white marble, in which figures turned and twisted like mythical beings turned to stone: two caryatids and two atlantes held the great roof, while all about them tumbled centaurs, Nereids, minotaurs, satyrs and gorgons with wings of gold, claws of brass and tusks of boars. Limbs wrestled with limbs, heads seemed to stop and turn and look at the viewer, griffins with the bodies of lions and the heads and wings of eagles flew against the screeching of harpies, and furies with the wings of bats hovered about a finely carved figure of the winged goddess Nemesis.

The eye travelled upwards, drawn by these creatures and their wars and alliances, until it reached an entablature between chimney piece and ceiling, where a long row of flags strutted from end to end. Aehrenthal glanced at them, invigorated as ever by what they signified. On certain days in the year, they took them down and paraded with them far away from prying eyes: the original Führerstandarte, Hitler's personal flag; a Deutschland Erwache standard, a battle flag bearing the iron cross; an SS HQ flag, the ever-popular swastika set on a white disc against a red field. Next to them hung the green flag of Romania's Iron Guard, on which lay a triple cross like prison bars, the red banner with four joined arrows that belonged to Hungary's Nyilaskeresztes Párt, and the Austrian Vaterländische Front's *Kruckenkreuzflagge*.

There was a loud scraping of chairs, and at the tables, everyone stood to attention before raising their arms in the traditional fascist salute. A deep silence fell and was transmitted down to the kitchens, where the banging of pans and dishes came to a halt.

'Gentlemen,' said Aehrenthal, 'you are most welcome. I trust our council will be a successful one. Tonight, we shall have our first session. I have important news for all of you. But first there are some matters to attend to here.'

He turned to Fodor, who was still standing next to him.

'This man,' he said, 'is called Ágoston. Ágoston Fodor. The Hungarians among you will know him well. Before I went away, I made him my deputy here at Vár Farkasnak, the Wolf's Lair. I told him to launch a hunt for some people who have defied me and gone into hiding nearby. They include the woman I have mentioned, the woman I wanted to introduce to you tonight.

'But today the woman and her companions escaped. Mr Fodor was in charge of the hunt, and Mr Fodor must be held responsible for its failure. He must be punished. I would have him shot, but he is one of our best men, and I have work for him in future.'

He looked Fodor up and down.

'Strip,' he said.

'What?'

'Don't question me! Take your clothes off. Or are you afraid I am a homosexual, that I intend to rape you?'

The menace in Aehrenthal's voice was

unmistakeable. The entire room shivered into silence. In the great fireplace, logs spat and roared up in flame, casting a shimmer of red and gold light across the assembly. Fodor obeyed his order and stood at last, ruddy with flame, naked before his fellows. His mind cast about for every possible punishment, but he could think of nothing that would entail his stripping beforehand. Perhaps this was the punishment, he thought, perhaps stripping was all.

Aehrenthal nodded at two men seated not far away.

'Here,' he said. 'Now, hold him. Take his arms. That's right. Hold him steady, don't let go for a moment.'

Saying which, he reached beneath his jacket and took out a Nieto sheath knife with a wooden handle, his constant companion when out hunting.

'Now, Mr Fodor, you will see what it costs a man to interfere with my plans.'

Bending slightly, he reached down and put his left hand on Fodor's penis, limp and shrivelled despite the warm air. He sawed breath through his nostrils. With his left hand, he played with the limp organ, stroking and teasing it as a woman might do until, in spite of Fodor's innate reluctance to respond, it did respond and grew slowly erect. He drew back the foreskin delicately, and the shaft of the penis elevated itself further.

'Please, sir, please, I'm sorry. It will never happen again, I will never let you down again. Don't cut off my penis, I can't live without it, please...'

Aehrenthal did not seem to hear. Leaving the penis in its half upright position, he grabbed Fodor's testicles and, with a single movement, sliced them away. He stood up, holding the bloody things in one hand and threw them, high over the heads of the staring diners, into the blazing fire. There was a sudden sound of sizzling, as though bacon were being fried, then a silence everywhere in the room, behind which the logs spat and cracked as always. Fodor screamed and slumped unconscious in the arms of the men who held him.

'Take him away,' shouted Aehrenthal. 'Someone clean up this mess. I have no time to lose.'

A servant hurried in and set about cleaning the blood from the glistening floor. The two men who'd been in charge of Fodor dragged him from the hall.

'I'm sorry if I have ruined your appetites,' Aehrenthal said. 'But there may be serious consequences for all of us as a result of Fodor's lack of control. He has been punished, and I take responsibility for that. You have all known, from the day you vowed to serve our Order, that it is an order of iron discipline and rigorous obedience.

'Gentlemen, we have reached a cross-roads. I have in my possession things you have scarcely dared to dream of. After so many years in our quest, and the quests of those who have gone before us, we can see and touch the unreal, and know that it is very real indeed. At midnight tonight, I shall parade them to you. I shall keep them with me at all times and in all places. All here will bear witness to the truth that gives life to this Order. All here will touch tonight the Spear of Destiny and the Crown of Thorns. I shall give you wine to drink from the Holy Grail. Your journeys have not been in vain, your sacrifices have not been wasted.

'But before that there is someone we have to find, someone who can lead us to the place where these things came from, to the bones in their caskets, to the bones and the dry flesh.'

He stopped and looked at the assembled acolytes. Their food sat in front of them, growing cold. The flames behind them devoured the logs and danced less brightly.

'I shall need twelve of you tonight,' he said, then reeled out the names of the men he wanted to help him.

They reached Sancraiu aboard three four-by-four vehicles, fitted with snow tyres and hunting lamps. Together, they drove into the main square and got down, leaving their powerful engines running. Aehrenthal had already given instructions. Each of his deputies was armed with an H&K G3 semi-automatic rifle.

They spread out through the village. Aehrenthal led two of his closest followers into a bar on the far edge of the square. It was filled with cigarette smoke, smoke from a beechwood fire, the sounds of men's voices, a woman's quick laughter, and the underlying smell of beer.

An old man was sitting near the fire, surrounded by his usual crowd as he dredged up memories. Aehrenthal recognised him right away. This was the town mayor, a much respected old soldier by the name of Bogdan Bogoescu. He held court in the inn every night, treating it as a sounding board for the opinions of local residents, and a place where they could listen to his recommendations on village affairs, together with his reminiscences about life as a soldier in World War Two.

Aehrenthal went up to him.

'You,' he said. 'Old man.'

Eyes turned to examine the newcomer. Most of them knew or guessed who Aehrenthal was. He spoke Romanian with what they took for a German accent, and he faced them down with frigid contempt.

The old man looked up at Aehrenthal like someone who had better things to do with his time. He noticed the two men with him, the way they swaggered with their large rifles.

'Can I help you?' he asked.

Aehrenthal's answer was crisp and to the point.

'I want the name of the person responsible for keeping the man and woman in the hunting cabin west of my castle. I believe it's a woman I'm looking for, and I want her name now.'

Bogoescu wasn't particularly frightened of Aehrenthal or what he considered his pomposity.

'Can't think who you're talking about,' he said. 'I never go up that way myself.'

Aehrenthal had expected this response. He didn't hesitate. Lifting his rifle, he blew a hole through the old man's head. Blood leapt in every direction, drops of it spinning like red wasps onto furniture, clothing, and skin. Fragments of skull flew back into the fireplace and rattled against the back. The woman screamed and threw up. The air was filled with exclamations. Aehrenthal stood stock still. No one here was going to attack him. He had nothing but contempt for the villagers, their way of life, their prejudices, their lack of concern for matters of higher importance, their lack of respect for someone like himself.

He turned his head and spoke to the first

man he saw.

'Perhaps you have a better memory than Grandfather here. I'm sure you understand that I'm impatient.'

The man trembled and wet his pants. His companions darted glances everywhere, wondering if there was anywhere for them to run, seeing Aehrenthal's companions blocking their way on both sides.

'Ilona,' came a voice from further back. 'Her name is Ilona. Her family name is Horváth.'

Aehrenthal spotted the man who had spoken.

'Very good,' he said, 'come with me, take me to her house.'

The man made to shrink back, but the nearest of Aehrenthal's assistants simply dived into the group he was with and dragged him out.

The house stood in a short street between the church and the Rózsavölgyi bakery. It had been freshly painted; a street lamp nearby cast a wash of dim light over its façade, as if varnishing the painted surfaces. There were lights behind the windows on one side, and from further in came the sound of a television. Someone was watching *Te crezi mai destept?* on Prima TV.

Aehrenthal had brought four men with him. One was a bodybuilder from Budapest, a tall man they called Samson behind his back. He seemed to do no more than lean against the door. It buckled under his combined weight and strength, and fell with a crash to the ground. He stood aside to let Aehrenthal lead the way, a pistol held in one hand.

The whole family was assembled in the living room. They had just finished dinner and were watching TV together: Ilona's father, mother, two brothers and sister. The brothers were aged fifteen and thirteen, the sister, a pretty girl called Ecaterina, just nine. Aehrenthal killed the little girl first, with a single shot to the head. The room was instantly in uproar. Ilona's father made to grab Aehrenthal's handgun and was shot summarily in the throat. He staggered, choking on his own blood, while his wife, terrified beyond endurance, made to go to him, only to be thrown backwards onto the sofa. The two boys, seeing their sister and father killed, began to whimper. Aehrenthal snapped at them.

'Shut up, you two! If I hear another peep out of you, you'll be next.'

He went across to Mrs Horváth.

'I want answers,' he yelled. 'If I don't get them, I will shoot your boys. And if you give me any false answers, I'll come back and burn this house down round you and these brats.'

The mother was close to hysterics, but the ice in Aehrenthal's voice and the imminent danger to her two sons acted as rods to stiffen her.

'Where has Ilona gone?'

No answer. She just looked wide-eyed at him, not knowing what would pacify his terrible rage. She was praying without words or the presence of God.

'I asked you where your daughter is. She left Sancraiu earlier today. Where did she go?'

He pointed his gun at her youngest boy, and she looked into Aehrenthal's eyes and saw no pity.

She could not answer. The words were trapped inside her, between fear for her sons and dread for her only remaining daughter.

Aehrenthal shot the young boy once in the head. The boy did not shake or jerk or fall backwards, but simply collapsed in a heap, like a toy whose string has been cut. There was no time for him to cry out. His brother shuddered and ran to hold the younger boy, talking to him as if he was still alive. He knew an end was coming. On the television, the programme that had been such a cause of mirth only minutes before rattled on like a tram down lines that would soon lead to a wreck.

Persuaded of the boy's vulnerability, Aehrenthal trained his gun this time, not on him, but on his mother.

'P-P-Putna,' the boy stammered. 'I heard

her say it. That's where she went. I wish I'd gone with her, I wish I was with her now.'

'Where in Putna?' But he had already guessed.

'The ... the mon-monastery.'

'Who will she see there?'

There was no answer, but Aehrenthal knew the name already. Many years before, someone had whispered it in his ear. He had put it to the back of his mind and forgotten it until now.

He reached out and put his hand on the boy's head. The boy flinched, fearing and despising him equally.

'Well done,' said Aehrenthal. 'You did well to tell me this. I'll see you are well treated. You and your mother. It is always best to tell the truth, especially when someone is angry. I have been very angry, and I apologise for it.'

He ruffled the boy's hair, then turned and left the room. His men were waiting for him by the open doorway. One of them was a young hopeful by the name of Ferenc. Aehrenthal took him aside.

'There are two left,' he said. 'Finish them off, then dispose of all the bodies. Do it all somewhere out of sight. Don't trouble me with it.'

Ferenc saluted and took his pistol from its holster.

Aehrenthal stepped out of the house into a

286

deserted street. His lieutenants followed him.

'We leave for Putna tonight,' he announced. 'Get cars and half a dozen good men. You have one hour to make things ready.'

His own car drew up at the kerb. As he started to get into it, a shot rang out behind him. For a moment its echo sounded in his ears. Then a second shot cracked. The silence that followed it was dreadful, and for a moment it seemed to hang over the town like the end of all hope. Then Aehrenthal's driver snapped the ignition on and took the car roaring out into the empty street.

CHAPTER TWENTY-ONE

A Stranger in a Strange Land

'You will not be surprised if I tell you that Egon Aehrenthal is an evil man. I think of evil in religious terms, perhaps you do not. But no one can deny he is a man of evil appetites and evil deeds.'

Father Iustin held a half-filled wineglass between his hands, but he did not drink from it. He had never had a need for liquor of any kind, though he enjoyed a good wine with his meals; but what he had heard tonight had so troubled him that he sensed danger in the wine, and in the oblivion he thought it might bring. Tonight, oblivion would have been welcome. But in the morning he would have to wake again and start the work ahead of him, and that he feared more than anything.

He sat with Ethan in the deserted dining hall, at the end of one table, still lit by candlelight. The great fires had died down, and it had started to get cold. In their cells, monks prayed alone, while others sang the divine liturgy in the church. Ethan wondered what had brought him to such a proper place, a place so quieted by centuries of prayer and meditation that it seemed as though polished by the hands of ten thousand monks. He had never set out for it. He was no pilgrim. But for now he was a stranger in a strange land, and he knew instinctively his journey would not end here.

'Ethan, what do you know about Count Laszlo Almásy?'

'Hardly anything at all. Wasn't there a film about him?'

Father Iustin nodded.

'*The English Patient*. Almásy was played by an English actor, Ralph Fiennes.'

'Yes, I remember. There was a cave in the desert, a cave with painted swimmers.'

'The Cave of the Swimmers. In Wadi Sura. In the Libyan desert.'

Ethan nodded.

'I remember now,' he said. 'Almásy was born in a castle in Burgenland. I nearly visited it. Burg Bernstein.'

'It was originally a Hungarian castle, before Austria took Burgenland from the Hungarians. Almásy was born there, as you say. He spent his early life there. And he became involved in a series of right-wing occult movements in his youth there. What do you know about the Nazis and the occult?'

'Nothing,' answered Ethan. 'Surely they were just a political party.'

'It depends what you mean by that. In their early phase, they were greatly influenced by a number of occult beliefs and organisations. There were movements like this everywhere: Germany, Austria, Hungary – even here in Romania. A lot of them were obsessed by the idea of a pure Aryan race, just like the Nazis themselves. Later, the party crushed as many of them as it could. But in the SS, there were two units that continued to devote time and resources to occult investigations.

'Around 1900, two important ritual organisations were founded, the Ordo Templi Orientis and the more racist Ordo Novi Templi – the Order of the New Temple. Many years later, Burg Bernstein, Count Almásy's castle which you nearly visited, became a centre for the Ordo Novi Templi. They regarded themselves as the descendants of the Templars, a heretical order of knights that was repressed by the Catholic Church in 1307. Some say the Templars possessed sacred relics such as the Holy Grail and the True Cross. You, I think, know better. But some occult-minded Nazis like SS Brigadeführer Karl Maria Wiligut went out to search for relics, including the Lance of Longinus, which they called the Spear of Destiny.'

Ethan took a sip of wine. The musky taste and the flickering of the candles brought back to him memories of Holy Communion in the church at Woodmancote. He had long ago given up on God and the dark mysteries of the Church. Yet now his life had been trammelled by godly weight.

'What has this to do with Almásy?' he asked.

'Do you not see? Almásy and his brothers were adepts of the Ordo Novi Templi. They got to know Lanz von Liebenfels, an ex-monk who owned castles in Austria-Hungary, which he used for occult rituals. Some people call him the father of the Nazi movement. Some of the occult societies sent expeditions to different parts of the world to search for the origins of the pure Aryan race. One expedition went to Tibet, another to Nepal, one each to the Arctic and the Antarctic, to Neuschwabenland, where the Germans had established a very remote colony. But von Liebenfels and others also despatched expeditions to seek for the Grail and the Spear of Destiny.'

Ethan felt small fingers cross his scalp. Was this the connection he'd been looking for?

The priest smiled. His face seemed as though built from shadows, shadows through which his white flesh and green eyes shifted like smoke.

'Almásy was the doyen of desert explorers. He knew the Egyptian and Libyan deserts like no one before or since. He travelled by camel, by jeep, by plane. The desert was his, it belonged to him, he possessed it the way a man possesses a woman, he made it his mistress. And it yielded up its secrets to him, it whispered sweet nothings in his ear, gave him all he ever wanted. It gave him caves painted with people swimming, breasting the waves of a sea that had long ago grown silent and dead, it gave him oases in an ocean of sand. But unlike what was shown in the film, he did not die, not then. He survived the war. British intelligence moved him to Trieste for a while, then to Rome, and finally to Burgenland, where he spent time in the castle, reading his occult texts, meeting with masters of ancient lore. Look, I know all this occult business is utterly ridiculous. I no more believe in theories of a hollow Earth than I do in their obscene notions of a master race. But such ideas have been powerful before, and they may become powerful again.

'Not long after that, Almásy went back to Egypt. He contacted his old friends, the desert scholars. In 1951 he mounted an expedition to search for the remains of a great army the Persians had sent to the Siwa Oasis. Herodotus tells us that fifty thousand men went out into the desert, and not one of them returned. They say they're out there still, their bones hidden by the desert sands. The official story is that Almásy became obsessed with the search.

'But it turned out to be his last adventure. Before it could get properly under way, he contracted amoebic dysentery. He was invalided back to Europe, where he died in a clinic in Salzburg.'

The priest paused. He was coming close to the heart of the matter.

'There is one strange thing about Almásy's death,' he said. 'When his brother went back to his apartment in Cairo, he found it empty: all the papers were gone, all the desert diaries, all the maps. The plans for the Cambyses expedition were missing, the records he'd kept about the Cave of the Swimmers. Everything had gone.'

'How does all this concern Egon Aehrenthal or, for that matter, me or Sarah?' Though the Libyan desert was far away on the other side of the Mediterranean, Ethan could feel its warm breezes brush his cheek. How had this happened? he wondered. To have gone to midnight mass in preparation for the greatest Christmas his family had ever known and woken to carnage, to have seen relics of the man Jesus and followed them to a place he knew only from vampire movies...

Father Iustin answered.

'I believe Almásy's papers found their way to Burg Bernstein soon after his death, and remained there until many years later, when Egon Aehrenthal stumbled over them. He found books and papers that stirred his imagination. But one thing in particular drew his attention. He read a tale about relics. Almásy had met your grandfather Gerald in Cairo, and had made contact with the other members of the LRDP unit who had been with Gerald when they found the lost city. Somewhere along the way, Almásy got wind of a place where relics of Jesus had been found, and perhaps more than relics.

'The hunt for the remains of Cambyses's army was a bluff. Over the years, more than one expedition had gone in search of the lost soldiers, and no one had found them. The desert out there is vast, it might have taken a lifetime, and he still might not have found so much as a bone.

'Almásy wasn't in the least interested in dead Persians. He suspected that out there, not so very far from the Siwa Oasis, he might find the bones of Jesus. In addition, he would be able to track down all the relics that had been taken from the city. He thought what this might mean to the Ordo Novi Templi and to the other semi-defunct orders and temples and cults and fellowships that held to the old beliefs. With the power of the relics, with the magic potency he thought rested in the sacred bones, there might be a revival. Not just of the occult demi-monde. He hoped for the revival of a belief system that had only recently terrorised the globe. A new Volk, a new Führer, a new Reich. I know he dreamt of it. But until recently, I thought his dreams had been buried with him in 1951.

'But I was wrong. My sources tell me that Aehrenthal bought everything from a relative of Almásy's while he still lived in Bernstein. Or perhaps he stole it, I would not find that surprising. In one way or another, he came into possession of the diaries and found a reference to your grandfather and what he had found. I don't think he knew too much to begin with. He may have assumed the relics were still far out in the desert, in the City of Wardabaha.

'That was when he shifted his interests to biblical archaeology and began to earn a living as an antiquary in that field. Stories came back to us from time to time, of certain searches he had made, of certain objects and manuscripts he had found.

'A few years ago, some of us became more concerned than usual about Aehrenthal. It started when I spoke with a man in London, a scholar working for the British Museum in Middle Eastern antiquities. He had come across Aehrenthal more than once, and on several occasions he suspected he'd been cheated out of an important discovery by him. This man still frequents St Dunstan's. He is not an Orthodox Christian, but an Anglican. However, he and I discovered that we had mutual interests. When I was a young priest, I studied Hebrew and Aramaic and took a great interest in biblical matters. We talked about biblical history and went from there to archaeology, about which I knew little.

'He told me that Aehrenthal had managed to get his hands on Almásy's papers. A few weeks earlier he'd met Aehrenthal in Jerusalem. Aehrenthal was in high spirits. He could barely restrain himself from laughing, and kept telling my friend that he was close to finding the Holy Grail. About a week after that, Aehrenthal headed for the Libyan desert. He employed half a dozen Tuareg guides. Word got around that he was planning to finish Almásy's expedition, the search for the lost Persian army. But weeks passed and nothing was heard of him or his guides, and people thought he'd headed into the empty places, that he'd joined Cambyses's soldiers, that he'd never be seen alive or dead again.

'But then he popped up in Tripoli. He had grown gaunt and more arrogant, he had been lashed by desert winds and emerged like a prophet or a man chased by demons. What he had seen he would not say, and perhaps he had seen nothing. He did not speak of a discovery, and he brought nothing out with him. But anyone who met him at that time said he was a changed man.

'My friend – the man I spoke to you about – went to Tripoli and met him. He offered to buy anything Aehrenthal had brought out of the sands, but he was turned down flat. Aehrenthal said there was nothing, not even bones or fragments of bones. No chariots, no harnesses of horses or camels, no armour, no spears, no swords, no axes. Just sand. But he let something slip: that he was looking for men in England, old men, men who'd been in the desert with Almásy, or without Almásy – it was never clear which. My friend asked about the Grail, asked what Aehrenthal had meant, but this time the man was silent.

'He went back to Austria soon after that, where he visited several organisations and met with various people. Then he returned here and took up residence in the castle where Miss Usherwood was kept prisoner.

That is his headquarters now; the Austrians are too watchful, their security services keep a close eye on his comings and goings. Here, things are more relaxed. Of course, there are plenty of old Nazis in Austria, and a great many new ones, but the state watches them. Here, in the forests of Transylvania, he can plot his plots and weave his webs.'

Ethan got to his feet. He wanted to walk and stretch his legs. Tiredness enveloped him, and though he expected little comfort in a monastic bed, he wanted to lie down and close his eyes, longed to be wrapped in sleep.

'I still don't understand what Aehrenthal wants to achieve, what his ambitions are exactly. I can see he hopes for some sort of Nazi revival, and that he plans to use the relics as symbols, as rallying points for his great endeavour. But why this obsession with Sarah? He has what he wanted from us, why does he have to waste time with her?'

Father Iustin stood as well and walked to the fireplace, where the embers still held a certain degree of heat.

'Ethan,' he said, 'I've been avoiding this question, but I don't think I have the right to hold it back from you. He wants Sarah, but he will have you just as readily. You know something he does not, and he will stop at nothing to extract it from you.'

'The location, of Wardabaha.'

'That's right.'

'But he has the relics. He can display them, open a museum to hold them, make a documentary about how they were found.'

'He wants much more than that. We only found out about this a year ago, and we weren't certain until...' He hesitated and reached out to take a poker with which to stir the embers into a little life. 'Well, quite honestly, not until you arrived this evening. There had been certain rumours, but what you and Sarah have told me seems to settle the matter.

'Until a few years ago, Aehrenthal was interested only in his Novo Ordi Templi and the various neo-Nazi groups he belonged to or was in contact with. He had ambitions to find the sacred relics from an early stage; that's why he became a biblical antiquarian in the first place. Every time a relic was mentioned on the grapevine, he would hare off after it. He has a collection of fakes in his castle up there.

'Then he got wind of your grandfather and his discoveries. Almásy gave him that. Almásy had met several of your grandfather's crew while they stayed in Cairo after the discovery. If it hadn't been for the war and their being sent off on further raids it's highly likely one or another of them would have done some sort of deal with Almásy to relocate Wardabaha. They might well have gone out there with him, and he might have made his name by bringing out the ... the relics your grandfather chose to leave behind. Then the war ended, Almásy died, several of the original LRDG patrol died as well, and it was all forgotten.

'I think Wardabaha remained a distant dream for Aehrenthal for many years. Then two things came together. He found out where your grandfather lived. And he read about cellular cloning. Or perhaps it happened the other way round. I don't think the link occurred to him for a long time.'

'I don't understand. Cellular cloning? Like sheep?'

Iustin rubbed his hands together. He too wanted bed, but he knew he would not sleep tonight.

'He wants to find the bones of our Lord. He hopes there will be tissue on them. He will extract the DNA. He will grow his own Christ, he will create a baby that will grow into the Christ child, and the child will grow to be a man, and the man will be Aehrenthal's creation. Not just physically, but mentally and emotionally. He will be a Christ who hates Jews, who despises blacks, who preaches Aryan supremacy. And his first act will be to announce a second holocaust.

'Long before that his followers will have started to gather at his feet. Aehrenthal will summon them, and they will summon others. Aehrenthal has the relics. There's no point in our looking for them in Romania: he'll take them with him to Libya, to rejoin them with the tombs. Soon he will have the bones of the entire family of Christ, the bones of some of his early followers, the bones of their children, and whatever is left of their possessions.

'There will be a new Reich, and Egon Aehrenthal will be its Führer.'

He put the poker back in its place. The burning embers had turned to ashes. Here and there lumps of blackened wood lay twisted and misshapen.

'It's time we went to bed,' Iustin said. 'We both have a lot to do tomorrow.'

CHAPTER TWENTY-TWO

The Road to Nowhere

They left the following morning long before dawn. Ethan drove in the darkness while the others slept. He'd been given a map, together with an address and instructions. The address was in his head, but he had to stop from time to time to consult the map by torchlight. Driving on again, he peered into a tunnel formed by the car's headlights, as though it carved its way through stone. Sometimes rain fell, sometimes balls of ice, sometimes snow.

They headed east for a short space, then turned south on a road that passed through Radauti. A little further brought them to the main road between Siret and Suceava. As they reached the outskirts of Suceava, the first light of dawn penetrated the darkness, and by the time they got there they could see the great bell tower of St Demetrius form itself like a ghost to see them past. Ethan pressed on for Falticeni.

Ilona had started to come round.

'God, it's cold. Where are we?'

'We've passed Suceava and are on our way to a place called Falticeni.'

'Falti-*ch*eni.' She pronounced it for him. 'Where's Father Iustin?'

Ethan changed down a gear to get traction on a slippery slope. The lights of other cars were passing them now.

'He decided to stay behind. I've got the name of someone in another monastery, outside a town called... I really can't pronounce this one! Pi-at-ra Neemt?'

'Not bad. Piatra Neamt.' She repeated the place-name slowly. 'Do we have time to stop in Falticeni?'

'We have to leave this good road after that. Maybe a short break.'

301

'Falticeni's not much of a place, but many writers and artists have lived there. There's a museum full of works by Ion Irimescu.'

'Never heard of him.'

'You English know nothing. Irimescu was a great sculptor. He lived to one hundred and two. We're very proud of him in Romania.'

Ilona wakened Sarah as Ethan found a parking space off the main road. They had come a long way from Sancraiu, but Ethan knew that Aehrenthal's order had eyes and ears across the country. They would have to watch every step of the way until they reached their destination.

Back in Putna, the *toaca* had begun to sound. In the 'bell tower', a young monk prepared to summon his fellows to the divine service. A long wooden board, the *toaca* hung from the rafters, facing the monk. He held two metal mallets in his hands, and slowly began to strike the board with them. What started as staggered bangs slowly acquired rhythm and form and speed. The simple strokes gave way to a stunning complexity of instrumentation as the monk's hands spun and danced, bringing the dead wood to life, sending out a pattern of blows and counterblows through the freezing air. He never missed a beat, never lost control of the rhythm.

Throughout the monastery grounds, monks and nuns turned from their breakfasts or their morning tasks and started towards the church to pray. The music of the *toaca* rose in the cold air, loud and persuasive, driving away sleep, quickening hearts and minds, blow falling upon blow in fast succession, like rivets driven into the steel heart of winter.

Marku Dobrogan stumbled into the open air, his eyes watering as they came into contact with the cold, his nose seizing up, his throat burning as if sprinkled with spices. Every morning he struggled against the temptation to turn round and head back into the dining hall for a few minutes more warmth. But he knew that if one of the older monks caught him showing such weakness, he'd be put to stand in the open for the rest of the day and sent off to attend divine service all night without supper. He'd known it would be a hard life in the monastery when he'd entered the novitiate, and with only a month left before he took holy orders, he hated to think that he might stumble towards the end.

His job every morning at this time was to refill the lights in the church, following the night's devotions. He had a can of olive oil and a bag of candles. The lights inside were never allowed to dim.

Little light entered the church from outside. Some fell through the lantern tower, but there were no high windows, no stained-glass panels to bring light and colour into the building. That was achieved by candles and oil lamps. Huge banks of thick commemorative candles studded the nave and clustered around the pillars. There was an aura of piety so thick and complete that it filled the young monk's lungs like a soothing smoke. Incense turned piety to fragrance, the scents of spikenard and hyssop, opopanax and sandalwood, onycha and myrrh. The church was wreathed in it still, the high roof and its saints lay hidden behind a thin, twisting veil.

Marku moved diligently here and there, following his morning routine, running prayers through his head to keep out the troubling thoughts that constantly threatened to intrude. As he filled one of the larger lamps about halfway down the nave, his eye caught sight of something. He wasn't sure what it was at first, but he knew it was out of place. Someone had left a large object in front of the iconostasis, something black that blocked the gold of the icons.

Fearing that one of his fellow novices might get into trouble for leaving the object where it had no right to be, he walked further down to see if he could take it away himself, before anyone else came in and noticed it.

He rubbed his eyes to clear more early morning tears, and when he opened them he could see more clearly. Too clearly.

The young man's screams could be heard above the hammering of the *toaca*, above the wind, above the cries of circling birds. He screamed and screamed until someone came at last. Kind hands went round his shoulders, and someone led him away.

They had torn Father Iustin's cassock open at the back and gagged him. Someone had lashed him with ropes to the iconostasis, and someone else, a strong man, had flogged him while a third man stood near enough to catch his words, if he spoke.

'Where have they gone?' the third man asked. 'You know who I am, you know there is nothing you or your friends can do to stop me. I have what I need, I just need your friends to take me to the place the relics came from. I want the bones, you see, as I imagine you have guessed in your interfering mind. Just say one word, old man, and I'll let you rest. I mean you no harm, but I will have what I came for. I do not mean to hurt you, but it is up to you if you suffer. Just one word, a direction, a hint. The whip in my friend's hand is a flogging whip, and he will flog you with it until you are within an inch of your life. Unless you tell me where they have gone.'

He said nothing, so they stripped him and lashed him to the iconostasis, on the gate, between an icon of the Virgin and a representation of St John the Baptist, and they put a wad of cloth between his teeth, so he could not cry out, and the man with the whip spat on his bare back. It was all done quite calmly, without moral dread or fear of consequence. Egon Aehrenthal did not have a conscience, not even a flicker of one, and he had instilled in others a sense that a conscience was a weakness to be suppressed in them, just as the monks in Putna fought against lust and greed.

The first blow came down heavily, driven by controlled anger. Iustin's skin cracked open and a gush of blood sprayed into the cold air. Aehrenthal watched as the beating went on, watched with fascination the crack and fall of the knotted lash, the spasms of pain that rustled like fire across the monk's body, the open wounds that started to lace his back, the blood that kept coming even when he seemed already drained.

'Stop,' Aehrenthal said, raising his arm. The whip halted in mid-air and was lowered. Aehrenthal reached for the soaking wad and pulled it from Father Iustin's mouth.

'I will stop this now,' he said, 'if you say just one word. A person, a place, a hint. You have suffered enough. Jesus barely withstood thirty-nine lashes. You have had a dozen.'

But all this time, though the priest's lips moved, all that came from his mouth were the opening words of *Ave Maria*.

Aehrenthal rammed the wad back in the old man's mouth. The priest would have to break soon, he thought, for he didn't look capable of withstanding the full weight of the biblical lashing. He nodded and the whipping started again.

It went on like that for over seventy lashes, and in the end Aehrenthal knew he would get nothing from the priest, but had him lashed anyway as a symbol of something or other, he didn't know or care what. Father Iustin died between one stroke and the next, and his back was torn to shreds, the skin gone from it and a red, bleeding mass left underneath. They left him like that and walked from the church as if they had just attended midnight prayers.

That was how the acolyte found him, like meat hanging in a butcher's shop. A symbol of sorts, but no one could rightly say of what.

They drove south to Piatra Neamt, in the northern part of Moldavia, the main town of the Eastern Carpathians. From the town, they headed north-west for seven kilometres before turning right onto the main road from Piatra Neamt to Bicaz. A few minutes later they reached their destination, the Bistrita monastery.

Inside, they asked for another monk,

Father Gavril Comaneci. They were shown into a bleak, unheated room and told to wait. Ten minutes or more passed, then a monk with a long white beard and hair growing from his ears and nostrils came in. He asked what business they had with Father Gavril, and Ilona said something long and persuasive. The monk frowned several times, then nodded and left.

More minutes passed. This time a different monk appeared. He was aged around forty and wore a black beard. His little round hat stank of fish glue, and his hands were stained with paints. Comaneci was an artist, and he was currently engaged in a complete re-painting of the frescoes throughout the monastery. Interrupted in his work, he looked irritable. He had eyes with peacock-blue irises, and a look that went through anyone he fixed them on. Ilona stumbled as she tried to explain who they were and what had brought them there.

But Father Iustin's name was enough. The moment it was spoken, Comaneci stopped Ilona and switched to English, telling them to accompany him.

As they left the unwelcoming welcome room, Ilona remembered that she still had not been able to get in touch with home. Her mobile battery had been drained, and she had left her charger behind. Father Gavril showed her to the monastery office, where the one and only telephone was kept. She rang home. She knew her parents would be worried about her. They would think she had simply disappeared, or imagine something bad had happened to her when she last went onto the mountain. Everyone knew that Aehrenthal kept several thuggish types up at the castle, and there had been cases – all unproved – of rape.

The phone went on ringing for ages. She thought it odd, knowing that someone was usually around after Christmas. Her mother spent most of her time at home anyway. A minute passed, then another. Ilona put the phone down. Puzzled, she decided to ring her grandmother, who lived two streets away. She lifted the receiver again and dialled the local code, 265, then her grandmother's number. The old woman (in fact, she was in her late fifties) had lived alone since her husband Petrica passed away five years earlier.

This time someone answered the phone within seconds. But it wasn't her grandmother.

'Hello?' said Ilona. 'Who is this?'

'Ilona? Is that you, Ilona?'

'Yes, who–?'

'This is Cosmina Bratianu, dear. Your gran's next-door neighbour. Were you trying to get her?'

'Is something wrong with her? Don't say

she's been taken ill. She was fine when I saw her last–'

'It's not that, dear. It's not illness, but ... she's staying with your other grandparents. I'm looking after her house. Ilona...'

Ilona noticed that the woman's voice was shaking. She had known her all her life, not well, but well enough. She didn't sound right at all.

'What's all this about?' she asked.

'Ilona ... you must brace yourself. I have very bad news for you...'

Later, when Ilona had been put to bed in the infirmary to be treated for shock, and a doctor had been sent for from Piatra Neamt, Gavril took Ethan and Sarah to the studio where he kept his materials and worked on anything portable that needed his attention. He found them seats and put them round a trestle table covered in a paint-smeared tarpaulin.

A novice brought glasses and a bottle of *vinars*, a brandy made in the monastery and popular throughout Moldavia. Sarah and Ethan were still deeply shocked by Ilona's news. Almost as shocking as the deaths was the radio news that no one in Sancraiu would tell the police who had been responsible for the killings. Aehrenthal had walked away from yet more deaths, as a man walks from a field where he has shot birds all day.

'Take your time,' said Gavril. 'I have lost good friends to this man. I know a little of what you have gone through. Start at the beginning. For the moment, there is no rush.'

By the time they reached halfway, they were joined by six visitors, all summoned by Father Gavril. Two were monks from Bistrita, the other four came from neighbouring monasteries, from Agapia and Secu, further north, near Târgu-Neamt, and from Papgarati and Horaita, nearer at hand. They were introduced in turn as they arrived, and Ethan forgot each name within minutes. He went on with his story.

Sometime just before noon, there was an interruption. Father Gavril was summoned outside and did not return for twenty minutes. When he did so, his face was ashen, and he had to steady himself as he took his place at the table again. He seemed not to recognise anyone at first, then he started speaking in Romanian. Whatever he said, it seemed to shock the other monks as badly as it had shocked him.

He looked up and caught sight of Ethan and Sarah, as if they had been ghosts and only become visible to him now.

'You can see there has been more bad news,' he said. 'This is a blow for all of us. Father Iustin has been murdered in Putna. They have flogged him to death. If you are

311

up to it, I would like you to join us and the other monks to pray for his soul. If he revealed anything about where you were headed, then we are all of us dead already.'

They spent over an hour in the church. Ethan and Sarah stood at the back, watching the monks and hieromonks gather to pray. Vast clouds of incense enveloped the nave, and beyond the iconostasis the voices of the mourners rose and fell.

They brought the sacred icon of St Anne that had been presented to the monastery long years ago by the learned ruler of the Byzantine Empire, whose son, Constantine XI, sat on the throne when Constantinople fell to the Ottoman Turks in 1453. The icon was reputed to work miracles, and as it was presented to each of the monks in turn, Ethan could almost believe it held some redemptive power. He held Sarah's hand, at first to convey a sense of comfort and, as time passed, with greater warmth than either of them might have expected.

At the end of the first hour, Father Gavril summoned his six companions and beckoned to Ethan and Sarah to come with them.

'We have to leave here now,' he said. 'I do not believe Father Iustin will have said anything. But not all of us are strong all of the time. Your young friend is not fit to travel; I spoke to the doctor earlier, and he was adamant. There's a small nunnery near here where she'll be well looked after. Someone will take her there.'

They said goodbye to Ilona, in moments snatched from the urgency of their departure. She seemed dead to them, her whole world ripped away. It was not simply grief she suffered, for she had lost what was beyond grief and the passing of nature. Her face was red and swollen, and she could say nothing to them in English. Ethan felt a terrible guilt, for he'd brought her into this ravenous thing without thinking. Her willingness to help had destroyed her life and the lives of her family. Sarah sat beside her on the bed, telling her of her undying gratitude, trying to explain what it meant for Ilona to have done so much towards putting an end to Aehrenthal and his insane mission.

'I'll kill him for you,' Sarah said, not knowing if she could. Ilona said nothing, but she pressed Sarah's hand. Next moment, they were gone.

They had enough cars to travel in, and the monastery supplied them with warm clothes and food.

'Where are we going?' Ethan asked.

'Back to Transylvania. Don't worry, I have no intention of taking you back to Sancraiu or anywhere near it. We will go to Sighisoara. You will like Sighisoara, it is very medieval, very touristic. You can walk in the streets and people will say, here is just another tourist come to look at the famous Clock Tower. You and Sarah can stroll hand in hand in Citadel Square like lovers.'

'Why would you call us that? Lovers.'

'Because when I saw you both at the back of the church just now, I sensed something between you. Just because I'm a monk doesn't mean I'm not sensitive to such things. Our priests marry here, like your Anglicans. Well, perhaps I was mistaken.'

'Why Sighisoara?'

'The Church has a retreat house just outside town. The last group left there about a week ago, and no one else is expected to arrive until the end of January. Maybe not even then if the weather is bad. I want to have a base to work from. Others will arrive to join us, once word gets out. We need to know what Aehrenthal is doing. If he cannot find you, he cannot get the coordinates to find the lost city. That will give us time.'

Ethan shook his head.

'Sarah started to keep a journal while we were in the hut near Sancraiu. It got left behind when we had to run. She was using it to get her head together, to help her make sense of the rapes ... of all that. But this morning she remembered something. She mentioned my grandfather's letter and the fact it held the coordinates. She thought it was still in England, in the library at Woodmancote where we left it. But I brought it with me. We have the coordinates of Ain Suleiman.'

CHAPTER TWENTY-THREE

A Call to Arms

The Wolf's Lair
Castel Lup
Sancraiu
Romania

To all soldiers of the Legion of Longinus, all Pauperes commilitones Christi Templique Solomonici, poor fellow soldiers of Christ and the Temple of Solomon, knights of the Novo Ordi Templi, troopers of the Nyilaskeresztes Párt, warriors of the Vaterländische Front, all you gods and demons of the new Reich, Illuminati of the New Day, Aryan upholders of true morality, all you who struggle with your hearts and souls to bring about the Day of Justice, the New Order, the Final Triumph.

Adolf Hitler was right. Right about the Com-

munists, right about the homosexuals, right about the Gypsies, right about the leftist intellectuals, the so-called writers, the poets, the painters, the jazz musicians. Yet what do we see all around us today? Rights for homosexuals, rights for women as if they are men, rights for intellectuals, rights for 'artists'. We see, do we not, the results of the British, American, and Soviet attacks in the WorldWar against the Reich. Fornication, sleaze, corruption, and fatal diseases spread by whores and gays and rapists everywhere. The rise of Russia, the spectre of communist China, the jumped-up Arab states, the arrogance of Israel.

Hitler was especially right about the Jews. Of all races, the most perfidious; of all peoples, the most corrupt; of all nations, the most tainted by lies and conspiracies and double-dealing. We read of them in Mein Kampf and in The Protocols of the Elders of Zion, where their scheming, their cunning, and their devilish conspiracies are revealed. Is there any war they did not provoke? Any rebellion they did not unleash? Is there any plot they did not contrive, any assassin they did not arm, any well they did not poison, any child whose blood they did not spill to make Passover matzos?

Hitler was right about the Jews, but his enemies defeated him in war and left him powerless. He killed six million of the devils; but he did not live to finish the job.

That is for us to do. That will be our first accomplishment. What the Arabs have failed to

do for over sixty years, we shall achieve in minutes. Do you doubt it? Can you doubt it? If so,
you are no friend of mine, and a traitor to our
common interest.

Why do I make such a claim in the first place?
Because I am a prophet? I have never said so.
Because God has bestowed unique insight upon
me? I think no such thing. Because an angel
comes and whispers in my ear? I have no such
pretensions.

I say it now because great things have come to
pass, and greater are expected soon. I have now
in my possession the Lance of Longinus. Not a
fake. Not some product of the Middle Ages. The
true relic. With it I have the Grail, fresh from the
lips of Christ. I have the Crown of Thorns. The
titulus. The nails.

But it will not end here. One of my trusted
lieutenants has just returned from England,
where he has found a journal, and in that
journal he has found the location of the place
where Christ is buried and where his bones lie to
this day.

It is time to make your preparations. The
leaders who have been at the Wolf's Lair will
now return to you in order to begin preparations
for phase one. The five relics will go with one of
them, for you to see and touch. They will be
taken from place to place so that all may share
in their power. In the meantime, I shall head for
the place where the tomb is situated. When I
return, I shall bring with me the bones of Christ

and the bones of his family.

This is our destiny. Our struggle. Our resurrection. A new order will arise from the ashes of the old, and we shall live to see it. The shadows of the old world are passing, and soon there will be bright sunshine for all coming generations.

Sieg Heil

Grand Master Egon von Aehrenthal

CHAPTER TWENTY-FOUR

Love Lies Bleeding

'If I'm to be honest,' said Gavril, 'there's not much our little society can do in the event that Aehrenthal steps up to the plate and starts batting.'

The monk had done much of his schooling at the American International School in Bucharest and had acquired an American accent, American mannerisms, and a brain full of American information, from baseball scores to the films of Bruce Willis. But Ethan had seen him speak in Romanian to his fellow monks. He was a tall man. His body bore not an ounce of extra flesh, his face was gaunt and ascetic, his eyes seemed to stare out of another world. When he spoke, a great passion seemed to be stored within him.

They were in a small room normally used for lectures during the retreats. Someone had painted the walls salmon pink, and in the watery light of mid-January, the room seemed bathed in its steady glow, as if the walls were coral and the three of them creatures of the sea. On one wall hung a brightly coloured calendar on which the main festivals had been highlighted in yellow.

'There are only two hundred of us,' he went on. Sarah sat across the table, her eyes resting on the stern monk, then moving away to rest on Ethan.

'We call ourselves Ostea Domnului, the Host of the Lord. We possess weapons, but we are not an army in any real terms. Aehrenthal and his associates make up a much more formidable force. We could never hope to defeat them in direct combat. And though it pains me to say it, we cannot defeat them through the power of prayer alone. I'm a priest, but I'm also a pragmatist.'

'What will they do if they find out where Wardabaha is?'

Gavril shrugged.

'They will take the bones. At the very least the bones of Jesus. But I suspect all the family, to give more chance of finding old tissue from which to start the cloning. They'll get them back here for that. Aehrenthal has a laboratory in Bucharest. He bought it several years ago, and he has had scientists working there since then. Very low-grade stuff to begin with, straightforward somatic cell nuclear transfers. But they've been learning. Rapidly. He brought in some researchers from the Kichijoji Institute in Kyoto and gave them all the money and all the toys they might need to take their work further. They have already cloned seven human embryos and grown them to six months. A second batch is on the way, and they are confident they will reach full term. They have human volunteers who have the foetuses implanted in their wombs at an early stage, and who carry them until they miscarry. Of course, all that will change when the first one gives birth. I believe there's some sort of competition between the women.'

Sarah shook her head. She couldn't see just where this was leading.

'Surely,' she said, 'surely half the genes would come from the women. They could be from anywhere. They might not even be Jewish, let alone...'

'Aehrenthal would never employ Jewish women, not even for this purpose. In any case, the women are irrelevant. One will be chosen to bear the Christ child, and it would be a great honour for her, but she would contribute nothing to the bloodline. The embryo will be created in test tubes before it's inserted into her uterus. If he can get cells from Mary's bones and Jesus's too, it would be an ideal combination.'

'Isn't this all years away?' asked Ethan.

'The cloning? Not at all.'

'No, I mean the child. He has to grow before it can mean anything.'

'Not for Aehrenthal's devotees. If they believe he has the Christ child in his possession, they'll throw themselves at his feet. He wants to rule himself, for as long as he can.'

'And if the child grows up ... well, like Christ?'

'Then he may well have an accident. Now – I have to attend weapons practice. You two should stay here.'

For the rest of that week, there were weapons training sessions in the hills above the retreat. Ethan had gone out with them a few times, and passed on his own firearms expertise, such as it was. Sarah had insisted on being shown how to operate each of the guns they used. There was no time for her to become proficient, but she mastered the basic techniques and could shoot anything from a pistol to a sub-machine gun with reasonable accuracy.

Gavril went out with the other monks. Their faces were grim. They knew that Aehrenthal must be aware that Sarah and Ethan were the only other people who knew of the existence of the oasis of Ain Suleiman and the lost city of Wardabaha that lay beneath its sands. Killing them and anyone associated with them would be one of his priorities. If he found them, they would have to fight for their lives against killers who cared nothing for any human being unlucky enough to get in their way.

The retreat was a ramshackle building with a wooden tiled roof, built in the 1920s in the traditional Moldovian fashion and designed by a pupil of Alexander Bernardazzi. The original building had been added to over the years. Twisting corridors branched from one another and branched again, doors opened onto unexpected passages, windows revealed fresh vistas. Most of the residents slept in a dormitory, all men or all women depending on the retreat. More senior residents had small rooms to themselves. And there were two bedrooms for married couples, which were used from time to time for visiting priests with wives. These last two had been given to Sarah and Ethan; the beds were larger and the mattresses thicker, they had two armchairs each, and little tables. The walls were studded with icons, like most walls in the house.

From the kitchens came the sound of pans clanging and cooks exchanging banter.

'Let's go down to the lounge,' said Ethan. 'I want to talk about Ilona.'

There was a room towards the front of the house that was used for silent prayer and meditation sessions in small groups. Usually, it was reserved for the senior clerics, but it had become a meeting room for Gavril and his friends. Unlike most of the other rooms, it had only one icon on the wall, a nine-teenth-century copy of the famous Holy Virgin of Vladimir, which shows the Christ child with one arm about his mother. This copy was heavily masked by an *oklad*, a gilded frame of metal that revealed only the faces and hands of the sacred pair, and the feet of the Christ child. Sarah had been captivated by it from the moment she stepped into the room.

The room was set as far away from the kitchens as possible, in order to preserve the silence so necessary for the monks' medita-tions.

An old sofa had been placed opposite the Virgin. They sat down wearily.

'Are you feeling any better?' Ethan asked.

'I think so. I feel better every day. Except for the nightmares. I still have those.'

'I've told you. I'm willing to sit with you at night. In case you wake.'

'I do wake. Several times a night. I don't

always dream, or I don't remember. It's all right during the day. I have you, for one thing. You make me feel safe.'

'Speaking of safety, they tell me Ilona's safe at the nunnery. They're looking after her well. One of them is a retired psychologist and is treating Ilona. Aehrenthal won't be able to reach her there. And you'll be all right here.'

She took his hand.

'I don't know what you mean,' she said, and her grey eyes looked at him and looked away again. 'I'm not happy when you aren't around. If I look up and you aren't there, I feel sad.'

He squeezed her hand.

'Don't worry,' he said. 'That will pass. It won't be long before you can get about perfectly well on your own.'

'Oh, for God's sake, Ethan,' she spat, tearing her hand away. 'You're the most perverse, obtuse, short-sighted creature I've ever come across. Why the hell I ever fell in love with you, I can't begin to imagine.'

He stared at her as if she had just confessed to a small murder or a gigantic perversion, the wilful killing of small birds or a longing to be whipped by slave boys wearing leather clothes.

She felt the sudden anger drop from her as quickly as it had come. His face was an exercise in perplexity.

'Don't tell me you didn't know,' she said. 'I've known what I feel about you for ages. Since Christmas Eve.'

His mouth fell half open. His eyes blinked as if he fought back tears.

'You were so... They hurt you so much,' he said, as if explaining.

She shook her head, then leant forward and kissed him softly.

'They hurt me a little,' she said, pulling back to look at him again. 'Now I need you to make things better.'

He drew her to him, one hand behind her head. There had been several women before this, he thought, several promising beginnings that had led to nothing. She was no more beautiful than any of them, no more intelligent than some, no more warmhearted than others, yet he loved her out of all measure. He had wanted her since that first night as well, and had only held back out of his original fear of incest.

He felt her relax, felt her mouth open to him, felt the warmth of her tongue against his. His heart was leaping, yet he felt calm. He felt an urgent need for her, not simply a physical need, but something crazier than that, something that shook him to his roots, like a man who kneels at a deep pool and knows he will never slake his thirst.

He unbuttoned her shirt with trembling fingers, undoing the buttons with one hand while he ran his other through her hair.

His hand cupped her breast, then slipped beneath her bra to caress naked flesh.

Her hands came up between them.

'Are you planning to have your wicked way with me, Chief Inspector?'

She was grinning. Her cheeks were flushed by his lovemaking.

He nodded.

'In that case,' she said, 'I think it's a good idea to move. It would be something of an embarrassment if the holy Gavril and his chums came back and found us humping away in here in front of the Virgin and Child in a manner to which they might not be accustomed.'

He extricated his hand, drawing his fingers across her nipple as he did so. She moaned and looked at him and smiled. He smiled back and started to button her shirt.

She unbuttoned it again herself the moment they were in his room. Tossing it on the floor, she reached behind her and unfastened her bra. He bent to her breasts, kissing and fondling them as though he'd never been with a woman before, and she arched her back while he licked her nipples. He cried out with the urgency of his need for her. She moaned, feeling her nipples harden and rise to his touch. His hands grown clumsy with need, he fumbled with the catch that held her skirt. It fell to the ground, and she stepped out of it, almost naked now. He thought he had never seen anything so utterly beautiful or so achingly desirable in his life before. And if her body stirred desire in him, her face, which he knew so well now, held that desire in balance, for he loved her and would not stop loving her.

She removed her pants and stepped out of them, then walked naked to the bed and lay down. He undressed, looking at her all the time. All the beautiful things in his life before this seemed to turn to ashes and crumble: the icon in the prayer room, the woods at Woodmancote Hall, all the women he had slept with, the voices of King's College choir, his mother's face – everything blurred into one thing and was devoured by flame, turned to ash by her.

Lying beside her, he felt like a youngster again, seeing a naked woman for the first time, touching her, preparing to make love to her. He ran his hands softly across her skin, and she gasped and reached out to bring him closer.

'Now,' she whispered. 'Come into me quickly.'

He ran his fingers between her legs. She was ready for him. Carefully, he rolled onto her, and positioned himself to push inside her.

The moment he did so, she cried out and pushed him away hard. He fell onto the bed, and she pushed herself to a sitting position. She was shaking and crying out.

'Get off me! Get off me!'

The words came flooding out of her again and again. Ethan lay watching, shocked by the suddenness of her reaction, then filled with understanding.

She was still shaking, but no longer crying out, when he moved higher on the bed and put his arm round her. She was staring at the ceiling as if he didn't exist, and tears were welling from her eyes and rolling unhindered down her cheeks.

'It's all right,' he said. 'You'll see. This was a mistake. It was my mistake to think you were ready. I didn't think, I was too full of needing you. Just rest. Take it easy. We'll do this later, at the right time.'

She did not answer at once. Time passed and she remained silent, and he feared she had returned to her earlier state. It was not so long, after all, he told himself, since she had been so brutally raped. He had thought that making love with him would erase the taint of it, but he'd been wrong.

The monks returned, and their voices could be heard in the corridors. Ethan did not seek them out. This was his business, and Sarah's. It was the one thing Gavril and his friends could not help with.

She stirred next to him, then turned and smiled.

'I'm sorry,' she said. 'You must have wondered what was going on.'

'I knew exactly what was happening. You don't have to apologise. There are more important things going on at the moment than us making love.'

She shook her head.

'At the moment, there's nothing more important. You can scarcely guess how much you mean to me, especially after ... what happened. I won't let Aehrenthal and his thugs take this away from us. You must have known I wanted you, you must have been able to tell. I don't know what happened, but I don't mean it to happen more than I can help. I'm going to move my things in here with you. You'll have to explain to Gavril. I'm sleeping with you every night.'

'I think they're back, by the way. Can I smell food?'

'They ate ages ago. I've no idea what they're up to now. I think it's time to get dressed and face the music.'

Gavril and the others were in the little room where they held conferences. They looked up with surprise when Ethan and Sarah came in, but no one said anything.

Gavril looked up as they entered.

'Ethan. Sarah. Come in and sit down. I have some news for you.'

They took their places in silence. It could

only be bad news, Ethan thought. What other sort had there been recently?

'We've just been talking about this,' Gavril said. 'The news was waiting for us when we got back from weapons training. Aehrenthal has someone in England. They went to Woodmancote Hall and found your grandfather's journal. They have the coordinates too. Aehrenthal is in Libya even as we speak.'

CHAPTER TWENTY-FIVE

Oea

Getting into Libya was one thing. Getting a permit to go exploring in the deep desert was something else. Sarah carried the fake passport that had been organised for her by Lindita. The three of them travelled with a group of six monks. No one wore clerical garb. They brought with them a sheaf of false documentation in the name of the Centrul de Istorie Comparata a Societatilor Antice, the Centre for Comparative History and Ancient Society, based in the history faculty of Bucharest University. The telephone number, fax number, and email address all led to an office in Piatra Neamt, where they would be answered by operators well-versed in the background and likely plans of the expedition members.

If getting to Ain Suleiman was hard, harder still was it to get hold of weapons. Gavril knew Aehrenthal's capabilities and knew he would not travel without guns. It was highly likely the two teams would meet at some point, quite probably at Ain Suleiman, should they get there. If fighting broke out, they had to be prepared.

One day Gavril asked Ethan to step outside the hotel they were staying in. They were staying in the capital, Tripoli, the ancient Oea.

As he stepped out, Ethan looked back and saw Sarah sitting by a downstairs window, gazing out at the street. A sand devil, come from God knows where after days without rain, danced teasingly in front of her, then went off spinning for a while among the traffic. She did not seem to notice it. If there were dervishes, they were in her brain, whirling like atoms in fancy dress. From a loudspeaker in the hotel came a burst of Arab music, bewildering and passionate, its plangent melody caught and given strength by the tap-tapping of a small drum.

'We need to slip away,' said Gavril. 'This is still a dictatorship. There are eyes everywhere, and they like to follow foreigners. Come this way. And try not to look as though you're doing anything suspicious.'

They walked away from the harbour, across to the entrance to the Old City, the Medina. Father Gavril – who wore jeans and a black leather jacket – had already visited this surviving district of the pre-Italian period, filled with winding *suqs*, artisan workshops, mosques and Qur'an schools. Ethan thought of his grandfather. Had he wandered down these same alleyways, bought bread at these bakers, passed these brightly painted doorways? It all seemed timeless, but for the plates in souvenir shops bearing portraits of Mu'ammar al-Qadhdhafi, or the tubes of Crust toothpaste.

Gavril guided them to an old cafe opposite the Ottoman Clock Tower. A boy offered to shine their shoes for one dinar each. No sooner had they sat down than the boy got to work, applying liquid polish and spit before stropping and buffing as though his life depended on the brightness of the shine he could raise.

At other tables, old men played backgammon, their fingers fluid as they moved the counters with bewildering speed back and forwards over antiquated boards. From time to time they would pause to smoke their *shisha* pipes, inhaling fragrant smoke.

Gavril ordered mint tea, a concoction of green tea in a silver pot stuffed to the brim with mint leaves and sugar. It was sweet beyond measure, but deeply refreshing. With the tea came a plate of baklava.

'Not a great place for diabetics,' declared Ethan.

Gavril nodded and took a sip of the hot tea.

'Ethan,' he said, 'I need your help. I don't mean you haven't been the greatest help already. But this is ... different.'

'Go ahead.'

'I've told you before that we need weapons. All my people are well trained in firearms, and knowing what we do of Aehrenthal, and knowing we could well bump into him, I don't want us to be unarmed.'

'But you can't just walk up to the nearest gun shop in Tripoli and come away with a little arsenal. Don't worry, I had to leave my gun behind at the airport as well, and I feel as naked as you do. How can I help?'

The shoeshine boy finished Ethan's feet. Ethan looked down and, to his surprise, he found himself gazing into a mirror. He parted with his dinar and thanked the boy, using one of his newly acquired Arabic phrases. The boy pocketed the money and moved on to Gavril's shoes.

'There's something only you can do, Ethan. I don't know how it will work, or whether you can pull it off, but I don't think we have any choice.

'There's a small office here in the Suq al-

Mushir. It's manned by three of your compatriots, two kids of about nineteen and one older man, maybe your age. The organisation they work for is a charity registered in the UK. It's called We Are Palestine, and its stated aim is the collection and distribution of money for various building projects in Gaza and the West Bank. In fact, very little of the money they collect reaches either place, at least, not in the form of building materials.

'We Are Palestine is a Hamas-backed front organisation whose real purpose is to buy and smuggle arms across the Egyptian border into the Gaza Strip and, by a more circuitous route, the West Bank. The border police couldn't give a damn what goes through, and Gaza is controlled by Hamas, so it isn't hard getting material through.'

The shoeshine boy halted and held out his hand. Gavril smiled and handed him twice the agreed amount. The boy grinned and went off in search of more customers.

'I'm a man of God,' Gavril said, 'or, at least, I'm supposed to be. Yet here I sit, talking about weapons while this poor child scrapes a living polishing my shoes.'

'How do you know all this?' Ethan asked. The tea was warming him inside. Though this was the Mediterranean, the weather was chilly.

'I've been preparing for this for a long

time,' he said. 'We've long known that tackling Aehrenthal would involve weaponry, so we've made provisional arrangements for several parts of the Middle East and North Africa. I want you to go to WAP's office and offer them a lot of money. We'll give you a cover story. Say there will be a lot more in future, but explain that you need some guns immediately, that you want to hit an Israeli target in southern Egypt.'

'And you think they'll give me the guns just like that?'

Gavril poured more tea into his glass and drank it all in one gulp. Opposite, people had started to head for a little mosque.

'We'll give you money. Some things endure in this world, and greed is one of them. Whether they really love the Palestinians or are just getting off on being out here on the cutting edge of left-wing activism, the money will get them moving. There are so many weapons passing from hand to hand round here, they won't mind handing a few on to you.'

WAP's office consisted of two dingy rooms at the rear of a flyblown Ottoman-era building that clung on like a ghost at the end of a long alleyway studded with firmly closed doors. Its wrought-iron window grilles and intricately carved doorway had seen better days. It had served as the city's largest

Qur'an school under the Karamanlis, then as a brothel for European women brought to these shores by Barbary pirates under the Ottomans, then as a halfway house for Sicilian peasants newly arrived in the *quarta sponda* during the Italian occupation, and finally as a trade union reserve office under Qadhdhafi's Jamahariya.

The sign on the door was in Arabic, badly written and peeling, *Nahnu Filastin*. Someone had taken a fibre tip pen and scrawled beneath it the initials WAP.

Ethan knocked on the door. He made it a loud knock. They had to think he was confident about turning up here unannounced. In fact, he had seldom felt so vulnerable. It reminded him of the times he'd knocked on doors as a beat policeman, never knowing who or what might lie in waiting: a Yardie with a gun, a pissed-off gangster with a baseball bat, a pit bull terrier on a short leash.

It took several knocks, then someone shuffled across the floor and opened up. Ethan's host was a man aged about thirty, on the scruffy side, smoking a very pungent reefer of locally grown *kif*. He looked barely alive, as though the hashish had wandered into dangerous recesses of his brain.

'*Sabah al-khair*,' he muttered, then, beneath his breath, 'Who the fuck are you?'

'I'm not the fuck at all, son,' answered

Ethan. 'I've come for a friendly chat, and it's time you woke up or missed the opportunity of a lifetime. Can I come in?'

Taken aback, Mr WAP tried to extend a limp hand, failed, and shoved it back inside his trouser pocket. He stood aside to let Ethan pass inside.

As he did so, a woman's voice came from the first room.

'Bob? What the fuck's going on. Who is it?'

To Ethan's surprise, the woman who emerged from the dingy, poorly lit office, was not the raddled harridan he'd expected, but a pretty young woman wearing a burnous and with henna tattoos on the backs of her hands. She had blonde hair, tied back behind her head, and twinkling eyes. Ethan guessed she must be about twenty-one.

'Sorry,' she said. 'Been to a wedding last night. I had my hands hennaed. Like them?'

Ethan smiled and nodded. Her slim hands seemed wrapped in brown lace.

'Would you like me to come back at a better time?' asked Ethan.

The woman shook her head.

'Better get it over with, eh? It's a bit of a relief to talk to somebody who speaks bloody English.'

She looked past Ethan to where Bob stood, bewildered, holding the door close to his chest as though he feared it might run away.

'Bob,' she said, 'why don't you close the door and go back inside and have a nice sleep?'

Bob hesitated for about five seconds, then recollected himself and went to a door in the far wall. It closed behind him with a heavy clunk.

'What can I do for you, stranger?' she asked, obviously taken by the contrast between Bob and Ethan. 'Why don't you take a seat? Over there, just toss the books off.'

She pulled a seat up beside him.

'My name's Ethan,' he said. 'Ethan Taylor.' It had occurred to him that even this woman, buried away in the heart of old Tripoli, might have heard of him and his devilish deeds.

'Helena,' she said. 'Helena Mayberry. I'm Bob's assistant, at least that's what they sent me out here to do. Bob's not very together at the moment. He thinks Pete Doherty sent him a message. Well. You'll have to put up with me instead. I hope that doesn't upset you.'

'It certainly doesn't.' Ethan had gathered from Helena's smiles and body language that Bob was probably dreadful in the sack, and that she thought herself an English rose languishing in the far, far realms of Barbary and just longing to be properly shagged. Maybe it was just as well, Ethan thought. He didn't fancy using the subtle arts of seduction on Bob.

They talked for over an hour. Helena was puzzled by Ethan's offer, and even more by his demand, but she was relatively new to the Palestine Aid game, and thought this must be the sort of thing that went on all the time over here. She knew all about the weapons smuggling into Gaza and the West Bank. They didn't take stuff across by sea much now. The Israeli boats didn't come this far across, but they kept a tight watch on the Gaza coast. The Italians had started patrolling in Libyan waters, to turn back would-be migrants heading for Europe. Most of the arms went by the desert route.

'Where are you staying?' she asked. She'd told him she had graduated from Bolton with a degree in post-structural literary studies. Her attempt to explain it was shipwrecked on her own incomprehension of any of the books she'd read or lectures she'd attended. She was one of those popular girls in a gap year, a 2:2 or a third in her pocket, yet never really educated, a party-pooper girl, all blotched mascara and bad judgement, her pale eyes and golden hair suffering under a too hot sun.

'I make it a rule not to give out my address,' he said. 'This is enemy country. You need to be careful. Mossad have been sniffing round, I think they're on to me. Keep your door locked and don't go out for a few days. You'll be all right once I leave Tripoli.'

'You wouldn't like me to come along, would you?' she asked. 'I'm a bit fed up here, to tell you the truth. I mean, the Israelis are pigs and that, and the Palestinians should have their own state, right? But I have to tell you, I'm pissed off with Bob. The next boyfriend will have to be a lot more together. And a lot more use in bed.'

She smiled a come-on smile and licked her lips. She was pretty enough and probably hot stuff beneath the burnous, but Ethan withdrew from her mentally. His thoughts were with Sarah. He hadn't spoken to her since the unfortunate incident in Romania, but as often as they met there was electricity between them. Their eyes would meet and pass, then return to each other and rest.

'I'd better get going,' he said. 'When should I come back?'

He'd left a list of arms that Gavril had drawn up.

'Give me till tomorrow night,' she said. 'Come here late. Come on your own.'

He shook his head.

'I'll need help to carry it all.'

She looked disappointed, then sniffed once and shrugged.

'Bring your fucking friends, then. We'll have a party.'

To Ethan's surprise, the arms were waiting for them when they turned up at the WAP office. Bob was nowhere in sight, but another man, a Libyan, handled the transaction smoothly while Helena looked on. His luxuriant black hair was combed back and fell down almost to his shoulders. He wore a white silk burnous and fingered a string of amber prayer beads while he talked. Helena eyed Ethan all the time, but he noticed that she sometimes let one nail-varnished hand rest on the Libyan's, and that he did not draw his hand away. He gave his name as Tariq, but revealed nothing more of himself. His English gave away the fact that he had spent some time in the United States.

Ethan had been accompanied by Gavril and two other monks. As they began to carry the weapons, wrapped in sacks, out to the alleyway, the Libyan turned to Ethan.

'I had things to see to in the new harbour,' he said. 'While I was there, I heard of someone, a German or an Austrian, I can't be sure, who was also buying guns. Perhaps he is a friend of yours. Perhaps you and he work together?'

Ethan shook his head.

'I know of no Germans,' he said. 'Though I'm sure there are many Germans who try to help the people of Palestine.'

They said their farewells. Gavril and Ethan waited till they were safely back at the

hotel before speaking. They knew Aehrenthal was ahead of them. They would have to
leave on the following day.

CHAPTER TWENTY-SIX

The Road to Kufra

After the coast comes the sand. Beyond a
certain point, the Sahara is inevitable. It
stretches right across, from Morocco in the
west to the shores of the Red Sea in the east.
It is not a sea but a vast ocean that has
swallowed worlds. It runs south to the Sahel
region, engulfing entire nations, gathering
their bones, turning men and animals and
stone to dust.

They drove by night, navigating by GPS,
their headlights dancing as they climbed tall
dunes and rolled down the other side. At the
top of each dune, the headlights would
point at the sky, like searchlights in search of
aeroplanes long vanished. Ethan wondered
if his grandfather had journeyed like this,
listening for German planes, twisting the
dial on his radio to stay in touch with base.

When they camped by day, they switched
off their engines and a silence fell on them
like no other silence. In that silence, they

thought they could hear the Earth turn. The silence, like the sand, went on for ever. Sarah could have lived in it an entire lifetime. She thought it cleansed her. The silence, and with it the great emptiness and the pure, pure air. When she breathed, she could feel the air reach her lungs, and she wanted to drown in it, to feel the perfect desert air reach inside her, driving out all the filth and contamination Egon Aehrenthal and his men had inflicted on her.

When she listened it was as if she listened to the most perfect music, to a singer with perfect intonation, a song with perfect harmony. The silence became a code for the desert itself, a place that could swallow whole armies and coffles of slaves without trace.

Sometimes a lonely bird would creep across the sky, its wings outstretched to ride on the air currents. Once she saw a kestrel, once a flight of ducks. She thought of the birds often, their freedom and mastery of the air. She would watch them soar, wondering where they had come from.

They drove south to Jalu, a palm-fringed oasis where they stopped for dates. They proceeded down along the *palificata* track, the old Italian route to Kufra. Here and there they saw signs of the Second World War: abandoned jerrycans, a rusted tank, strands of barbed wire, a telegraph pole –

the detritus of a conflict over territory on which no one would ever grow a fruit tree or flowers.

Ethan followed Sarah late one afternoon after they woke, walking beside her along a flat alley between high dunes. In winter, the desert was cold and more bleak than at any other time, but the further south they travelled the warmer it grew.

There had been few opportunities for them to talk. If they weren't in the jeeps, they were bivouacked in a circle of monks in leather jackets, while a guard watched for bandits or Aehrenthal. Behind them, at the camp, the monks were saying morning prayers.

He looked at her. Time was healing her, but after what had happened in the house at Sighisoara, he could not be sure she would not slip back to her horror and self-disgust. Feeling his eyes on her, she slipped her hand inside his.

'I'm all right,' she said. 'What happened before... I'm sorry about that. I didn't doubt you, don't think that. I wanted you, I have never wanted a man so much. You must understand that.'

'I was too fast. You need to recover. Aehrenthal, that whole crew, they aren't behind you yet. Who knows, it may take years, your entire life, to be over it.'

She walked with him a few more steps.

'Don't say that,' she said. 'You forget that I love you. You forget you love me. That has already made a difference. Sometimes I have nightmares, and I dream I'm being raped again, and it terrifies me, you can't imagine how much. But other times I have good dreams, and I mostly dream about you, and sometimes I dream we're in bed.' She grinned.

He grinned back, then took her in his arms. She made no attempt to resist, letting herself fall against him, with her head on his shoulder. They stood like that, defying everything, for a long time, while all around them the desert grew dark and the moon and stars grew bright in a cloudless sky.

Someone beeped a horn, calling them back. It was time to go.

They stayed in Kufra only long enough to restock on food and water. Apart from the Italian fort that towered over the oasis, and the stark contrast between green fields and the ochre shades of the sand, there was nothing to keep them in the oasis. Gavril didn't want to draw attention to the expedition, so only he, Ethan, and their guide went in.

Gavril wanted to find out whether Aehrenthal had passed through Kufra. Unfortunately, he had no photographs of the Austrian, and no idea how large his party might be. He instructed the guide to ask the most obvious people in the oasis, people who might have supplied a party heading west towards Rebiana and the great sand sea beyond it. No one knew anything, or so they said. Ethan spotted some tourists and overheard them speaking English. One, he guessed, was German, another Scottish. He walked over to where they were haggling for a can of petrol.

'I heard you speaking English,' Ethan said. There was a pretty girl among them. She smiled at him and looked away.

The Scottish man, whom Ethan put at about twenty-five, dressed in a thermal vest and stained blue dungarees, answered.

'Piss off. We dinnae want any fucking hash. We've got more than we can smoke already.'

'You're welcome to it,' Ethan said. 'But I'm not here to play games. How long have you been in Kufra?'

'What's it tae you? If you're polis, this is no your country.'

'It's not yours either, chummy.' Ethan walked right up to him. He had handled hard cases like the Scot from the first day he went out on the beat.

'Listen to me, sonny,' he said. 'Very carefully. You talk to me politely, you tell me the truth, and you walk out of Kufra with both fucking legs. The same thing goes for anybody with you. I have jeeps out there and men with guns in them, and believe me, they will hurt you if you try to mess with me.'

'Sonny' went red with anger, but the flare-up lasted only seconds. Adding things up, he melted like butter. Without another word, he slouched over to join the girl. She shifted out of his way and started talking to another one of their party. Ethan turned to the man he thought was German.

'I want to know if you've seen a second party like ours. An expedition heading into the deep desert. All men. Tough-looking bastards. Their leader is a tall man with a scar on one cheek.'

'I saw someone like that. He was speaking German, that's why I noticed. Is your man German?'

'Austrian.'

'Of course. His accent.'

'Where did they go?'

The German waved his hand in the vague direction of the west.

'Out there somewhere,' he said.

'How long ago was he here?'

'Maybe two days. Yes, I'm sure – two days. And you're right, they were tough-looking bastards.'

CHAPTER TWENTY-SEVEN

The Sand Sea

All was not lost. Just because Aehrenthal had gone into the desert in search of Wardabaha, there was no reason to suppose he would arrive there ahead of them. There were no roads where he was going, just acre upon acre of sand, whipped up into high dunes by the wind. A wrong turning, a false intuition could take a car far out of its way as it dropped down from an unclimbable dune and was forced to drive between the high sands until a gap opened up to let them through. Even then, there might still be repeated twisting and turning before they could get back to their original route.

Ethan spoke to their guide, a young Arab from Tripoli who had been born and bred in Kufra and knew the desert well. His name was Ayyub. He was a tall, good-looking man whose green eyes looked out on everything with a wide, searching gaze. He spoke good English with a strong accent.

Ethan asked him if there was a specific route another guide might have sent them on. Ayyub shook his head.

348

'There are no routes,' he said. 'The desert is a sea, a sea of sand, *bahr ramal*.'

Ethan persisted.

'Even at sea there are shipping lanes. There are routes that avoid strong currents, routes through narrow channels. There are dunes out there. Some are as tall as mountains.'

'The sands shift. Wind comes and lifts the dunes, it blow and blow until is nothing where was once something, something where was once nothing.'

He looked out to where the sun was extinguishing itself in the western sands, on its way to drown in the waves of the Atlantic.

'One day, even this desert will have vanished, even the sun will dry up and shrivel and become blackness.'

Ethan could not tell whether he was smiling or not. 'It's time to get going,' he said.

The going got tough very quickly. The moon was almost full, and galaxies of stars like candy floss augmented the light it cast, throwing a blanket of silver across the humped and lawless sand. This was somewhat to the good, but the stark shadows the moonlight created made it hard to navigate between dunes or to tell which were safe to climb or likely to collapse the moment the spinning wheels of the first jeep touched them.

Ethan travelled in front with Gavril and the guide, Sarah took the rear with two monks called Claudiu and Flaviu, neither of whom spoke a word of English.

Outside, light and darkness turned the desert to something very like the surface of the moon. Sarah felt herself crawl across it, an alien being on a world without fixed points. The slow passage of shadows, the turning of the stars and the steady passage of the moon all dimmed her eyes. She started to doze, then fell fast asleep.

When she next woke, they had stopped in a broad wadi. They had started unloading the Hagor fast-up tents and were hauling sleeping bags and other equipment inside. When everything had been stowed or left behind, the monks assembled, as they assembled every morning, to sing matins. Ayyub looked on from a distance, disapproving.

The last stars passed away on the bright horizon. Camping tables were laid out, and soon the smell of supper wafted through the dunes. Just as it confused everyone to sing matins before sleep, so everyone had a stomach unable to cope with the changes a night-time existence thrust on them.

No one slept well that day. The bright sunshine proved unbearable, the tents retained an unaccustomed amount of heat, sand crept into the folds of everyone's skin and even seemed to work its way down into the pores and behind the eyelids.

They struggled through noon, and were out of their tents soon after, preferring to drive on than remain in misery. Ayyub agreed there were now few benefits to travelling by night. In daylight, they had a much better chance of finding their way or spotting Aehrenthal. They decided to stay awake by day and sleep once the sun went down. The caravan was reformed and they set off once more.

On the following day they came to another wadi surrounded by five-hundred-foot-high dunes. Sunset had already touched the sky with red and pink, gold and green. They were all exhausted. They got down stiffly, their bodies aching from the profound hammering they'd received during the day's journey. There was a chance they might find the lost city in another day.

They wolfed down their food, then checked their weapons. If they did reach Wardabaha, there was a chance they'd come across Aehrenthal and his men. Tents snapped open across the floor of the ancient river bed. The monks chanted early vespers together, under Gavril's direction, then headed for their beds.

When Sarah ate, her digestive system was in such disorder that she could barely keep food down. The shock of her abduction had never really left her, and this latest journey and the knowledge that Aehrenthal was somewhere around revived those earlier sensations.

She sat up for a while, talking with Ethan. It was the only time of day when they could find an opportunity to be with one another, and with every day that passed it grew more important to do so. They talked of hopes and fears, of memories good and bad, of relatives, of whatever came to mind, but of Sarah's pain they said nothing. Each day, more and more, they returned to their love for one another, and how precarious it felt, yet how necessary to them both. It was not a matter of whispering sweet nothings or inviting seduction, or inciting lust. They both wanted time for that, but they knew that their love and its fulfilment depended utterly on the outcome of this expedition and the downfall of Aehrenthal and his plans.

As they parted, Ethan noticed that it was darker than usual for the time of day. It was far too early for him to have learnt the rhythms of the desert, and he knew he could not trust his own judgement. Only Ayyub was properly attuned, and Ethan did not trust him.

He looked up and saw clouds scudding across the sky. Most seemed to be grey, but here and there clouds of a distinctly blacker hue moved at a slower pace. There was a little breeze at ground level now, that picked up the finer sand and carried it along.

Sarah stepped inside her tent. Its sides were stretched like a drum against the growing wind. Thoughts of Oxford came to her. The spires, the river, the colleges were all vivid in her mind, but in the way matters of dreams are vivid. The whole city seemed to her nothing more than a setting for an episode of *Morse* or *Lewis*. Whatever she saw in her mind's eye was accompanied by snatches of classical music. She preferred Amy Winehouse or Joy Division. Here in the desert, her best memories turned to sand. If she had ever wanted drama, she had found it in abundance.

She lay awake in the dark, her mind spinning with thoughts of what the following day might bring. She still could not sleep. There was no help for it, she thought, but to get up and go outside for a walk. She dug out a bag of clothes she'd bought in Tripoli expressly to wear at night: woollen socks, a heavy Benetton pullover found on a stall in the *suq*, and above it a man's *jelabia* that Ethan had bought for her in the area where men's clothes were up for sale.

It had grown colder than usual, and the darkness had increased by several degrees. She went inside to retrieve her torch, then set off down the wadi. Within minutes, the contours of the landscape had inveigled her away from the wadi floor up onto a channel between two dunes whose height she could only guess at. Walking on the loose sand was far from easy, but something drove her upwards and away from the camp, a need to walk, to push herself to exhaustion. Her thighs soon started to ache. She had not yet recovered her strength after her ordeal, and even if she thought she was up to a walk through the dunes, the truth was that her muscles had not regained their elasticity.

She decided to sit down for a spell. Nobody would miss her, after all, and the sand was more comfortable to sit on than walk over. As she sat, she yawned and looked up at the black sky. The clouds tumbled like clothes in a drier. In the end, she turned her eyes away, finding herself made almost giddy by the dark movements. She yawned again, more deeply this time, and to her surprise her head started to drop. Jerking awake, she decided her objective had been attained and started to get to her feet in order to work her way back to the camp. But as she moved, her thighs protested. It felt comfortable in the little dip she had made for herself in the sand, so she thought she'd stay some minutes longer, until her legs were properly rested.

She yawned again, then a second and a third time. Next thing she was on her side, fast asleep and snoring.

Afterwards, she could not guess with any accuracy how long she'd been out. It was a deep sleep, she knew that, and she knew that she'd only come round from it with difficulty. What wakened her was the sensation of rain falling on her head. Heavy rain. Cold heavy rain that soaked her hair in seconds and ran in rivulets down through her collar and onto her back and chest. When she moved, she could feel fast-flowing water on either side of her. It was cold water, and it sucked at her, as if eager to pull her with it, to drag her downwards.

She scrabbled about, knowing she had to find her torch, that without it she'd be lost till daybreak. There was no doubt in her mind what was taking place. In the winter, there can be heavy downpours in the desert. They could be highly uncomfortable, but they never lasted long. But in that short time they could kill, creating flash floods in places like wadis – dried-up river beds. Even now, she saw that water was moving down from the peaks of the dunes, skimming fast over the sand, and heading for the lowest regions.

Fighting down growing panic, she switched on the torch and tried to find her way back. But everything had changed. She found a channel that headed downwards, and followed it, feeling the chilly water tugging around her ankles and rising higher.

She had to find Ethan, had to warn them all of the danger they faced. People died in flash floods, swept away before they knew it, from a place where they had never expected to see water at all.

Down in the wadi, they already knew the risk. Ayyub had warned them the moment the rain started to hit the tents. Moments later, the first water started to flood the wadi, and the monks had started to tumble back out of their tents.

'Don't waste time on the tents,' shouted Ayyub. 'Get into the vehicles and drive out of here.'

Ethan couldn't see Sarah anywhere. He grabbed Ayyub as he was scurrying past.

'Have you seen Sarah?'

'The woman? Yes, she's with her two monks, Claudiu and the other one. The jokers.'

'Where are they? Quickly.'

Ayyub saw Gavril leap aboard the jeep he shared with Ethan. The engine started up.

'There's no time,' he shouted. 'The flood will sweep us all away.'

He tore at Ethan's arm in his panic, and forced him aboard the jeep before leaping in himself. Gavril saw they were aboard and put his foot on the accelerator. For half a minute their hearts were in their mouths while the tyres spun, unable to get traction on the wet sand. Then the back wheels caught and, with a terrible roaring of the engines, the jeep leapt forward and tore into the darkness. Behind them, a second and third jeep pulled away. There was a roaring of water as the wadi filled.

CHAPTER TWENTY-EIGHT

After the Rain

The rain fell for two hours then stopped. One moment it was pouring down, the next it came to a stop, as though someone had turned off a giant tap. It was still dark, and floodwaters still lay in low places, where they waited for the unwary.

Several hours more of darkness passed, during which everyone stayed on board the jeeps and did what they could to sleep upright.

Out to the east, over Lebanon and Israel, and down along the Western Desert of Egypt, a ball of fire rose above the rain-sodden sands, and quickly set to work drying off the surface water. On the desert, fine vegetation was triggered into brief life. Jerboas, roused from their holes, scampered across the desert floor. Long-eared fennec foxes ran over the dunes, keen to eat anything in sight. And high overhead, its engines humming softly, an aircraft crossed the desert from north to south.

'Egon,' said Iorghiu Bogoescu, his second-in-command, waking Aehrenthal from the deep sleep he'd fallen into during he rainstorm. 'The rain's over. Mohamed wants to talk to you. He says it's urgent.'

Aehrenthal yawned and stretched.

'I need to piss,' he said, opening the door and stepping out. He went to one side, unzipped his trousers, and unleashed a stream of pungent urine onto the side of a dune. When he went back to the cars, his guide, Mohamed, was waiting for him.

'Good morning, excellency,' he muttered. He held his hand to his side, preferring not to shake the hand of someone who had just urinated standing up, holding his organ in that filthy manner of the unbelievers.

'Iorghiu tells me you have something to report.'

Mohamed nodded. He was a young Tuareg from Ghadames called Mohamed ag Ewangaye. Mohamed had never revealed his face to anyone in the group, but his fierce eyes said as much about him as a nose or a mouth might have done. For several years he had lived in Kufra, where he made his living taking adventure-seeking Europeans into the deep desert, to search for the

Cave of the Swimmers or investigate Second World War battlefields. He had heard tell of Am Suleiman, and that there might be Tuareg there, but never a word of Wardabaha.

'Sir, I climbed up this dune' – he pointed to a tall dune to their right – 'to the very top. I wanted to see how everything looks after the rain, whether the road ahead is dangerous. But the first thing I saw was an oasis, maybe five miles west of here. I am sure it is Ain Suleiman. The Spring of Lord Solomon. We shall be there this morning, *insha' allah*.'

Aehrenthal received the news with equanimity. His quest was as good as over.

'Pass word round,' he said. 'We leave after everyone has eaten.'

As Aehrenthal busied himself with maps and GPS devices, Mohamed hung around restlessly. Finally, Aehrenthal swore and asked him what he wanted.

'You didn't give me time to finish, sir. When I was on top of the dune – it is a very tall dune, you must understand – when I was atop this great dune, after I have spotted Ain Suleiman, for I am sure it is Ain Suleiman my eyes have seen, then, sir, I spy out the rest of the desert and in the east, I see more cars. I cannot tell how many, for some were behind dunes, and the ones I saw disappeared about a minute later. I stay up there many minutes, but they do not reappear. Perhaps it is another expedition. They are a day, two days from us.'

Aehrenthal's first reaction was to shrug. Plenty of expeditions came out here. Thinking it over, however, he'd been reliably told that they didn't come in this direction. There was nothing for them out here, or so they thought.

'Thank you,' he said. 'Now, take my binoculars and go back up there, and see if you can spot them again. Stay there fifteen minutes, then come down. I don't want to waste time in getting to Ain Suleiman.'

Sarah had been cast adrift, like a sailor after long voyages, on a sea of sand. Escaping the flash floods had forced her higher and higher, but she had climbed in the dark, and when she woke after a fitful sleep, all the world was strange. By some mischance, she had strayed into a field of very high dunes, each one of which blotted out her vision whichever way she looked.

She realised with a pang that she had no water and no food, not even a compass. Her orienteering skills were limited to those she had learnt in the Oxfordshire countryside during her first year as an undergraduate. Using the sun, she could get a rough idea of the four compass points. What she couldn't do was work out a path through the dunes, whether to take her back to Kufra or further on to a city that had been lost for decades, a city that might well lie buried beneath centuries of sand.

After the soaking of the night before, her limbs ached. Any movement caught her short with muscle pain, and she feared getting cramp. But she knew she had no choice but to move. If she stayed here, lying on her side, she would die. She had no idea how long that would take. The sun could be hot, even in winter, and she had no protection from it. Even now, its rays were growing uncomfortable.

She scanned the very narrow horizon around her, trying to estimate which of the many dunes in her neighbourhood was the tallest. It wasn't easy. In the end, she decided it didn't matter too much if she selected the tallest dune or not. It would be enough to climb one close and to use that eminence as the first step to finding a way to safety. If she was lucky enough, she might catch sight of the expedition and make her way across to it. They'd be looking for her, she knew that. Ethan would not give up the search.

She got to her feet and made her way stiffly towards an ochre-coloured dune to her right.

The floods had not just swept down wadis, carrying everything in their path, but they had caused landfalls from many of the dunes, rearranging the landscape to suit themselves. Ethan's expedition had paid no heed to direction, but pushed on in the dark, praying loudly, twisting, reversing, punishing their engines in a desperate bid to avoid the flash floods.

Now they watched as water sank into the thirsty sand or steamed under the hot rays of the sun where it cut through gaps between the dunes. The sky had cleared completely. A haze had settled across the surface of the sand, giving the landscape an eerie, unsettled look. It had become a place where the jinn might walk on an inner plane between the worlds of men and angels.

While Ayyub performed the two voluntary and the two obligatory prostrations of his morning prayer, Ethan and Gavril got out the navigational equipment and began to work out where they were. They had strayed from their original path by about two miles, but that diversion had taken them nearer Ain Suleiman. Despite that, their first goal was to find and rescue Sarah.

'Let's climb that dune,' Ethan said to Gavril. 'Bring the binoculars and let's see what we can find.'

It was the hardest physical exercise either man had undertaken. The waterlogged sand made the going extremely difficult. It was hard not to slip back. Each foot was a conquest to be made and held. The dune was about four hundred feet high, and before they were halfway both men's thighs felt as though another step would finish them. They rested for ten minutes, then started again. They had to rest several more times, growing weaker the nearer they came to the summit.

At the top, they lay down to recover from the climb, hoping their legs didn't freeze. Ethan was the first to get to his feet and train his binoculars on the terrain below. Off to the west, he immediately picked out the palm fronds surrounding the Ain Suleiman spring, and the spring itself rippling blue in the gaps between the trees.

Sarah passed the day in growing discomfort. With only herself for company, her fears expanded to fill her heart and mind. She feared the sun, the desert, dehydration. More than that, she feared Egon Aehrenthal. She felt certain he was close, for they had come within striking distance of Am Suleiman, and she thought he might be there already, or on his way, and that she might stumble into him behind the next dune.

The day passed and night came, and she was left with the moon and the stars. Without cloud, the desert was bitterly cold. The moon moved through the stars like a misshapen disc of chalk. Her feet were freezing, and she wished the sun would come back, for all it would burn her and increase her raging thirst. The stars were not English stars, she thought. For one thing, it dazzled her to see so many of them, to see such a profusion of pure light. She knew nothing of their names, and only a few of their constellations: the Plough, Orion with his belt. They were the loneliest things in creation, and the most aloof, and watching them she felt herself drift. Out on the dunes, she thought she saw ghosts, but when she blinked her star-dazed eyes the ghosts flickered and blurred, and she was left alone on the sand, cold and lost and constantly on the brink of tears.

She must have slept at last, and deeply, for when she next opened her eyes, the sun had already climbed some way into the sky, and everything was growing hot again.

It seemed beyond her strength to climb another dune, but she knew she had to if she was to have any chance of spotting the expedition or Ain Suleiman. She dragged herself to her feet and found a suitable dune about two hundred yards away. It wasn't very high, but she didn't think she could find the energy to climb anything else.

As she struggled upwards, the dune wall faded from her sight. She was moving sightlessly, guided only by the sensations of her feet biting into the sand and pulling out again. Suddenly, her left foot encountered open space, and she went tumbling for-wards, all four limbs sprawling across the dune. Had it not been for the way her right leg became entangled with the left, and the bracing motion made instinctively by her arms, she might have continued tumbling down the other side and landed back at the bottom, with the dune to climb again and quite beyond her strength to do it.

By luck more than balance, she landed about a yard below the top of the dune. It took several minutes for her to fight off the dizziness and catch her breath. When she was more herself, she looked down and blinked.

At first she found it hard to make out what lay below her. Just sand, she thought, more bloody sand. Then she squeezed her eyes and looked again. No, she thought, she was wrong, there was something down there, too far away to distinguish clearly, and blurred by shade.

She let herself slide down about one hundred feet, and the blur became a jeep, and the two smaller blurs beside it became men, though she couldn't make out who.

She cried out, 'I'm here!', but her voice caught in her throat. She stood, then fell backwards, and continued her way down on her back, like riding a sledge when she was nine. She felt ecstatic, euphoria cascading from her like rain from a dog's back. To be rescued, to know she would see Ethan again, to be within a short radius of the most precious objects in the world, and to create a new life for herself through their discovery. It all raced through her veins in the short space it took her to slide to the bottom of the dune.

She got to her feet and stood up, a smile broadly visible through her cracked lips and reddened face. A happy schoolgirl on a Christmas break, safely back with her family and friends.

When she cleared her eyes of sand, however, and looked towards the jeep, her heart skipped a beat. She did not recognise the two men. One was an Arab, the other wore a uniform she had never seen before. And as she looked, a door opened and a third man stepped out. All hope failed her. This man she did recognise. He was the end of her world. In him all things fell to their destruction. In him, she was in hell. He spoke to her, and his voice seemed to echo through the banks of sand as though he was everywhere, like a king of the jinn made physical at last, or Satan come to earth in a black uniform. She reached out for something to hold on to, but there was nothing, and she fell unprotected to the ground while her mind reeled and was replaced by blackness.

Ethan took turns at the driving wheel. His heart had not stopped beating since they discovered Sarah was missing. Only the tight grip he held on the wheel and the pressure of his feet on the pedals helped relieve the tension. It was like driving on Mars, boxed in by a landscape that belonged on a dead planet.

They had gone several miles when Gavril ordered Ethan to stop.

'It's time one of us went up again, just to take another look. She could be in the next valley and we could miss her.'

Ethan volunteered to climb a nearby dune. At the top, while he was still catching his breath, the silence was broken by a single sound. A gunshot that seemed to come from all directions at once. A crack uttered by a pistol that seemed as near as it was far. A single bullet. For all he knew, a single death. He felt his legs give way. Fear descended without pity. Silence returned.

CHAPTER TWENTY-NINE

King Solomon's Spring

Aehrenthal's chief advantage lay (though he did not know it) in his guide, Mohamed. Unlike Ayyub, who knew the desert only as far as his tourist clients ventured, which was not far at all, Mohamed was a Tuareg and a descendant of Tuaregs. The desert was in his blood, its patterns, its labyrinths, its signs and disclosures, its mysteries and its dark secrets. The Tuareg knew everything and said little. Mohamed's knowledge of the desert was the result, not just of his lifetime's work, or that of his father and grandfather passed on to him, but of generation upon generation of veiled men who had lived their lives on the margins of survival, men who understood the long sands the way sailors know the sea or farmers the soil or soldiers the blood.

Although he had met and talked with plenty of foreigners, Mohamed was still profoundly unaware of their ways. When Aehrenthal explained that the woman he had taken on board and whose hands he'd tied with tape was, in fact, one of his wives who had been snatched by another expedition, Mohamed believed him and approved of his stern measures in restraining her before he was sure of her unchastity. If Aehrenthal wanted to kill her, Mohamed would recommend a single shot to the head, since rocks were not easily come by in this part of the desert and bullets were expensive. A knife across her throat would work as well, but it would be messy.

Using their most recent tracks to guide them, they made their way back to the rest of the unit without difficulty. On Aehrenthal's orders, they had stayed put, using a radio signal to transmit their position across the dunes.

Aehrenthal was hungry and thirsty. He dragged Sarah from his jeep and pushed her across to where a long shadow stretched beneath a dune. The others followed him. Someone brought water. They were more confident about using their supply since they knew the oasis was only a short distance away. Aehrenthal's cook set up a large camping stove on which he prepared eggs and bacon for everyone. They ate in silence for a while, then someone switched on a radio. He spun the dial for a few moments, finally picking up LJB Radio Benghazi, broadcasting in Arabic. There was a brief discussion. Mohamed told them it was about the Second World War and the struggle against the Italians and Germans.

'Now they are going to play music from that time,' Mohamed said. Next thing, the radio blared out. Sarah recognised it at once, as though she remembered it. Lale Anderson singing 'Lili Marleen'.

'Vor der Kaserne
Vor dem grossen Tor
Stand eine Lanterne
Und steht sie noch davor...
Wie einst Lili Marleen.'

Aehrenthal's men, though none was old enough to remember the wartime years, all knew the song as a German forces number, and could whistle along to it.

One of the men, whom Sarah recognised as one of her rapists from the castle, licked his lips and set down his plate.

'Sir,' he said, addressing Aehrenthal, 'I suppose you'd like us to teach this young woman a few lessons. Teach her not to run off the way she did. I've been feeling an itch since we left home, if you know what I mean. I'd like permission to take her behind one of these dunes and give her a seeing to. Maybe we can all have a go, relieve our itches before we head on for this oasis.'

Aehrenthal stared at the man, a sergeant in his own guard unit. Serghei Comeaga was not an unintelligent man, and if he felt a stirring for female flesh, he kept it well under control.

'The woman is out of bounds, Serghei,' said Aehrenthal. 'If anyone touches her, I touch her. She is my property. You do not steal my property. Later, I may give her to you, but for the moment I want to keep her with me. She will help me decipher the inscriptions, she will help me authenticate the contents of the city, and one day she will meet with museum curators to persuade them of the truth of what they see. When enough money has been paid, we will have the funds to begin our project. She will not matter so much then. You can all have her, you can all fuck her until she is blind and insane, for all I care.'

Serghei was not satisfied. He remembered the Englishwoman only too well. Once she stopped putting up a fight and lay back and opened her legs, she'd proved sweeter than any woman he'd ever had. He'd had her several times, she'd teased him with her little moans and cries, and he'd known she'd wanted him, and that when she squirmed, she wasn't fighting to get away, but giving way to ecstasy, for all her pretence to the contrary.

'Listen to me,' he said, addressing Aehrenthal, but not reading him, not noticing the little twitch beneath his right eye, the stillness with which his leader received him.

'You bring us out here to a fucking wilderness, you half starve us, you almost get us lost, you nearly get us drowned, and now you tell us we can't get a little physical relief to take our mind off things. Maybe you're above a sweet little fuck, maybe you're feeling tender for the little lady's feelings. But you're not God, you're not Jesus Christ, and you're not even Adolf Hitler. I'm not putting up with your bossing us around for another minute. The woman is mine until I finish with her, then the rest of you can have her.'

Aehrenthal had his pistol in his hand and a bullet in the chamber before Serghei even noticed.

'I'm in charge of this expedition,' Aehrenthal said. 'And I'm the commander of the Legion of Longinus. You are an insubordinate piece of shit. Kneel down.'

He raised his arm and gestured with the gun. Serghei refused to move.

'I said kneel.'

There was a stubborn streak in Serghei that overrode his obedience to his order, his unit, and his leader. His mouth was dry and there was little enough spit, but what there was he spat onto the sand, where it was swallowed up.

Aehrenthal lifted the gun and shot Serghei low in the belly. For a moment, the man stood still, assessing where he'd been shot and evaluating how he felt. There was a lot of pain, but he didn't feel dead or on his way to death. Then the pain mounted and he slumped forward, landing on his knees.

'Let's get out of here,' said Aehrenthal, pulling Sarah by the arm again and pushing her into his jeep.

No one questioned the shooting. No one suggested taking Serghei with them or leaving him food or water. No one hazarded a guess as to how long he would last. The engines roared into life. Within moments, Serghei was lying alone on the desert floor, watching blood flow from his abdomen in a long stream that worked its way into the sand.

CHAPTER THIRTY

Maryam

At fourteen, Maryam ult Hana was the youngest of Masud Tegehe-n-Efis's four wives, the prettiest, the one with breasts that did not sag and private parts that held him tight. He had come to favour her over his other wives the way a young man comes to favour a Mehara camel over its peers, or an older man, grown weary of camels, finds one date tree, one half in shade, the other in sunshine, that has the sweetest fruit, or the most plentiful crop, or the darkest shade.

She had already borne him one child, a male child, and when she slept with him, her womb leapt for the next child, and the one to follow him. Her body was still young and firm, her little breasts grew day by day. Masud liked to undress her in the light of oil lamps and to look at her before he entered her. He was not the young man she had hoped for when she was a girl, but he had camels and grown-up sons.

Taking her baby in her arms, she started to make her way down to the holy city. The other wives would have gone there before her, and most of the other women. Her age did not permit her to seek precedence, even if she was her husband's favourite wife and had borne him a healthy child. She wore her head-wrap tight against her hair, and on her chest she carried a talisman against the *tugarehet*, the ever-present evil eye. A camel started braying, its raucous voice trumpeting as though to announce a coming. That was when she first heard it, a sound so faint it might have been the buzzing of a mosquito. She listened for a while, but could make no sense of it. When she looked round, the *taklit*, her female slave, was there, waiting to walk with her to the city.

The great doorway was open, and lamps had been lit all the way through the interior.

It was a festival for women today, to prepare for the wedding of Aisha ult Hamid to her cousin Agwilal. From inside, she could hear the sound of ululation. The bride-to-be would be in the holiest place.

The slave made a way for her through the press of women and children. Her husband was an important man in the oasis, and other women deferred to her. When she walked among them, she feared the evil eye. She had gone only a few yards inside when the ululation came to an end. In the silence, she heard the sound again, like the buzzing of flies, somewhere in the desert. Was something evil on its way? she wondered.

It was about an hour before sunset when Aehrenthal and his gang finally arrived at Ain Suleiman. All was quiet, but somewhere beyond the trees a woman was singing. She sang a lilting song, then more women joined in.

'They're preparing for a wedding,' said Mohamed. 'In a moment the drums will begin. For now, this is for the women.'

The light changed from pearl to pink to red. In the sky the first stars quivered. The moon had not yet risen, and as the sun sank lower it carried the world with it into darkness. In the oasis oil lamps flickered like stars of a different universe.

The singing continued for a little while,

then one by one the voices stopped until the women had all stopped singing, and all their silences came down and filled the chambers of Wardabaha.

Outside, the moon had risen, shedding a white light across the blue water of the great pool. It tipped the leaves of the palms with silver.

As the soldiers of the Legion of Longinus walked down the slope that would bring them to the edge of Ain Suleiman, they saw dark shapes gather ahead of them. The men of the oasis had heard the jeeps arrive, and one old man, who had been a child on that wartime day, had told his son, 'They've come back.'

The men of the Kel Ajjer waited in a line, watching the newcomers. Mohamed ag Ewangaye walked ahead, all but his eyes wrapped in blue and black cloth. When he reached the tribesmen, he stepped up to a man in a high headdress, whom he knew to be the chief Imashaghen.

'*Al-salam 'alaykum*,' he said in greeting. '*Oy ik.*'

The chief mumbled a reply.

'*Alkher ghas.*'

'*Mani eghiwan?*'

The same reply.

'*Mani echeghel?*'

The same reply. Mohamed turned to Aehrenthal.

'I have enquired about himself and his family, and I have asked about his work. All are well.'

'I'm glad to hear it. Now, tell him we've come to see the holy city.'

The chief, a man called Idris agg Yusuf agg Yaqub Iskakkghan, looked at Mohamed, then at Aehrenthal. The moonlight etched Aehrenthal's face. One glance at it and Idris knew all he needed to know.

'Are you British?' he asked. 'English?'

Aehrenthal hesitated. What did this man of the desert know of England? He was much too young to have met any of the Usherwood expedition.

'If you are British, you are very welcome. It was British soldiers who came here when my grandfather Yaqub was still a little child. He was dying of the jaw sickness and they saved him. There was a doctor. Do you know if he is still alive?'

Aehrenthal nodded and, speaking through Mohamed, answered that his father had known the doctor.

The moonlight reflected off Idris's smile. Then he spoke again.

'You cannot go into the city tonight. There is a wedding tomorrow. The women are there tonight.'

Aehrenthal said nothing. He knew Usherwood and his friends were behind him somewhere, and he knew he needed time to

go through the chambers with Sarah Usherwood, if she would cooperate. But, then, he
thought he had the perfect means of
persuading her to do that.

Instead, he asked for food, and an hour
later he and his men had sat down to a meal
cooked by the servant girls. They ate while
the singing recommenced. The Tuareg
watched them with sharp eyes, intrigued by
the little implements they called 'spoons',
which had come from their vehicles. They
did not join their guests. The Anislem, a
descendant of the priest who had harboured
murderous thoughts towards Gerald Usherwood and his men, busied himself by
writing talismans made up of six-pointed
stars inscribed with fine Tifinagh letters as
old as the rocks.

They ate outside, squatting on the ground
around a fire. The fire had been lit out of
respect for the visitors. It would not last
long: wood was a scarce commodity in the
desert. Above them, the stars formed a net
of light.

Aehrenthal put his spoon down. The goat
had been stringy, the stew thin, the wine just
water from Solomon's spring. His men had
started to complain about the repast, some
volubly. There was a sense of violence in the
air. He was growing impatient. He knew
someone had followed him here, and Sarah
Usherwood's presence told him who it was.

He wanted out of Ain Suleiman before Usherwood got here with reinforcements. It was dark, and it would be darker still inside the city, but his expedition had come well equipped with torches and lamps that could be powered from the engine of a jeep.

He stood up and went to where Idris agg Yusuf and his fellows were seated. The chief had dropped the lower half of his veil to eat, revealing a narrow chin and straggly moustache. He looked old, but Aehrenthal guessed he might be no more than thirty. Life in the desert was incredibly hard, Mohamed had told him, and no one lived very long except the Anislem, who led a more sheltered life than the rest.

Aehrenthal spoke to Mohamed.

'Tell him we are grateful for his food. But our time here is short. We came here to see the city of Wardabaha, and my men are growing impatient. We want him to take us there tonight.'

A brief exchange followed. Mohamed turned to Aehrenthal.

'He says that, with respect, he cannot tell the women to stop their celebrations. He asks you to have patience. Nothing will leave, nothing will change. Wait till morning. The women will leave in the morning.'

Something snapped in Aehrenthal. He had waited so many years for this, for something to come to the point of revelation, of contact. He had at last set foot in a place he had long thought legend or a mirage. He was come like a wise man from the east, a barbarian in awe of a dead king. But the only gifts he bore were death and fear.

He got to his feet and stalked across the circle of diners until he was in front of the chief.

'I asked you to take us to the city. I didn't expect you to fuck me around like this.'

Idris looked at him in puzzlement.

'Tell him!' bellowed Aehrenthal. All around him, the Tuareg were growing agitated. No one was eating. The slave girls scampered away, sensing trouble in the offing.

Mohamed told the chief in polite language, but he knew he was already on unsteady ground, that the insult had already been mouthed. He noticed that Idris was already surrounded by a bodyguard of Imashaghen and that they had raised the *agedellehouf*, the lower half of their veils, over their noses and mouths to signify both the end of the meal and the end of hospitality. To break off hospitality was a signal for guests to depart, since it might be understood as a token of war. The last time someone had insulted one of the Kel Ajjer had been in Ghadames fifty years earlier. No sooner had the offending words been uttered than the Kel Ajjer had used his sword to cut the other man's windpipe. He had drawn aside so swiftly, not a drop of blood touched his clothes.

Some of the younger men let slip their swords. There was a glimmer of hardened steel, a quivering of light. Their elders told them to put the swords back in their sheaths, but the young men, who felt they had the impetuousness of youth on their side, would not comply. They stood firm against the insult that had been offered their leader and, through him, the Imashaghen altogether.

Lord Idris staggered to his feet. Not once in his life had he been spoken to like this. He decided it would be best if the strangers left. Turning to Mohamed, he called out loud.

'Tell them I order them to leave. Take them into the deep sands and lose them. See they never come here again. When it is done, come back here and make your apologies to me.'

Mohamed stood frozen to the spot. He had formed a clear idea of the nature of Aehrenthal and his friends, and he knew they would not back off. He opened his mouth to explain all this, but Lord Idris was already walking away.

One of Aehrenthal's bodyguard lost his temper at this snub. He ran up behind Idris and made to put a hand on his shoulder, to pull him round. But before he could get within several inches, two of the Imas-haghen had their swords in their hands. One slit his belly from crotch to breastbone, the other came behind and sliced his throat from side to side, and the man fell to the ground like a slaughtered animal.

Two shots rang out, and Lord Idris's defenders dropped lifeless next to their victim. Then the killing started in earnest. The neo-Nazis were all armed with sub-machine guns, Russian-made Bizons carrying 9 x 19mm Luger/Parabellum rounds. Watching their companion killed brought to the fore all their atavistic terrors of dark-skinned races.

An Austrian named Helmut Kiesl had good night vision. He lifted his Bizon, clicked off the safety catch, and started firing.

He was followed within seconds by his companions, and in just as many seconds the men of Ain Suleiman lay bloody and scattered across the cold ground. Lord Idris, spangled with bullets, lay among them. The guns fell silent, and the little massacre passed without notice. Above, the moon moved and the stars twinkled, but no comet fell.

They left their victims lying where they had fallen. Aehrenthal appointed six men to keep an eye out, in case there were other Tuareg in the oasis, who had not been at the dinner. They followed the sounds of singing. These were faint at first, but grew in intensity as they stumbled through the dunes, out into the desert surrounding the oasis. In the end, the music brought them to their heart's desire or, since it was much the same thing, to Egon Aehrenthal's obsession. He had long ago persuaded them that what he wanted was what they wanted, and that glory for him would bring glory for them. They walked in silence, well-built men without pity, in black clothes carrying black guns.

Some of the women had heard the brief stutter of the guns and were now hurrying along the track between the old city and the encampment. None of them had heard a gun fired before, let alone an automatic weapon. They feared the jinn and the shayatin, not human beings. There were children with them, and they walked quickly. Behind them, the city was silent. At first they thought the men coming towards them were their husbands and brothers, then they saw their outlines against the sky and knew they were not.

Aehrenthal ordered their hands tied behind their backs and told two of his men to take them somewhere safe, where they wouldn't see their dead relations and panic.

'These savages can get agitated,' he said. 'If they see their men lying dead, they'll go hysterical. I can do without all that squawking. Now, you can all do what you want with them later, but it's time we got ourselves over to the tombs.'

He knew their supplies were running out. They could replenish their water cans here, and a certain amount of food, but there would be no petrol or oil, no fresh fruit except dates, no wheat flour, no eggs. They might survive, but the floods had held them back. He wanted to get as much on board as possible, bury the bodies well out of sight, and get moving again.

By now, the women had begun to guess that something was not right with their menfolk. Their crying grew in volume and meaning.

'If they give you any trouble,' said Aehrenthal, 'shoot them.'

CHAPTER THIRTY-ONE

Sarah

Sarah sat rigid, watching the sky. She was cold, hungry, and scared to death. She had no way of knowing where Ethan had got to, and had abandoned hope that he would arrive at Ain Suleiman in time to do anything. Or, if he and the others did turn up, there would be a shoot-out and another bloodbath.

Tired of stars, she tried to sit up straight. They had tied her hands in front of her, so she had to rock back and forwards on her buttocks to come more or less upright. As she moved into position, she noticed that one of the Tuareg men had fallen inches away from her. He was lying on his back. His headdress had been dislodged and had rolled several feet away, exposing his naked head. In his right hand, he held his sword, and this lay well within Sarah's reach.

She looked for the guard and saw he was sitting with his back to her, watching in the direction Aehrenthal had gone with his men. Making as little noise as possible, she bent sideways to get the sword, then held it fast between her legs while she used it to saw through the ropes around her wrists. Cutting her legs free was only the work of seconds. Thinking quickly, she tiptoed to one side and picked up the Tuareg's headdress. It unrolled in a long blue strip. She took some of the ropes along with it.

Still clutching the sword by its leather handle, she inched towards the guard. He hadn't heard her approach and sat, a little bored, wondering what was happening with his comrades. Sarah put the sword on the ground. Taking the strip of blue cloth, she braced herself then slung it over the guard's head, pulling it tight over his eyes, blinding him. He cried out, but she tightened the cloth behind him and pushed him face down onto the ground. She got her knee in his back and took a hank of rope with which she started to tie his wrists. He struggled, but he couldn't see. She took the sword from its scabbard and held the point to the back of his neck, drawing blood. Taking a second rope, she tied his ankles together, then stretched the cord up to his neck and round, making a noose. If he tried to struggle, he would choke himself. It was less than he deserved. His sub-machine gun was lying beside him. She took it and slung it over her shoulder.

She had already heard the women's voices, though she could not be sure what had happened to them. She decided the best thing she could do was to follow the voices until she found the women and whatever men were with them. It would not have surprised her to find they were being raped.

First, she went back to the jeeps, where she found a padded jacket that fitted her. It was identical to the jackets worn by the men, and she hoped it would disguise her, along with her short hair.

The moonlight made her passage through the oasis simple, and she soon saw the group of captive women up ahead. Her suspicions were quickly fulfilled when she saw that two men had taken a woman each and were now busy raping them. Howling children and infants were everywhere. She moved swiftly, singling out the man on her left. She sneaked up behind him and, as he reached his orgasm she kicked him hard in the ribs, pushing him off his victim onto the ground. Scrambling to his feet, he reached for his handgun, but it was in a holster attached to his trousers, which were round his ankles. Sarah lifted the sub-machine gun and pointed it at him. She grinned to see him so ridiculous. She could have shot him, his death would not have mattered. The woman screamed, thinking another man had come to rape her. Sarah smiled and put a finger to her lips. The woman's cries subsided. A second woman crept towards her. She had rescued her goat earlier, and now she removed the palm-fibre cord from round its neck. She gestured to Sarah, who nodded.

While the Tuareg woman tied the man's hands behind his back, Sarah took the gun from his holster. It was a Glock 19, short and functional, with a ten-round magazine. She'd been trained on a different gun, but it took only a minute or two for her to grow accustomed to its balance. She made sure the safety catch was off and strode to where the other man had slumped across the body of his woman, oblivious of what had just happened to his companion. She forced him up onto his knees, jabbing the barrel of the

Glock into his back. Terrified, he put his hands behind his head. Sarah had him at her mercy, but she had no more rope with which to tie him.

The other woman finished tying up the first guard and walked over to join Sarah. Taking in the situation at a glance, she gestured to the sword Sarah had thrust into her waistband. Sarah did nothing to stop her as she took the sword in one hand, weighed it, then thrust it hard into the guard's chest, above his heart. He died at once. The woman withdrew the sword and returned it to the scabbard.

Sarah reckoned that Aehrenthal must have started out with seven men and the guide, Mohamed. Aehrenthal himself had killed one man, leaving six, and now two were tied up and another was dead, leaving three. The odds against her were still high, but she reckoned they were not insuperable. She put the handgun into the band of her trousers and felt it nestle there.

Suddenly, she heard several bursts of machine gun fire. She guessed they came from the ruined buildings. Not knowing a word of Tamasheq, she wondered if any of the women spoke Arabic. She asked them if they knew how to find Wardabaha, but they showed no recognition. Her knowledge of Arabic was limited, but she knew it was sometimes close to Hebrew, so she tried some words in that language. To her surprise, she got a response from the young woman who had just killed the guard.

'The *proseuchê* is near here,' the woman said, speaking in a curious blend of Greek, Hebrew and what Sarah guessed must be Tamasheq. She knew that *proseuchê* could mean synagogue in Greek, but what could that possibly mean to these Muslim Tuareg?

The woman pulled her sleeve. 'The killers are in Wardabaha,' she said. 'We can all escape. Come with us. Don't stay here.'

Sarah shook her head.

'Show me the *proseuchê*, then take all these women somewhere safe.'

Even as she spoke, she scarcely knew what she was saying. Aehrenthal and his three remaining men were in there, all heavily armed. It would be suicidal for her to go there in an attempt to fight back, whether for herself or the Tuareg women and children. But she had come this far and suffered this much, to do nothing was unthinkable. This would probably be her only chance.

The woman went into the little crowd and removed the turban from a little boy. Taking the sword in its scabbard, she fastened it to her waist with the long strip of fabric. Suddenly, she smiled at Sarah, then embraced her. Still smiling, she led Sarah through a lacework of shadows and moonlight, beneath a channel formed by palm trees, across sand gouged by the passage of innumerable feet. Sarah wondered what the woman saw. Was the world any less for her, any less precious, because she had been born in this most remote of places, a place with so few possibilities, with so little variety, with such a limited range of companions? When the woman looked back, her face was made clear in the white light of the moon. She was young, Sarah thought, perhaps still in her teens.

'What's your name?' she asked.

'Marta,' said the girl. It was not an Arab name; Sarah recognised it at once as either Hebrew or Aramaic. Yet again, she thought how interesting it would be to do a study of the language spoken here at Ain Suleiman.

They came to a half-open door at whose back a dune had formed. They almost took a step too far, but just as they came within several yards of the doorway, a shadow moved and Sarah saw a man standing near the entrance.

'Go back,' she said to Marta. 'Make sure the others get to safety. Wait for me when it gets light.'

She didn't know at first how much of what she said made sense to the girl. Marta looked thoughtful, but she made no effort to leave. Then she came close and whispered in Sarah's ear. Sarah listened, discovering that Marta's language had a lot in common with

Aramaic. Nowadays, Aramaic was only spoken by Assyrians, Syriac Christians and some others; but it was a different, more modern Aramaic than Marta's. And the words Marta spoke had an air of the Bible about them. At first, Sarah made to ask her to say no more, but the young Tuareg would not be denied, and it soon dawned on Sarah that this might be the only hope for them to survive.

She laid down the machine gun and walked slowly up to the guard. She recognised him as one of the Austrians, and remembered that his name was Günther.

'*Guten abend, Günther,*' she said.

He frowned and stepped forward to block her way. He had recognised her.

'You were put under guard,' he said. 'Where is Herzog?'

She took a step forward.

'Trouble with the women,' she said. 'He told me to fetch help.'

She kept him talking. Slowly, she moved sideways so that he turned his back in the direction from which she had just come. He lifted his gun, as if afraid she was about to attack him. But she smiled reassuringly. He opened his mouth to speak again, but as he did so Marta slipped one arm round his head, clamping her hand on his face while she used the short sword to cut through his windpipe. He fell lifeless to the ground, and a rivulet of blood spilt from the wound, where it was briefly made translucent by the moonlight before being absorbed by the thirsty sand.

'Let's hurry,' Marta said, as she wiped the blade of the sword on her robe.

Sarah picked up a torch Günther had placed at his feet and switched it on. She studied the designs on the door, a Jewish menorah on one side, a cross on the other.

They stepped through into the entrance hall. Sarah let the beam of her torch play on the walls and ceiling. She saw the image of a building on a hill, perhaps the first really accurate depiction of the Jewish Temple ever made, and possibly executed by men who had worshipped in the real temple before its destruction. She looked up at angels and wings the colour of bright sunlight, saw the trumpets in their hands and the halos about their heads. She shivered. There were ghosts here. Ghosts that had been waiting for her.

In the next chamber was the synagogue. She and Marta went in together. Sarah's heart skipped beat after beat, seeing the synagogue build itself in section after section as she swung the torch about, revealing now banks of seats, now the bimah, now a golden cross. And whether it was fancy or physical, she thought she could smell a scent of incense; myrrh, perhaps, or sandalwood, amber or opopanax of Solomon.

A voice came out of the darkness, freezing her.

'Günther? *Was machen Sie da?*'

Her hands were cold, and her fingers shook out of fear, knowing she could be shot at any second. When she looked round, she saw that Marta had vanished into the shadows. She hoped the young woman would stick to her side of their agreement. The guard was a shadow, but he played his torch beam on her. She heard him swear. Quickly, she unzipped her jacket and shuffled it off. In a smooth motion, she pulled off her heavy jumper, dropped it, unfastened her bra, and tossed it to one side.

Her naked torso produced exactly the effect she'd known it would.

'Why don't you come over here?' she asked, hoping he understood enough English.

Whether or not the man understood her, he chose to interpret her striptease in the fashion that suited him best.

She lowered herself to the ground, and as she did so, he stepped towards her, letting the torch play over her naked flesh. The guard was riveted by her breasts and all that he thought they promised. When he came up close, he squatted down beside her and reached out a hand to grope her.

She felt panic start to grow in her. His hands were on her breasts, then on her stomach, heading for her groin. And then they fell away. He uttered a gasp that grew into a moan. She picked up the torch she'd let fall and pointed it at him. Marta was standing behind him and her sword was protruding from his stomach. He was still alive, but only just; he no longer posed a threat to them.

Her heart racing, Sarah struggled for several minutes to catch her breath and to fight down the panic. Marta helped her to her feet and held her in her arms, the sword dangling from one hand. Sarah's mind was whirling, her thoughts raw and confused. She knew she had to hold it all together. If she was right, Aehrenthal was down below with the last of his men.

She looked round once more, to make sure there were no other guards lurking in the shadows. As her torch beam played past the doors and up towards the bimah and the Tables of the Law, she had to bite back a cry of horror. Beside her, Marta cried out. Heaped in the central space where the first builders of the synagogue had once prayed, lay piled the bodies of the women who had been inside the building celebrating the coming wedding. Sarah remembered the chattering of a sub-machine gun, and realised that must have been when this small massacre had taken place.

The two women made their way across to

where the bodies lay piled on top of one another, their blood seeping through their clothing from one to another. They worked their way through them, feeling for a pulse here, a hint of breath there, pressing their fingers against wrists and necks until they identified three women who were still alive, though they could not say how near or far from death.

With great difficulty, they dragged them to a sitting position against a wall. Sarah could not be sure it was the right thing to do, but it would make it easier to identify them. She still hoped against hope that Ethan and the others would finally find their way to the oasis. Whispering, she told Marta this, that help was on its way. Marta nodded, but asked nothing. Sarah guessed that out here in the middle of the desert it was best not to rest one's hopes on outsiders. If the tribe could not help you, you could only rely on yourself.

She grew aware that Marta was sobbing quietly, crying her heart out yet fighting to suppress all sound of it. The bodies they had found were not strangers to her, but friends and relatives. Sarah took her hand and held it tightly. Five minutes passed, then Marta took her hand away. Her tears had dried. When Sarah looked at her face again, the woman's eyes held nothing but a firm resolve, a resolve that was mixed with something Sarah could not grasp. Not hatred. Not quite revenge. Not exactly contempt.

Together, they headed for the steps that would take them to the crypt below.

CHAPTER THIRTY-TWO

The Angel of Death

The angels seemed at once alien and as homely as the winged creatures on Christmas cards. Seeing them brought back the Christmas at Woodmancote, with that brief carol service at the parish church, vivid now against all the ugliness and unquietness that had followed. What had brought her to this? she wondered. And the answer came at once. For most of her journey from Woodmancote to this place, she had gone passively, crying out against her fate but unable to lift a finger to stop it. Now, with Marta's help, she had become her own mistress again. Even if she died, it would be on account of her own actions, of risks she had chosen to take. She let her fingers run over the precious stones on the angels' crowns.

She pushed open the door and was assailed by light. Aehrenthal had brought almost all the torches here, along with a little generator from which to run a series of small floodlights.

She saw them at once, Aehrenthal and another man. They were piling bones into boxes. She saw their carelessness, smelt Aehrenthal's arrogance as she watched him snap orders and strut about, pointing now at this ossuary, now at that, as though everything belonged to him and had always been his to treat as he pleased. As each box was filled, he bent down to write on it.

Aehrenthal remained oblivious to them, but his companion looked up from his work and caught sight of the two women, held in the harsh glare of the floodlights. As they stepped forward, he whimpered with fright, seeing what had just entered the chamber. Marta's hair was long and hung loose about her shoulders, there was blood on her clothes and hands, and she held a bloody sword by her side. Next to her stood a white woman, naked to the waist, with bloodied breasts and hands. The room the man was in, and the chambers he had passed through to get there, had already scared him stiff, and if he thought two demons had appeared in the form of two stony-eyed women with blood-smeared hands, it did not surprise him. A sub-machine gun lay on the floor next to him. He bent to pick it up. As he straightened, Marta came from behind

Sarah, sword in hand, running to strike him down. He held the gun at his hip and opened fire. She went on running, but the sword flew from her fingers. Her hands reached for him. He fired again and she pitched forwards onto her face.

Sarah put two shots in his chest, a double-tap that sent him staggering into a white marble tomb, where he collapsed and died. Going to Marta, she pushed her onto her back and saw at once that she was entirely lifeless. She got down on both knees and kissed her.

When she looked up, Aehrenthal was standing behind Marta's body, a look on his face that seemed somewhere between amusement and scorn. Before she could react, he swung his foot forward hard, hitting her hand and sending the gun flying across the stony floor.

'How nice to see you again, Miss Usherwood. You're looking a little rough. I hope none of my boys has been mishandling you. They're good men, you know, proud and upright. I find it regrettable that you've seen fit to kill Emilian here. Emilian had once thought of becoming a priest, you know. He was a pious man, and now here he lies with the bones of Christ, and all because you could not accept that you and your friends have been defeated. I hope you've not killed any other of my men. For each one, you deserve to be punished. Or perhaps I should hurt you by killing ten of these Tuareg women for every one of my men you have killed. What do you think of that? Does it please you? Does it not seem perfectly equitable?'

She remained silent. What would be the point of arguing with a man like this? What excuses for violence might he not take from her protests?

'You've been very foolish,' he said. 'If you'd cooperated, I would have made you director of the greatest museum in the world. Think of it. All the relics of Christ, the bones of his family, his own bones in their ossuaries. This little city of Wardabaha rebuilt, pilgrims pouring in from all round the world.'

Stung, she could not help making a riposte.

'You did all this, killed all these people just to turn this place into a tourist destination? With a luxury hotel and a golf course, no doubt. Drink a few cocktails and visit Jesus to while away a few minutes. Is that all this comes to?' She spat.

Irritated, he took a couple of steps in her direction. She pulled herself to her feet and retreated towards the wall. Her hand still stung from the kick he'd delivered earlier. As she steadied herself, she glanced to one side and noticed that Aehrenthal had indeed brought the relics with him, as they'd expected. They were all there, the long Lance of Longinus most visible where it stood upright against the wall.

'Do you think I have no respect?' he asked. 'What would you have done with all this? Packed it up and taken it off to the vaults at Oxford University and allowed privileged scholars to write learned disquisitions on Wardabaha and its contents? Kept the true believers at arm's length? Told everyone Jesus was a Jew? My Saviour a filthy Jew? Made him a mockery on account of it? Who gives you that right, you or any of your professors? I will do far more than you and your archivists could ever achieve. I will bring him back to life. And his mother and father, brothers and sisters. The Holy Family walking the earth again, Jesus Christ with us in the flesh in a new Reich led by myself as God's new führer.'

He paused and took a long knife from a sheath he carried on his hip.

'I don't need you any longer,' he said. 'I can find other scholars, men with greater experience than you. You threw away your chance. Stand still. I don't want a struggle.'

He stepped forwards, one hand reaching out for her, a smile playing on his lips.

Later, she could not remember the actions that followed. Her right hand reached along the wall and found the *pilum*, the Spear of

Destiny, and she grasped it tightly, bringing it to her front, swinging it forwards and buttressing it with her left hand; she braced her feet, the right ahead of the left, and thrust, throwing her body after the lance and taking him hard just beneath the heart, stopping him. The knife clattered to the floor, and he gave out a long sound, wordless and without echo. He remained standing and put his hand on the lance that had last pierced the side of Christ. He pulled it from himself with great effort, but Sarah kept her grip on it and pushed it back. He stood facing her, disappointed and angry to know he had been bested by a woman. He would have moved for his handgun, but she raised the spear again, and this time it penetrated higher up, piercing his heart with great force. For a moment she kept him suspended there, then she pulled the *pilum* from his chest, so that his legs gave way and his body fell to the ground and was still.

All around her, the skulls of the dead in their niches watched. They might have been saints, they had more probably been ordinary human beings caught by the tribulations of life. Sarah could look them in the eyes, and if they seemed to smile, she could bear it, for she could see no difference between them and her.

She walked among the tombs, identifying

the sarcophagi one by one: the tombs of Simon and Alexander, the ossuaries of Joseph and Mary and their children, and finally the Christ tomb, the holiest thing in the world, if not to her, then to millions.

For a long time after that, she sat in the centre of the charnel house, as though communing with the dead. Not far away lay the bodies of the freshly dead, and the weapons that had killed them. She understood everything, and she understood nothing.

At some point in the night she thought she heard breathing. Later, when she had fallen into a light sleep, she was wakened by a different sound. A baby was crying among the tombs. And a girl's voice was hushing the child to sleep.

CHAPTER THIRTY-THREE

Jesus

Ethan and the others finally reached Ain Suleiman towards noon on the following day. Their arrival sent the women into a state of near hysteria. Even though their guide, Ayyub – who knew a little Tamasheq – called to them reassuringly, they vanished among the palm groves and would not come out. The other guide, Mohamed, was nowhere to be seen.

The monks got out, weapons in hand, searching for Aehrenthal and his gang. They knew they would have been alerted by the sound of their engines as they arrived. But as they started to spread out, they came across several bodies. Clearly, something had happened here.

And then a voice called out.

'Ethan! Gavril! It's all right, you can put your guns down. Aehrenthal is finished. His men are all dead.'

Ethan swung round. Like a bird, his heart escaped him and took flight. Sarah was walking towards them across a stretch of sand. On one side of her walked a Tuareg man, on the other a young Tuareg woman carrying a child.

'I thought you were dead,' he said. His cheeks were wet with tears, but he barely noticed.

'I'd given up hope,' she answered, and then she was crying and falling into his arms. He clung to her, as if to turn her ghost to flesh. He wanted to sing or dance with her, or to sit with her in silence, holding hands.

After a long embrace, Sarah led them to a place by the pool where they could refresh themselves. Their cook brought food, and the monks sat at the water's edge, eating and gulping down mouthfuls of fresh water that

Flaviu and Claudiu had drawn from the spring. While they ate, Sarah told Ethan and Gavril as much as she could remember of what had taken place. The deaths, her visit to Wardabaha, Aehrenthal's death.

'I've walked around a bit,' she said. 'This city is much larger than the synagogue and tombs your grandfather found. They're probably the most important part, but it will take teams of archaeologists decades to excavate the whole thing. Who knows what's hidden here?'

She smiled to herself. For many hours now she had been hugging herself inside. Not for Egon Aehrenthal's death, which she considered a minor thing. What was Aehrenthal set beside the bones of Christ or the Lance of Longinus or the Crown of Thorns? But more than that, she knew something that would shake half the world to its foundations. It was not a relic, not a tomb, not a collection of bones.

She let her hand fall in the open water, felt it ripple across her skin. Later, when it was dark perhaps, she would come down here and take a bowl of water and strip naked, so she could wash it all away, so she could cleanse herself of Aehrenthal's filth and abuse. She smiled gently.

Next to her sat the young woman she had found in the tombs the night before, the woman with the baby. For some time, the woman had been in deep conversation with Mohamed, the Tuareg guide.

On her other side sat Ethan and Gavril. They were getting ready for their first venture into the city, which was being emptied of the corpses of Aehrenthal's men and the bodies of the women who'd been slaughtered there.

'Ethan,' Sarah said. 'Gavril. I want to tell you something. There's no easy way to tell this. The young woman beside me is the youngest widow of Idris agg Yusuf, who was the chief of this settlement when Aehrenthal arrived. His body is out with the other men awaiting burial.

'Idris is Arabic for the prophet Enoch. Yusuf is Joseph. All the leaders of the Tuareg here have carried the names of Jewish prophets or holy men. The names are the same as those used by Muslims, so no one has ever noticed anything odd. But all the men in general carry Jewish names. It is quite possible that this group are not Tuareg at all, but direct descendants of the Jewish Christians who settled the oasis in the first place. Some of the men have survived Aehrenthal's massacre. In time, the line may be reestablished. But there is more. Ask this young woman what her name is.'

Ethan exchanged glances with Gavril. Neither man could understand what Sarah was up to.

Gavril spoke first.

'Mohamed, will you ask this woman what her name is?'

The reply came without hesitation.

'Maryam.'

Mohamed nodded.

'The name Maryam mean Mary,' he said. 'Her name Mary.'

'Ask her mother's name.'

He asked her.

'Hana,' the girl said.

'Her mother's name in English is Hannah.'

'Now ask her the name of her baby.'

'Isa,' she said.

Mohamed looked at Gavril and Ethan.

'Jesus,' he said. 'Her baby is Jesus, like the prophet, *salla 'llah 'alayhuma wa sallam*.'

There was a long silence as the truth began to sink in. Finally, Gavril spoke.

'I don't understand,' he said. 'How does this work?'

Sarah smiled.

'I don't really understand it fully yet myself. It may take a long time working with linguists and genealogists. But I think it works like this. There appears to be a sacred lineage that has continued at Wardabaha for a long time. Two thousand years, perhaps. Since the time the first Jewish settlers arrived here around AD 70. The line goes back further than that, though. If I'm right,

Jesus fathered children, both sons and daughters. When Jerusalem was burnt, both lines left the city and wound up here. The female line took precedence, as it always has done among the Jews. Mary tells me that the women in the female line are always called Hannah or Mary, alternating. And when they have a male child, he is called Jesus.

'You'll be able to make DNA tests. But if I'm right, this little baby is in a direct line from Jesus Christ, through his daughter Hannah.'

Tears were streaming down Gavril's cheeks. He had never dreamt of such a thing, but even imagining it was too much for him.

'What do we do with them?' asked Ethan. 'Do?'

'Do we take this young woman out of the only home she has ever known, take her child into an environment where he'll become a target for every sensation-seeker on the planet? Look what happens to a mere celebrity like Britney Spears, how publicity destroys what it creates. This baby will be proclaimed the Son of God and who knows what. He will never know a moment's peace. Before very long, the world will crush him.'

'What do you suggest, then?'

'Let's find a way to re-establish this settlement. We leave the relics here. We find a few young Tuareg men who will agree to come here to marry and have children. They will be placed under oath never to reveal the existence of Ain Suleiman or Wardabaha. The women here and the male survivors will instruct them in the stories of their ancestors. But this place will slip beneath the sands as it did before. In time, Jesus will marry and have sons or daughters, perhaps both. The lines will continue.'

It took a long time for Gavril to answer. His hopes had been dashed and fulfilled almost at once. He was seated a few yards away from the new Christ child. He could not guess what these people knew or what they did. Did the boys called Isa perform miracles? Did they raise the dead and heal the sick? Would the men and women Aehrenthal had murdered come to life if this little baby walked across to them and put his hand on them? Or did it not work like that?

'Yes,' he said, 'I think you're right. We'll come back here again, just to make sure things go well for them. I would like to come often, to see Isa grow up. I would like to bring him gold, frankincense and myrrh. Or perhaps something more useful.'

The baby began to cry lustily. His mother Mary started to shush him. She gave him her breast, and he calmed down slowly.

When the crying stopped, Gavril noticed something. The wailing of the women, that had been unbroken since the previous evening, had vanished like a cloud before the sun. A deep stillness pervaded the encampment. It rippled through the palm leaves and across the surface of the blue water, before heading out into the unending wasteland of the desert.

Mary stood up and handed her baby to Sarah. She looked at Sarah and spoke for some minutes.

Sarah cradled the baby and summed up what Mary had said. 'I asked you before why you have no children, but I did not understand your answer. You said you are twenty-five years old, and that you have no husband. It must be a very strange place where you come from. I have asked God to give you a husband, and for the husband to have a large penis and to give you many children. I have lost my husband. Now you must have one of your own.'

There was much amusement when this was translated. Sarah handed the baby back to Mary, then turned, still laughing, to Ethan.

'Well, Ethan Usherwood, what do you say to that? Are you big enough for the job?'

She took him later to the synagogue that was halfway to being a church. They went down finally to the crypt underneath. Some of the monks had gone down before them to take away the harsh lights brought by Aehrenthal's team and replace them with hundreds of candles.

The monks were praying silently, using the Jesus Prayer of the Eastern mystical tradition. Knowing what had taken place in the chamber not many hours earlier, Sarah shivered. The blood had been washed away and incense was burning everywhere, giving out clouds of spikenard and onycha and styrax. Later, there would be masses and prayers to cleanse the place of its newly come horror.

They watched for a while, then went back and out to the open air. There, she told him how she had pierced Aehrenthal with the *pilum*. When she finished speaking, there was a cold wind. The wind carried fragments of the voices nearby, the women and their keening.

'Will you marry me?' he asked.

'You don't have to ask.'

'You are sure about that?' he asked.

'If you ask me that again, I'll call it all off.'

'You haven't said "yes" yet.'

She looked at him.

'Yes,' she said in a whisper, 'yes.'

Gavril married them that afternoon in the church-synagogue. Mary was there with her baby, with others of the women, and a choir of monks. There were clouds of incense, and candles in ancient candelabras, shedding a light that had not been seen in centuries. Neither Ethan nor Sarah understood a word of the Romanian rite, but they had passed far beyond understanding by then. Mary had given them rings to exchange. The women had taken Sarah to a private place, stripped her naked, washed her and hennaed her hands before sending her to be married in Tuareg robes. And when the service was finished and the last words spoken, Ethan kissed his bride while the women of Ain Suleiman broke the silence with loud ululations. Not of grief this time, but of joy.

The publishers hope that this book has given you enjoyable reading. Large Print Books are especially designed to be as easy to see and hold as possible. If you wish a complete list of our books please ask at your local library or write directly to:

Magna Large Print Books
Magna House, Long Preston,
Skipton, North Yorkshire.
BD23 4ND

This Large Print Book, for people
who cannot read normal print,
is published under the auspices of

THE ULVERSCROFT FOUNDATION